CW00569861

# Montana DANGER

JOSIE JADE

MONTANA DANGER: RESTING WARRIOR RANCH

*This book is dedicated the men and women of the United States
Armed Forces…
Freedom is never free.
Thank you for your service.*

# Chapter 1

*Grace Townsend*

The writing on the paper in my hand swam in front of my eyes. I couldn't seem to comprehend what the words said even though I felt as if I'd been staring at them forever.

Or was I intentionally refusing to focus on the letter? Because if I did, then the desire to hit something might overwhelm me, push me over the brink. And I didn't want to break anything.

I could really use one of the punching bags over at Resting Warrior Ranch right about now. If I told my good friend Evelyn that I needed to beat the hell out of something when I showed up at the ranch, would she let me into their impressive gym for a few minutes?

Evelyn was dating one of the former Navy SEALs who owned the local ranch. They raised and trained service animals to help those suffering from PTSD and held the respect and admiration of people all over the state of Montana for the work they did. So any of them would understand my need to take out my aggression on a punching bag.

One in particular would gladly help me punch something. But I was avoiding him the same way I wanted to avoid the letter I was slowly crumpling in my hands.

No.

Taking a deep breath, I smoothed out the paper. I would need it eventually.

For a moment, raw emotion welled in my chest. I pushed it down. I was fine. I was in control. This wouldn't break me. I would accept it and deal with it the way I had accepted and dealt with everything else since my husband Charles had died.

*Dear Mrs. Townsend*, the letter began. But that's about where the consideration ended. It was a summons to court. A hearing about whether the state would take away Ruby Round. My ranch. My home. Charles's home. In two days. Was the state even allowed to move that quickly? Charles had only been dead a few months.

I knew damn well this had nothing to do with the state. I took the letter and stuffed it into the drawer of Charles's desk—my desk now. I would deal with it when I got home from dinner with my friends. The same place I wasn't going to go punch anything.

The setting sun painted the Montana mountains around me a russet gold. To the east, I could barely see the fence at the property line, but I knew what lay beyond it. The source of all my trouble: Dominion Ranch. More specifically, its owner, Wayne Gleason.

I made a face as if I could see him walking the fence line. He did it every damn day, always circling my property like a vulture. I wasn't sure if it was a habit he used to check for fence breaks, if he was pining after all our land, or if he did it to mess with me.

Knowing Wayne, it was every one of those reasons. Nothing about him would surprise me. But I would never give him the satisfaction of knowing he was the reason I made sure one of my late husband's shotguns was loaded and within reach every night.

Glancing at the clock, I sighed. I needed to leave soon for the Resting Warrior Ranch, where I'd been invited to dinner tonight. The drive wasn't long, but I wanted to be there early. Evelyn and Lena would be there early too, and…everyone else would arrive later.

Being early would give me the fortitude I needed if *he* showed up. Harlan Young. Former Navy SEAL. Former owner of my heart.

He didn't scare me like Wayne Gleason, but he was dangerous on an entirely different level.

I shook my head as I swept my hair back into a pony-tail. I needed to stop acting like I was going into battle every time there was a chance I was going to see Harlan. He knew where we stood, and I knew he wouldn't cross the boundaries I'd set.

Especially after the last time.

I'd slapped him so hard his head had spun to the side —something not easy to do with someone as big and strong as Harlan.

I'd seen how fast he could move. He may not be active duty anymore, but he was still a warrior. He could've caught my wrist and stopped the slap. But he probably would've had to hurt me to do it.

So he hadn't.

I cringed at the memory of the whole event. When he'd kissed me all those months ago, I should've stopped him. Should've stepped back and calmly told him to leave me alone. No matter our past, Harlan hadn't deserved the way I'd reacted. He may have broken my heart a lifetime ago, but he hadn't deserved for me to slap him the way I did.

But in that moment, I'd felt as if I wasn't in my own body.

And even worse—even more surprising—I hadn't been able to forget about that kiss since. What was wrong with me?

Climbing up into my truck, I laid my forehead on the steering wheel. I felt the familiar circle of grief and guilt pull me down. Those emotions were a swamp. The minute I stepped into the muck, it started to drag me under until it took a nearly Herculean effort to crawl out.

Grief that I was alone after so long of being married to Charles. Guilt that I hadn't paid more attention to him and the workings of Ruby Round Ranch while he was alive. Grief that I didn't know what had happened to him the day he'd died. Guilt that I'd let another man kiss me so soon—

I stopped the thought in its tracks. Charles would laugh if he were here to hear my errant thoughts. Our marriage hadn't been a romantic one—neither of us had been looking for a sexual partner in the relationship—so the idea that he would be upset about my kissing someone else after he was gone was ludicrous.

Especially Harlan, the very reason I'd married Charles in the first place.

But that wasn't the way it had looked to anyone on the outside. And no matter the real mechanics of our relationship, Charles had been a good man. He had been good to me. I didn't want to smear his memory by being the unfaithful widow.

The truck mirrors were perfectly aligned, but I checked them anyway. And then a second time. I tested the seat belt by tugging on it, and I tapped the brake pedal to feel the pressure.

It was a routine I'd adopted these past six months since I'd gotten the phone call that Charles had driven off the road and was in the hospital. Brain dead. There was no saving him. Three days later, he was dead.

We had no idea what had caused the accident. Garnet Bend's police chief, Charlie Garcia, had looked into the accident himself. I let out a sigh. Charlie and Charles. They'd always joked that they were twins. Charlie had been Charles's good friend. But even my late husband's good friend investigating his death hadn't given us any answers.

I started the truck, satisfied there wasn't anything else I could do to make it safer, and pulled out of the gate. Tonight would be good. Normally, the Resting Warrior communal dinners didn't feature alcohol. But there weren't any guests at the ranch right now, only our group of friends. Evelyn had assured me that drinks would be flowing tonight, and I needed one after that letter.

That led me to another question. Should I even tell them about the letter?

My friends were wonderful. But the second I admitted that there was a problem, they would try to help me fix it, and there wasn't anything that they could do. They couldn't find the documents that proved I was the legal heir to Ruby Round. They couldn't explain why the documents were missing. They couldn't provide answers about why Charles had suddenly become joyous in the days before his death.

And when they discovered there was no way to help, they'd be sad and frustrated. I'd be more of a burden than I had been these past few months.

But the idea of keeping it all to myself felt awful too.

I didn't know what to do.

That seemed to be my mantra lately. I never knew what to do. *What would you do, Charles?*

Our relationship may not have been sexual, but I'd respected Charles. Loved him. He wouldn't roll over. He would fight. Ruby Round Ranch was his everything. And he wouldn't let someone like Wayne Gleason take his property on a technicality.

I pulled up to the Resting Warrior gate and entered the guest code. After Evelyn's violent ex-fiancé had stalked and nearly killed her, none of the Resting Warrior team took any chances. I didn't blame them.

Laughter flowed out to me from the main lodge as I climbed the stairs. The sound lifted my spirits as I'd hoped it would. For tonight, I wanted to put my problems aside and not think about them. Not feel guilty or sad or stressed. There would be plenty of time for that once I got back home.

Cheers greeted me as I joined the party. This was what I'd needed. What I wanted. Fun and laughter, not people giving me worried looks like they would if they knew what was going on. I definitely wasn't going to tell them. I painted a smile on my face.

"You're here!" Lena jumped up out of her chair and nearly tripped in the process.

"Are you guys drinking already?" I asked, laughing as my friend crushed me in a hug.

"A little," Evelyn said, raising her glass of wine. "We're saving the good stuff for later."

"Noted. I really could use a drink." I looked at the third woman in the room. "Hey, Cori."

"Hi." She grinned at me. "I was here checking out a few of the dogs, and these two roped me into staying for dinner."

Cori was the local vet, and I saw her often. She was sweet but shy, so it was rare to see her at things like this. "What did they bribe you with to make you stay?"

She swirled the deep-red liquid in her glass. "Tonight, the wine was enough."

"I get that. Believe me."

"Well then, allow me." Evelyn poured me a glass of wine and held it out. As I took the glass from her hand, I realized her forearms were bare.

She saw me notice her short-sleeved shirt and smiled. Normally, she covered herself from neck to ankle to hide the scars marring her skin, courtesy of her deranged ex-fiancé. The man who had kidnapped her, tortured her, and buried her alive. The scars were a visible reminder of the suffering she had endured.

But she had survived.

Showing her scars wasn't easy for my quiet friend, but it was a huge step in putting the past behind her. I raised my glass. "To short sleeves and everything they represent."

Evelyn clinked her glass against mine. "Thanks. A little at a time."

Lena winked. "Soon, we'll have her in a bikini on Flathead like the badass she is."

Evelyn almost choked on her wine. "I highly doubt that."

"You underestimate my power of persuasion." Lena laughed loudly, flipping her hair over her shoulder. She'd added brand-new red highlights. They looked great. She looked great. Her laugh sounded great.

But I recognized the subtle signs of strain wearing at her edges. Being so much larger-than-life meant people often didn't see what Lena worked so hard to hide. But I saw.

Evelyn's stalker had taken Lena too. The sicko had made

Lena watch as he'd hurt Evelyn. Lena was still working through the trauma that replayed in her night terrors and yanked her from sleep. She'd stayed with me for a while so she didn't have to go through it alone. Evelyn had had Lucas, but Lena needed someone for herself, and I'd been glad to help.

I wasn't going to ask Lena how she was doing in front of everyone, but I needed to check on her soon. Her trauma was just as real as Evelyn's.

I sat and took a sip of wine, then drained the glass. Moderation was not the name of the game tonight.

"Damn, girl." Evelyn reached over and refilled my glass before I could ask for more. "What kind of day did you have?"

I weighed the possibilities. If I was going to tell them, now would be the perfect time. But it would kill the mood, and the conversation would be entirely about me. I was tired of thinking about it, so I forced a smile. "Mundane ranch stuff. Soooo boring."

Lena rolled her eyes and looked as if she was about to pry deeper when the door opened, and Lucas stomped in. He headed straight for Evelyn. In a blur, she was out of her chair and wrapped in his arms as he kissed her.

After everything they'd been through not so long ago, Lucas never seemed to take a single moment with Evelyn for granted. Their public passion was nothing new, but I still looked away. Seeing them like that made me envious, and that wasn't fair. They'd walked through hell together and made it out the other side. Still, my chest ached when I saw Lucas tenderly trace the scars on her arms, whispering words meant only for her ears.

Grant and Jude, two more of the Resting Warrior team, joined the group. Jude shook his head and grunted. "Okay, you two, get a room."

Lucas shot him the bird, and everyone laughed.

"Now that we have that out of the way, what's for dinner?" Grant asked.

Evelyn smirked at him. "You mean there's supposed to be food? We were only told to start drinking."

The men's faces fell like they'd been given tragic news. Evelyn laughed. "I'm kidding! There's lasagna in the oven, and Lena brought fresh garlic bread. Everything will be ready in half an hour."

"I'm game for that," Grant said as he fixed his gaze on Cori. "But for the record, I'm a damn good cook."

Cori hid her blush behind her wineglass.

Lena's eyes never left Jude as he crossed the room to fix himself something stronger than wine. The mostly silent man didn't seem to notice.

The combination dining room-kitchen at Resting Warrior was bigger than most, but when filled with the big men—former Navy SEALs—and their guests, the space felt downright cozy. The delicious aromas of the almost-ready meal permeated the space, and the alcohol flowed, loosening tongues. I let the camaraderie fill me. It was nice to be surrounded by people.

My house was too big for one person. It had been too big even when it had been two of us living there, and every night I could feel the empty, echoey space all around me. Six months after Charles's accident and it still felt strange to be alone after so many years with him.

Even if our marriage hadn't been normal, it had been ours.

The front door opened again, and another chorus of greetings resounded. Harlan stepped into view, and my breath caught. I'd hoped maybe he wouldn't be here tonight.

Yeah, right. Whatever part of me didn't want to see him…a bigger part did.

He looked good. Freshly showered with still-wet hair, shirt with sleeves rolled up to show corded forearms, and jeans that were just the right amount of tight to draw a woman's eye.

Harlan Young was strong and rugged and rough around the edges.

And everything that I felt guilty for wanting.

## Chapter 2

*Harlan Young*

I swung the sledgehammer over my head and brought it down with enough force to drive the fence post deeper into the Montana soil. The reverberation sent an ache through my arms and shoulders, and using the heavy tool over and over was causing a burn in my muscles, but I didn't want to stop.

We had machinery and tools that could do this work much more easily too, but I didn't want that either.

Normally, I loved damn near everything about the Resting Warrior Ranch, even the relatively boring fence-mending duty, which the guys and I were on today. I loved the wide-open space all around us, loved the animals we raised and trained. Loved that we had taken our own PTSD and figured out ways to help other people wading through the same hell we did.

But today, I wanted the pain and burn. It gave me

something to focus on besides all the shit swimming around in my head.

Not to mention the pretty, pretty princess talk going on around me.

"I can't get Evelyn a traditional engagement ring, not after what that bastard did to her. So I was thinking about getting her an engagement *necklace*." Lucas Everett hoisted a fence railing over his shoulder and walked it from the truck to where our friends Grant Carter and Jude Williams waited to attach it to the posts I'd just finished planting in the ground.

"Yeah, after what she's been through, I think that's a solid plan." Grant held his end in place, while Jude attached the other. He grinned up at Lucas. "Or a tiara."

Lucas chuckled before flipping his hammer up in the air, catching it with each spin, and looking back toward the main lodge on the property. He knew that was where Evelyn was right now. It was still a little difficult for him to leave her alone after what had happened with that psycho who'd come after her.

I couldn't blame him. He'd come so close to losing her. And we'd come close to losing him.

And the fact that I'd almost been too late to stop it all had been dragging me back down into a past I couldn't forget or seem to do anything about.

I swung the sledgehammer down again and again, breathing through the burn and the pain.

"Yo, Harlan, you want me to take over sledge duty?" Grant asked. "That work is miserable."

I took off my hat and wiped my arm across my sweaty brow before replacing it. "No."

I swung again.

"Usually we have to draw short straw for who has to

work posts." Lucas waited until I was between swings. "Why the hell'd you volunteer?"

All three of my friends were looking at me now. Grant and Lucas were going to keep on me until I answered. Jude didn't say anything, as was his way, just studied me with eyes that saw way too much.

"I needed the workout." I swung again.

Grant pointed at my bruised knuckles. "Looks like you've been doing a lot of working out in the gym too. Punching bag pick a fight with you?"

I knew the guys were concerned about me and wanted to help. Hell, that was why they'd all come out here for fence-mending duty when it could've been handled by an outside company or just a couple of us.

We looked out for one another. That's what we did here. Offered whatever support we could when one of us was struggling.

But right now, I didn't want their help. There wasn't anything they could do.

"If the punching bag doesn't want me hitting it, it shouldn't throw out insults as I walk by." I forced a half grin onto my face. "What's a man supposed to do?"

The guys chuckled and went back to work and talking about Lucas's plans to propose to Evelyn. Crisis averted. Even though Jude was still watching me with those eyes that said I didn't fool him.

Hell, I didn't fool any of them. But we'd learned when to push and when not to. Any one of these guys would kick my ass if I needed it, if I really started spiraling. But we weren't at that point.

Yet.

I swung the sledgehammer again.

We had been *so close* to being too late to save Evelyn and Lena. I'd seen the look on Lucas's face, and I'd known exactly what he was feeling. If we hadn't made it, it would have haunted him for the rest of his life. Haunted me. Again.

That was what it was. That was what I was trying to burn out of my system by swinging this sledge and beating the punching bag until my knuckles were multicolored.

I was afraid of being too late. I was always fucking too late. Or in the wrong place. And coming so close to disaster had exhumed a few skeletons I had worked so hard to keep buried.

Skeletons involving Grace Townsend. All the things I'd screwed up and had no idea how to fix.

I swung the hammer again. And swung. And swung. The guys left me to it.

Eventually, we finished the work, and everyone was ready to head back to the lodge. Jude and Lucas got into the cab of the truck, and Grant and I hopped in the back.

Grant's gait was steady today. His limp was subtle enough that you would never notice if you weren't looking. But those of us who knew kept an eye out for the signs that he was in pain. Today seemed to be a good day for him. I was glad.

Lucas began driving slowly toward the lodge.

I leaned back against the inside bed of the truck. "I think I'm going to skip dinner. Just make something at my place."

"You think that's a good idea?"

"I'm pretty shit company."

Grant shot me a half grin. "We're used to it by now, Miss Congeniality. Just put on your tiara and come get out of your own head for a while. Evelyn is cooking. We're all eating together. You need people."

We hit a bump, and Grant winced before he could cover it. He was in more pain than he was letting on.

"How bad?" I asked him. I didn't need to elaborate. He knew what I was talking about.

"Manageable. How bad for you? I know how much time you've been putting into the gym."

I shrugged. "Don't tattle on me. I'm trying to dig myself out."

"I won't tattle, but come to dinner. Sitting alone isn't helping. Beating the shit out of that bag only helps so much. Come, even if you sit in the corner chair and brood."

I didn't want to go, but Grant was right. I nodded. "Can I sip whiskey while I brood?"

He smiled. "Of course. It's the Montana way. Better leave your tiara at home, though."

We got back to the main portion of the ranch and headed toward our separate living quarters. I tossed my gear into the laundry bin and stepped into the shower. My sigh as the water hit me was almost sexual in nature. After years of taking quick, cold showers in the SEALs, I never took the luxury for granted.

Maybe Grant was wrong and I didn't need people. Because right now, spending a few quality hours standing in the hot spray seemed like a good idea.

After I'd put off the inevitable as long as I could, I dressed and jogged over to the lodge. The sounds and smells hit me the moment I walked in. The chatter and laughter assaulted my ears, seeming harsh after so much time inside my own head. I forced a smile and waved as my friends offered greetings.

Lucas and Evelyn had wound themselves around each other to the point it was difficult to tell where one ended and the other began. Everyone else was spread across the large living room, talking and laughing. But my eyes immediately found one person as if they were caught in some sort of tractor beam.

*Grace.*

My heart slammed into my chest wall. She was here. Now I regretted not speeding through the shower. I didn't need to be around people; I needed to be around Grace. She injected light and life into my veins like nothing else.

Her eyes locked on mine, and I watched her gaze travel all the way down to my legs and back up to my face before she looked away, ignoring me.

This was a challenge I could handle. Grace's smile was like the sun coming out from behind rain clouds, and by the end of the night, I hoped to see it.

While she looked away, I drank in every bit of her. Long dark hair that I wanted to sink my hands into. Pale skin that I was amazed didn't tan from ranch work and the brash Montana sun. I knew she had legs that seemed to go on forever and curves she never showed off, sadly.

Grant nodded to me, acknowledging that I had made the effort. I jerked my head toward the wet bar, and he joined me as I poured both of us a drink. "You know all you had to do to get me here for sure was to tell me that Grace was here."

"I didn't know she would be," he said with a wink. "But noted."

Grace sat down in one of the two armchairs by the fireplace, and I quickly moved to claim the seat beside her. "Hi."

She didn't respond.

"How are you, Grace?"

She glanced over at me, and I saw it. The pain she covered so fast most people wouldn't notice…unless they were in pain too. "I'm fine, Harlan." She turned away from me again.

"Usually, this is the part of the conversation where you ask how I am."

She turned her body fully toward mine and took a sip of wine. "I thought I'd made it abundantly clear that I don't care how you are."

"Ouch." I pressed my hand to my chest. "A shot from point-blank? That's cruel."

"Honesty isn't cruelty."

I grinned. "I suppose that really depends on who you talk to."

She rolled her eyes. "Did you swallow a fortune cookie or something?"

"Maybe. We'll see if I get lucky by the end of the night."

"Sometimes I don't know why I talk to you." She drained her wine and stood, stalking to the bar I'd just come from.

"In case you haven't noticed, Gracie," I said when I reached her, "awful jokes and cookie-cutter wisdom are the only ways that you'll talk to me these days. Are you surprised?"

"Or you could, I don't know, not talk to me at all."

There was silence. She poured the shot and tossed it back. "Are you driving?"

"Jesus, Harlan. It's the only shot I'll have, and I'm done with the wine. I don't need a babysitter."

I clenched my teeth. "Forgive me for looking after a woman whose husband died in a car crash."

"Harlan—" Her body wilted.

"Listen, I can take what you throw at me. It's the game we play. But I'll stand up for myself over common decency."

A long beat passed where both of us took a breath. The rest of the room was quieter—I wasn't sure if she noticed. All of our friends were having superficial conversations while they watched what happened between us. Grace was being rude; they all knew it. And it was so out of her nature.

She saved all her rudeness for me. Not that she didn't have a reason for that.

She stiffened as she realized she'd become the center of attention. She never liked to have a group focused on her, but especially not for something like this.

"You're right." She hung her head as she whispered, "I'm sorry."

I couldn't bear this. I could take her snarkiness, mostly because I deserved it, but also because she only gave it to me. Whether she liked it or not, it tied us together.

And what did everyone expect when she went at me? An obnoxious reply.

"Hey, you're not going to throw yourself at me, are you?" My voice was loud enough to make everyone else aware they were not minding their own business. Immediately, they all turned back to their own conversations, taking Grace and me out of the spotlight. "I might think that you're starting to like me."

Grace scoffed. "Not a chance."

But I saw the flash of gratitude in her eyes before she moved away. I didn't follow her this time.

"If she slaps you again, please tell me." Jude appeared like a wraith behind me as I watched her go. I was no longer surprised by how silently the giant of a man could move.

"Why? You got money on it or something?"

A shit-eating grin covered his face. "Exactly that."

"How much?"

"A hundred."

I cursed under my breath. "And which side are you on?"

"If you get slapped, Lucas and Daniel owe me."

"You guys are ruthless."

Jude waggled his eyebrows. "We've all got to make a buck somehow."

Would Grace slap me if I kissed her again? It would be worth it every single day of the week to find out. She'd packed a wallop, but I'd seen the heat in her eyes before the blow.

"Food's ready," Evelyn called. "The shy go hungry."

Grace ignored me all the way through dinner, but I felt better than I had in days. Grant was right; being here was good for me. I'd definitely needed to be around people.

As I watched Grace while we ate, I realized I wasn't the only person who'd needed this gathering tonight. Something was wrong. She was going through the motions of talking and smiling, but it wasn't quite authentic. Not a single one of her smiles made it to her green eyes.

Had something happened?

We all ate and cleared the table. It wasn't long before Grace was announcing her departure. "I have an early morning, y'all. I've got to get home."

"Aww, are you sure?" Lena asked. "I didn't get you nearly as drunk as I promised."

Grace laughed. It wasn't her real laugh, but God, I'd missed that sound. She never laughed around me anymore. She used to laugh around me all the time, but that was a very long time ago. "I'm sure."

"Okay, but come make cookies with me this week. I need some more assistants."

"I will."

A chorus of goodbyes followed, and I waited until she went out the door before I got up and started after her.

"Protect your face this time," Lucas called, and I threw up my middle finger at him without looking.

"Grace," I called as I got outside.

She was already at her truck. Her shoulders visibly sagged as she heard me. "I don't want to fight right now, Harlan."

I stopped a few feet away. "I didn't come to fight."

She turned, angry tears in her eyes. "Then what do you want?"

*I want to kiss you again. I want to help you with whatever weight you're carrying. I want to go back in time and change how I handled things.* "I want to fix this, Grace. Fix *us*."

Grace was silent for a long time. Then she turned and opened the door to her truck, keeping her back to me. "Some things can't be fixed, Harlan. You need to stop trying."

# Chapter 3

*Grace*

Lena dropped the cold washcloth over her eyes and groaned. "Why do I do this to myself?"

I smirked into my coffee. She'd poured me the cup before declaring she needed ice and dramatically flopping into one of Deja Brew's overstuffed armchairs to recover from her hangover.

"Do you want the real answer or the friend answer?" I asked.

Deja Brew was in the midst of its morning lull, so Lena had decided to take a break and give Evelyn one too. They deserved all the breaks they got. Lena worked harder than anyone I knew, and it paid off. Deja Brew was the go-to place in town for coffee and any kind of baked goods you could imagine. Including the glazed orange swirl that currently sat on a plate beside me.

"Real answer," Lena moaned.

"You drank too much because you were simultaneously

trying to forget that Jude was in the room and getting up the courage to try to jump him."

She didn't respond.

I softened my voice. "Or you were pretending that you're more recovered from the ordeal with Evelyn's crazy ex than you are, and you're trying to prove it to both yourself and us."

"Ouch," Lena said. "I changed my mind. I want the friend answer."

I couldn't blame her for not wanting to face either of those. "Because the Resting Warrior Ranch gang is a lot of fun and you love hanging out with them."

She pointed at me. "Yup. That's the answer I want. Right there." Then she groaned again. "Everything is too loud."

"How much did you drink after I left?"

Evelyn walked out from the back of the shop. She looked pretty bad off as well. "I really don't think you want to know."

I laughed. "Probably good I headed out early, then."

"Yeah. And I'm dying to know what happened after you did." Evelyn plopped down beside Lena.

"What do you mean?"

Lena pulled the cloth off her eyes. "She means she wants to know if you slapped Harlan again."

"Why?"

Evelyn could barely contain her grin. "Lucas, Daniel, and Jude have a bet on whether he'll push you enough to get slapped again."

"No, I didn't slap him again," I said, rolling my eyes. "No matter how much he deserved it."

And I definitely wasn't about to mention that I still thought about the kiss that had provoked the slap. The slap had been a knee-jerk reaction, and I regretted it. I should never have hit Harlan.

But that kiss was still haunting me even now.

"Grace, you know I love you, but what is your deal with Harlan?" Lena got up and went to retrieve her own cup of coffee. "I know you guys have a past, and I've never asked about it. But he's a good guy, and though he's not my type, I can objectively say that he's attractive."

"I can second that," Evelyn said. "Hell, I think even Lucas would say that."

I looked at both of my friends, and all the details of Harlan's and my past together were on the tip of my tongue to tell them. But pain cut through the middle of my chest, the same way it always did when I thought of that history. It didn't matter how much time had gone by; the emotion hit me the exact same way.

Harlan had left a ragged hole in my life, and having to be around him all the time now on top of everything else was too hard. Every time I saw him, I had to ignore that pain. Especially when he tried to be nice to me.

At least when he was teasing me or poking a sore spot, it was easy to focus my anger. The anger masked everything, and it hurt less than *this*. Seeing him was a reminder that he had left me. And the fact that it hurt so much all these years later made me feel more guilty about Charles.

Because after all this time, Harlan walking away still hurt more than my husband's death.

That made it hard to look in the mirror sometimes.

Charles had taken me in and saved my life in the only way he could, though it meant giving up any kind of romantic life or real wife for himself. I owed him everything. He deserved to be grieved properly. Not for me to be fantasizing about the man who'd left me and broken my heart.

My appetite completely disappeared, the coffee already in my stomach swirling uncomfortably. "I have to go."

"No, wait," Lena said. "We're sorry. We didn't mean to push or give you a hard time. Please don't go."

"It's not that." But I saw the hurt in my friends' eyes. "I promise, it's not you. I'll tell you about Harlan and me sometime. I'm dealing with some things at the ranch right now, and I can't..." I rubbed my eyes. "I can't handle thinking about both."

"Are you okay?" Evelyn sat up at the edge of the couch. "Can we help?"

"I wish you could." I forced a small smile. "But no. I need to handle it."

Lena wrapped me in a hug. "You know that if you need us, we're here, right? Like, I'm hungover as shit, but I would still kick some ass for you."

I hugged her. "I know you would, slugger. But I'm okay."

I wasn't okay, but I wasn't going to announce it.

Evelyn gave me a little wave before I left. I felt bad about leaving so quickly—it wasn't the first time I'd done that—but I couldn't handle it. Yet another one of my failures.

*Stop it.*

I forced myself to straighten my spine, square my shoulders, and breathe as I hopped into my truck. I wasn't a failure. This was nothing more than a bad time. Everyone went through them, and Charles would be disappointed if I called myself a failure.

I was glad I would have most of today alone to prepare myself for the hearing in Helena about my ranch. I wasn't looking forward to that or the long, nerve-racking drive. All I wanted to do right now was go bury myself under the covers and hope my problems would go away. But that wasn't going to happen.

I tightened my hands on the steering wheel as I drove by Resting Warrior Ranch. Its security gate stared at me as I passed. Was Harlan in the gate? Sometimes the guys took turns running security. Or maybe he was outside working with some of his beloved animals.

I'd left my friends because I didn't want to talk about Harlan, but he was going to dominate my thoughts anyway.

I didn't hate him. I wanted to—had wanted to for years —but still didn't.

He wanted to fix what was broken between us. But where do you start to fix something so completely broken? Besides, *he* was the one who had left. *He* was the one who had disappeared without so much as a goodbye. *He* was the one who had broken all the promises he'd made to me.

They were silly promises—I knew that now. And he probably wouldn't have been able to keep them, no matter what. But we could have figured it out together. Instead, he'd left me crushed.

So no, we weren't fixable.

I shook my head. I couldn't afford to focus on this wound that never seemed to heal. It was like picking at a scab—all it did was make it worse. But today, especially, I didn't have time to think about Harlan.

Tomorrow, I'd have to stand in court and explain that Ruby Round was mine by right, but I couldn't fully prove it. And that alone was enough to give me a headache.

Stepping out, I slammed the truck door a little harder than normal, and it felt *good*. Maybe I should sign up for some gym classes—burning the extra energy and making myself too tired to think sounded pretty damned good right now.

I slipped my key into the lock…and met no resistance.

My breath caught in my throat as the door swung open a bit. I was positive I'd locked it when I left. Locking the door was part of my routine, practically an obsession, that I couldn't leave home without completing. I knew I hadn't missed it.

Every sense I had went on high alert. Was someone in my house? The adrenaline suddenly made things feel clearer. My heart pounded in my ears. For a second, I thought about calling someone to check the house, but I immediately dismissed it. That would take too long. One of Charles's shotguns was in the closet. It would only take me a few seconds to reach it.

I slowly opened the door wider, careful not to make a sound. I surveyed the living room. Empty. I quieted my breathing and listened. Nothing. But that didn't necessarily mean much. In three quick steps, I grabbed the open shotgun from the closet and loaded it as fast as I could.

I snapped the gun shut, its echo reverberating through the silence. The sound comforted me. If someone was here, they'd know I was armed.

I crept around. Nothing looked amiss. Everything was exactly where I'd left it, but I checked every corner of the first floor carefully. Still no sound, still nothing missing or moved. The second floor was the same. Except for the office.

I might never have known.

The folder for tomorrow sat on the desk, and it had been moved. Barely, but I'd laid it down differently. As soon as I checked the rest of the house, I came back to it. The documents—the few that I had—were in a different order. Someone had looked at these. Moved them.

Someone had been *in my house.*

I shoved down the panic crawling up my spine. They weren't here now. I was safe. But the house suddenly seemed too big and too full of shadows. Was it Wayne? Someone who worked for him? That would make sense, but there was no way to prove it. It couldn't be a coincidence that it happened today, the day before the hearing. But the main question was, what did I do now?

## Chapter 4

*Harlan*

Deja Brew always smelled so good, I wanted to bottle it up and keep it in my house. I suppose I could take up baking, but it wouldn't be the same—not to mention the shit I would take from the guys. And this kind of smell only came from the scent of coffee and bread seeping into the walls and floor. The building breathed it.

And right now, I was happy to sit and take it in.

Jude was at the counter, getting the ranch's weekly supply of bread and pastries that we kept in the lodge for snacks and sandwiches. It was something he did every week, usually alone. But today, Jude had dragged my ass into town.

The guys were all taking turns keeping an eye on me, making sure I didn't sink any lower. I couldn't even be pissed—we'd all been on PTSD duty for one each other at some point, helping one another make it through whatever was going on. Evidently, it was Jude's turn to babysit me today.

I drew in another deep breath of the bakery's scent and took a sip out of the cup in my hand. At least the coffee was good.

The phone rang, and Lena smiled at Jude before she stepped to the side and answered it. I didn't know why they didn't admit what was between them. If a woman smiled at me like that, I'd be done for.

Not any woman. If *Grace* smiled at me like that.

"Are you okay?"

Lena's startled voice on the phone drew my attention.

"Holy shit, Grace, you left early. What if they'd been there when you got home?"

I was on my feet without realizing it. It was Grace, and something was wrong. My whole body went on full alert.

"What's going on?" I asked.

Lena held up a finger. "Do you want to stay with me tonight?" She listened to the answer in silence. "Okay. Well, that's an open invitation. And I'm going to call Charlie."

I could hear Grace's protest through the phone.

Lena's face went tight. "The hell it's fine. You need someone to take a look. I'm not taking no for an answer, and I know you won't call him."

I gripped my hands into fists. If whatever was happening with Grace was something needing the town's police, then it was something important. I barely held on to my temper as Lena finished talking to Grace.

"What happened?"

Lena gave me a level stare. "I don't know if Grace would want me to tell you."

I swallowed down my frustration. Lena was protecting her friend.

But there was no way in hell I wasn't going to find out what was happening if it was something bad concerning Grace.

"I can drive out there and find out for myself, and don't doubt that I will. Telling me now won't make a difference, it will just help me help her better."

She sighed. "Someone was in Grace's house. The door was unlocked when she got there, and some stuff had been moved. She's fine but freaked out."

"Shit," Jude muttered.

"Grace doesn't want to make a big deal about it, but I'm going to call Charlie so he can go check it out. You guys have everything you need?" She gave Jude that smile again. And once again, he totally didn't recognize it for what it was.

Jude nodded. "Yeah. Thanks, Lena."

"Any time."

I rushed out the door, and Jude was right behind me, knowing he'd be walking home if he wasn't. Every second I wasn't where Grace was, was one second too many.

She was fine. She was safe. I kept telling myself that over and over. This wasn't like before. I wasn't going to be too late again.

I wasn't going to miss being there for her.

"You okay?" Jude asked when I threw the truck into drive.

"I'm fine."

He side-eyed me. "Bullshit."

"I'm fine enough, okay? I need to get to Grace."

Jude went quiet for a second. Quieter. He was always quiet. It was how he was, and part of the trauma that he didn't like to share. "Even if she doesn't want you there?"

I gripped the steering wheel tighter. "I'm not leaving her to deal with this alone." Never again.

"Fair enough. You want help? I'll come with you."

"No. She won't want a bunch of people there." She wasn't even going to want me there.

"Harlan, it's been a rough few weeks for you since Evelyn's attack. You haven't been talking about it."

I shrugged and took a turn toward the ranch. "What's there to talk about? I wasn't hurt. Evelyn and Lena bore the brunt of that. Lucas almost took a knife to the gut."

Jude glanced over at me. "But that's the problem, isn't it? You feel responsible, like you didn't do enough. It's the same way you feel about your past with Grace, isn't it? That you didn't do enough for her."

Didn't do enough. Wasn't there when she needed me. Too late. Caused her pain.

Step right up and spin the wheel of *How Many Ways Can Harlan Young Screw Up*. There's a winner every time!

And it wasn't just with Grace. The same thing had happened with my unit—I didn't do enough, wasn't there when they needed me either. And because of that, two of them had ended up dead. The others who had survived, like Jude, were still living with the daily nightmares.

But I didn't say any of that. What was the point? The silence stretched until we were almost at the gate.

"Look, you don't have to work through this alone," Jude finally said. "All of us get it. We're not going to want to paint your toenails or braid your hair if you want to talk to us about what's going on in your head. Or hell, if you want to make an appointment with Dr. Rayne."

I didn't answer. Maybe I would make an appointment with the good doctor, even though it wasn't really my thing. She'd helped everyone at one point or another. But right now, I just wanted to get this truck headed to Grace as fast as possible. We skidded to a stop in front of the lodge, and Jude got out. He turned, intentionally not shutting the door so I couldn't peel out the way I wanted to.

"I'm not trying to kick you while you're down, Harlan. I know you're itchin' to get out of here, but if you want to be with Grace—and everyone in the world knows that you do—you can't use her as a Band-Aid."

"A Band-Aid for what?" I locked my jaw and looked away.

"For being unwilling to forgive yourself for things you didn't have control over."

The words damn near gutted me, but I couldn't think about them right now. I had to get to her. Jude gave me a nod and closed the door. I barely waited until he'd stepped away from the truck before slamming it into reverse and spinning back onto the road.

It was good Charlie was already on the way to Grace's house because it meant he wouldn't be on the road to pull me over for speeding.

His patrol car was in Grace's driveway when I arrived, and Charlie and Grace stood on her porch.

My eyes drank her in. Lena had said Grace wasn't hurt, but only now when I could see it for myself could I believe it. The pressure that had built in my chest since overhearing her call with Lena finally deflated, even though it was obvious Grace wasn't happy to see me.

Charlie nodded as I walked up. "I'll take a look around in the office, all right?"

"Okay." Grace rounded on me. "How did you know about this?"

"I was at Deja Brew when you called Lena."

She massaged the bridge of her nose. "Of course you were. That's my luck."

"I'm here to make sure you're okay."

"I'm *fine*. I told her that. Nothing was taken. Lena

didn't need to make Charlie drive all the way out here for nothing."

The way she held herself—arms wrapped around her stomach, weight shifting—said otherwise. My fingers itched with the need to touch her skin, help her know she wasn't alone anymore. She didn't have to hold herself together.

"Someone was in your house, Grace. I'm sure that was terrifying."

She pressed her lips together and nodded just the slightest bit.

"What confirmed someone had been in there?"

"The front door was unlocked. I never leave it unlocked. And someone had gone through my file for tomorrow." Her body went rigid as soon as she'd spoken, as if she'd made a mistake.

"What's tomorrow?"

"It doesn't matter—"

"Obviously, it does," I said. "If someone broke in to your house to look for something related to it."

Grace scrubbed her hand down her face. "I have a meeting in Helena. A hearing. To prove that Ruby Round is mine, so that the state won't take it."

That didn't make sense. "Why would the state take it?"

She shrank. "Because I can't prove it. All the documents I need are gone. The deed, Charles's and my marriage certificate, it's all gone. All I have are the documents that show my name change and a few other things. And my neighbor that way—" she nodded to the east "—has been trying to get a hold of this property since before Charles died."

I tried to process all she'd said. It was obvious she'd been dealing with this—alone—for a while. If she'd told anyone, I would've heard about it in passing by now. Her husband had died six months ago. She'd pointed to the east when she'd mentioned the neighbor. "You think Gleason is behind it?"

"How did you know that's who I meant?" She actually seemed shocked.

I shrugged. "Small town. That is who you were talking about, right?"

She hugged herself tighter. "He's probably the one who instigated the hearing. Responsible for the break-in too, but I can't prove either."

Charlie appeared in the open doorway. "You're right. They were careful. I can dust for prints if you want, but we won't have the results by tomorrow."

Grace shook her head. "You don't break in to a house for something specific and make the mistake of not wearing gloves."

"I agree," Charlie said. "But I'm glad Lena called. We'll file a report, and if you have any other trouble—no matter how insignificant you think it is—you call me, okay?"

The sassy, confident woman who had told me to go to hell so recently was gone, and that hurt as much as the snark that had rolled off her tongue so easily.

Charlie laid a fatherly hand on her shoulder. "Charles was one of my best friends. You're my friend too, and we both know Charles would track me down in the afterlife and kick the bejesus out of me if I let anything happen to you."

She covered his hand with hers and squeezed. "Thanks, Charlie."

He turned to me. "See you, Young."

I raised a hand goodbye before I turned back to Grace. She had wrapped her arms around herself again. The afternoon light caught the natural brown highlights in her hair where they framed her face.

"There's no way it's a coincidence," I said softly, as if speaking to a spooked horse.

"No. Probably not." I hated hearing her voice so small.

Something clicked in my brain. "How long have you known about the hearing?"

"I got the letter yesterday."

I frowned. "That's short notice. No wonder you weren't yourself last night."

"You don't get to say that. You don't know me anymore."

My spitfire was back, and right now, I'd gladly let her work out her frustrations on me. I raised my hands in a gesture of peace. "I'm sorry, I phrased that poorly. I just noticed something was bothering you even though you weren't letting anyone know."

She swallowed and stared at me for a long minute. "Why did you notice?"

*Because I can't help but notice everything about you. Because I can't seem to look away even though you don't want anything to do with me.* "You know why."

The air went taut between us, tension that hadn't been present in forever because this was two-sided. Tension that I *missed*.

I needed to walk away. Jude was right; Grace wasn't a Band-Aid. But being here felt right when nothing else had. I didn't want to lose that now. I straightened, breaking the tension. "After everything with Evelyn, nobody likes taking chances. Including the small stuff like this."

"I know."

"You should come and stay at Resting Warrior tonight. Or if not, at least with Lena."

She stiffened. "I'm not a coward."

"No one thinks you're a coward. It's about being smart."

"This is my home, and no one is going to scare me out of it," she said.

"Then I'll stay here tonight." The words sprung up in my brain and tumbled out of my mouth without going through the filtering process. Jude was about to make his hundred dollars off the bet.

But Grace didn't slap me. She looked at the sky for a moment and shuddered. "Okay."

My eyebrows rose into my hairline. "I didn't expect that."

"Honestly, neither did I."

If Grace was voluntarily letting me stay, she was more scared than she was admitting. But I wouldn't take that small trust for granted. "I don't love the idea of you going to Helena alone either."

"Not a chance," she scoffed, turned on her heel, and disappeared into the house.

I grinned. This was familiar ground. She rolled her eyes when I followed her inside and she saw my smile. I sat down on the couch I assumed was going to be my home for tonight. "We'll see in the morning."

## Chapter 5

*Grace*

I couldn't sleep. Every time I closed my eyes, I kept thinking about how in just a few hours, I would need to convince a judge that I didn't know where the most basic documents of my marriage and home were. I imagined the incredulity on the judge's face when I said I couldn't find my marriage certificate.

How could I not know? Embarrassment mingled with shame. It made me toss and turn, unable to find a comfortable position.

And of course, Harlan was in my house. If there was ever something that was going to keep me up at night, it was that. I shouldn't have let him stay. It was dangerous to have him so close. But the idea of staying here *alone*, knowing someone had been in here already…

I didn't want that.

What if the state took Ruby Round away from me tomorrow? Where would I go?

I flopped back on the pillows and stared at the ceiling. The familiar cycle of thoughts started, and I closed my eyes, already exhausted.

Charles and I had had a unique relationship. He'd appeared exactly when I needed an escape, and he'd provided one. My life had been dangerous, and I'd needed to get out. But it hadn't been enough. I would have been dragged back into hell if there hadn't been something legal keeping me safe. So Charles married me. I was barely out of high school, and he was in his forties. We'd been on the receiving end of plenty of strange and worried glances those first few years. But there was never anything else between us. Just...protection. And a quiet friendship.

We'd basically existed in the same space for a while. I'd made friends and helped on the ranch. I spent time outdoors and spent a good portion of the years we were married healing. From Harlan. From everything.

But a few days before he died, Charles had been exuberant. I'd never seen him so happy. He'd told me things were going to be different, and he wanted to take me to the city to celebrate. He'd died the day we had planned to go. He'd left to "take care of some things" and didn't come back.

I never figured out what had made him so happy, and it gnawed at me.

My skin suddenly felt hot, and I shoved off the blankets. No way I was going to get any sleep like this. I needed to do something. Anything.

Tea. I would make some tea. It would give my hands something to do and hopefully soothe me enough to get to sleep.

Slowly, I snuck down the stairs. I knew where all the creaky bits were and how to avoid them. With Harlan sleeping so close, I didn't want to wake him. As I passed the living room, I peeked in and saw an arm thrown over the end of the couch. Good.

I quietly lit the stove and flipped the top of the kettle up so it wouldn't whistle. Then I waited. I rubbed my hands over my face. This was so fucked up. My stomach churned with nerves. Would I be homeless tomorrow?

"Can't sleep?"

"Jesus." I braced myself on the counter, recovering from the startle. "I thought you were asleep."

Harlan ran his hand through his sleep-tousled hair. "I was. But I'm a light sleeper. Something a lot of us Resting Warrior guys have in common."

"Is that so?" My heart was taking its sweet time returning to its normal pace.

"When you have to get rest and also be able to wake at a moment's notice, you get good at listening. Even when you're asleep," he explained patiently.

He flicked on the lamp near him, and I froze. Harlan hadn't bothered to put on his shirt. The small lamp painted him like a picture—all smooth skin and muscle. Something I hadn't seen from him in a long time. I remembered back to when Resting Warrior had first opened. I'd seen him working outside without a shirt, and that sight had been burned into my brain for weeks.

I had no doubt this would be the same. Maybe even more memorable. Because this time, he was shirtless *and* in my house.

The small amount of light from the lamp was enough to see by, but not enough to fully banish the darkness. It felt safer like this, in the half-light. As if the two of us weren't real, making it easy to believe this was nothing more than a dream.

And in that safety, I looked at him. I looked at him the way I *never* allowed myself to. My gaze always slid away because of the pain, or I tried to find someone else to focus on. But here, I saw all of him. The impression of the couch cushion on his cheek, his body casually leaning against the doorframe, and those piercing eyes looking straight at me. Suddenly, this safe darkness felt more like intimacy, and the thought had my heart and mind racing.

Lena and Evelyn were right. Harlan was attractive. They didn't know that I'd always thought he was the most attractive man in the world. And this safe darkness didn't diminish the sting of that memory.

"It's been a long time since we've seen each other this late at night." His voice was even deeper, sexier, with sleepiness.

I glanced at the clock. It was nearly one in the morning. He was right. The last time we'd been together this late had been— "I don't want to talk about that. Or think about it. I'm not ready."

"When will you be, Grace? I've been here two years, and you still don't want to talk about it."

I turned and flipped off the burner, poured the water into a mug, and plunged the tea bag into it. "Does that really surprise you?"

"I know I fucked up," Harlan said softly. "I did. And I'll do whatever I can to make it right, if you tell me what that is."

"Harlan—"

"If I'd had *any* other way, any other *choice*, I never would have left you. Just tell me."

Something snapped inside me. All that loneliness and exhaustion, all the energy trying to keep this ranch alive for the past six months and to keep it *mine*. All the guilt and the grief. They came racing out at once. I whirled on Harlan.

"Just tell you. *Just tell you?*" My volume rose, and I didn't bother to keep it in check. "You're the one who left me. You *left* me. You disappeared without a single word. And you're asking me to tell you what you can do? *Now?* There's nothing you can do, Harlan. There's nothing you can possibly do that will erase the years of not understanding why.

"You ripped my heart out of my chest. Do you get that? You can't fix it. You can't make that right. You *broke* me." My voice cracked on the word. "I've barely managed to put myself together again, and every time I see you, it's like that wound in my chest gets torn open all over again, and it never heals. You wonder why I can barely look at you? It *hurts*."

I hated how sad my voice sounded, and I hated that there were tears in my eyes. But I was done pretending I could keep doing this. "So don't you dare put this responsibility on me. You're here. I can't change that. And we have to be around each other. I get it. But I can't tell you what to do because I have no fucking idea how to fix this years-old hurt."

Harlan didn't move the entire time I yelled at him. He looked at me and took it. But now, he stared at me with intent, and he crossed the room to me without hesitation.

The last time he'd kissed me, I'd slapped him. This time, I knew that I wouldn't. Being around him had lowered my walls too far. I could try to stop him if I really wanted to.

I didn't.

Harlan leaned in and captured my lips with his. And seconds later, he sank his hand into my hair. After all these years, his kiss was achingly familiar. The way he molded his lips to mine and teased them open. The way he tilted my head and pulled me closer.

And it was all so, so much better than when we were

young. So much more than I remembered. And I remembered it being perfection.

He slipped his arms down around me, and his heat soaked into the thin fabric of my T-shirt. It was so overwhelming, I couldn't breathe. Couldn't do anything but fall into the way he kissed me.

It had been so long since I'd been touched. *Really* touched. And I'd told myself that I hadn't cared—that I made my vows for a reason. But my body was starving for the simple pleasure of hands on my skin, and this was the only man I had ever wanted to touch me.

Harlan slid his hands down my hips and lower, and then he lifted me like I weighed nothing. He set me on the counter, angling his hips between my legs. We were pressed together in ways that we hadn't been in so long.

He'd been my first...my only. Breath caught in my throat. No wonder I'd never recovered from him. He owned a piece of me, and he always would.

Hands glided up the tops of my thighs, fingers teasing the edge of my T-shirt and the skin underneath it. Barely a touch, and still, goose bumps raced across my skin. My nipples hardened under my shirt, my body reacting to him viscerally.

I wanted him. It was impossible to ignore the way heat built deep in my core. Harlan's tongue traced mine, curling around it in a dance that reminded me of other things. Produced images of us tangled together far more intimately. Moans and breaths in the darkness. Buried under blankets and sheets.

My legs were curled around his hips, arms around his neck. I held him as close as I could, the tightness in his jeans obvious. He wanted me too. If I let him, he'd carry me upstairs to bed, and we'd—

What was I doing?

The reality of my life came crashing back down on me like those giant anvils in Saturday morning cartoons. I was a widow. I was fighting for my home. And the man in my arms had hurt me. That memory stole my breath and left me wrecked.

I pulled back, pushing on his chest with my hands.

Harlan didn't resist, as if he knew it was coming. He stepped away and quietly finished making my tea exactly the way I'd always liked it. Two scoops of sugar and barely a dash of cream. I sat on the counter and watched him.

"I want to tell you something," he said as he handed me the mug. "There's nothing on this earth that will make me leave you again. Nothing. Whatever you need, I'll be there for you. And hopefully…" He looked like he wanted to touch me but didn't. Good. I wasn't sure every defense I had against him wouldn't crumble again if he touched me. "Hopefully one day, you'll realize I mean it."

He turned away and went back into the living room. I heard him settle on the couch again. My heart pounded in my chest, and the mug shook in my hands. I slowly got down from the counter and started back to my room when it hit me.

Harlan had said a couple times now that he hadn't had a choice when he'd left. He made it seem as if there were things I didn't know. And because of everything, I'd pushed those words aside. But…was it possible?

The only fact I'd ever known was that he'd left and taken my heart with him. I'd never asked him why. Part of me wanted to shove that thought back into the hole it had come out of and never think about it again. But the rational part of my brain knew that, now that I'd had the thought, I wouldn't be able to ignore it.

I stopped halfway up the stairs. "Harlan?"

"Yeah."

"Why did you leave?"

A long moment of silence passed in the dark before he spoke. "I left to save your life."

I stood there, unsure of what to make of his words, before finally turning to walk back upstairs. I had a feeling the tea wasn't going to help me sleep.

## Chapter 6

*Grace*

I was a coward.

I desperately wanted to know what Harlan had meant, and yet I couldn't face it. There wasn't any part of me that could understand how my life would have been safer without him. He'd been my safety—my refuge. What could have happened to change that?

I couldn't deal with it right now. Not with the hearing this morning and everything bearing down on me. I would ask him again. When I could handle it.

I showered and gathered the things I would need. The few documents I had. Charles's death certificate. Pictures from our wedding. A list of witnesses who would attest to the fact that we had been legally married. Bills from the ranch and proof that I'd been paying them and that all the accounts were now in my name. The paperwork for me changing my name.

And that was it.

I looked around the office again, hoping to see something I'd missed in the past six months, but I didn't. Hell, once in desperation, I'd poked at a few floorboards to see if any were loose. I'd looked at every piece of paper in this office, and I hadn't found anything. Which meant I was left with the documents in the folder.

I'd procrastinated as long as I could, but it was time to leave. Harlan was downstairs, and after last night, I didn't know how to look at him. The way he'd kissed me was everything I'd ever wanted—and everything I shouldn't want. Along with the things I wasn't ready to talk about, seeing him made me feel vulnerable. As if I were made of glass. Glass that had been smashed and pieced back together. Sort of.

But I couldn't wait any longer if I was going to make it to the hearing on time. I gave an extra-hard tug on my big-girl panties and marched down the stairs with as much bravado as I could.

Bravado that all but dissolved when I spotted Harlan in the kitchen. The scent of coffee filled the entire downstairs. For a brief moment, it all seemed so abnormally normal. As if we'd been a couple all these years, and this was nothing more than our daily routine.

"Morning." That single word broke the spell. He jutted his chin toward a travel mug on the counter. "It's ready to go."

It was the exact color I usually fixed for myself. "You know how I like my coffee?"

He looked as if I'd caught him trying to sneak a treat before dinner. "I try to pay attention."

I took a breath before stepping into his space to cover the coffee.

"Grace—"

"If you want to talk about last night, I can't," I said quickly. "Not with everything else today."

"All right." His voice was quiet. "I'd still like to go with you to Helena."

"No," I said quickly. Maybe too quickly. "No."

"I can help."

"It's not that," I said. I was about to tell him how, that if he were with me, I wouldn't be thinking about what I had to do for Ruby Round. That I would be thinking about him. And I could not afford to do that. "I… Please don't force this, Harlan."

I met his eyes and saw the understanding. "Okay. But know that I'm here for you. Whatever you need."

I pressed my lips together and nodded. We didn't exchange any more words as I gathered the rest of my things and headed outside. Harlan followed me, and he stood there as I got into the truck, watching as I checked and double-checked the seat belt and mirrors.

He was still standing there when I was done, so I rolled down the window. "Yeah?"

Harlan reached through the window and slipped his hand behind my neck. Softly. He guided my gaze to his. I hadn't realized I'd been avoiding looking at him again. Merely looking him in the eye opened me up in a way I wasn't ready for today. "Please be careful."

I thought he might lean through the window and kiss me, and I wouldn't have stopped him. But he didn't. "If you need me, call."

Yesterday, my response would have been acidic, automatically telling him I didn't need him. Instead, I nodded. "Thank you. I'll be careful."

I watched him in my rearview mirror until I turned out of the front gate. It filled me with both relief and dismay to see him disappear. Now I was alone and on my way. With the coffee Harlan had made me for company.

I walked into the courthouse in Helena and immediately wondered if I'd made a mistake. Wayne Gleason sat outside the courtroom listed for my hearing. It was brazen of him to show up here, especially given that I suspected him of breaking in to my house yesterday.

For a moment, I wished I'd let Harlan come with me, but I knew I had to stand on my own two feet in front of Wayne. He'd barely respected Charles. Now that I was alone, and a mere woman, showing me any kind of common decency was beneath him.

If he was here, that meant he wasn't finished trying to take my ranch from me. I didn't know who he had pressured to make this hearing happen, but I also didn't doubt it was entirely his doing.

"Wayne," I said as I approached the doors.

"Grace." He seemed surprised to see me. "What a coincidence."

"Is it? Do you have business in the capital regarding your property? Or are you here to take mine?"

"Oh, Grace," he said. "I don't take things that aren't free for the taking."

"Good. Ruby Round is mine by right. Back the hell off and stay on your own property."

A slow smile crossed his face. One that made me want to run away without looking back. I stood my ground. Scared? You bet, but I didn't show it as I brushed past him into the courtroom.

I had to wait for a few cases before mine was called, and my stomach churned with nerves.

"Grace Townsend," the judge said after my docket number was called. "You're here to—" he examined the paper in front of him "—respond to a summons regarding Ruby Round Ranch."

"Yes, Your Honor."

He looked at me over his glasses. "Says here that you're illegally inhabiting the property after the owner's death, and that the state intends to repossess the land. You wish to protest that?"

"I do, Your Honor. The land is mine through survivor's rights. My late husband owned the property."

"You have documents?"

I held up the folder. He waved me forward, and I handed it to him. "I don't have all the paperwork I think you'll need, but I'm here to ask you to consider my claim, regardless. My husband died unexpectedly, and the documents that you'd expect to find are missing. Our marriage certificate, the deed to the ranch. His will. They exist— Charles Townsend was a conscientious man, and I not only signed the marriage certificate, I witnessed the will that names me beneficiary. But I haven't been able to locate them in the time allotted."

The judge looked through the documents in the folder. I folded my hands together in an attempt not to fidget as I waited. Finally, he looked at me again. "Well, I see what you're aiming to prove with these. Unfortunately, I can't rule the ranch is yours in the absence of the appropriate paperwork. But I can put the process on hold until they're located. You may occupy the property in the meantime."

He lifted the gavel, and the relief that poured over me was real. I would have time, at least.

"Excuse me, Your Honor."

The relief was gone before I had a chance to enjoy it. Wayne's voice grated on my frayed nerves. The judge looked at him skeptically. "Can I help you?"

"I have more information about this case before you declare all the processes on hold."

The judge looked at me—could he see the terror on my face? What could I say? That this man had been trying to steal my ranch from me, and I suspected he'd broken in to my house yesterday? I supposed I could get the police report, but I still had no evidence. "Do you know this man?"

"He owns the ranch next to mine, Your Honor."

The judge sighed. "What information do you have? Do you know something about these missing documents?"

Wayne stepped forward. "No, Your Honor. But there's a statute that you may not be aware of."

I appreciated the look of annoyance on the judge's face. "Get to the point, then, and don't waste my time. Or I'll look less favorably on you speaking out of turn in my courtroom next time."

Wayne plastered a charming smile on his face. He knew how to mask his true self when needed. "Yes, sir, Your Honor. The city of Garnet Bend has a home charter. It has since 1936. I'm sure you know that home charters have the same force and effect as state laws, provided that they don't explicitly contradict the state constitution."

"I'm aware."

Wayne held up his own folder, and the judge waved him forward. "As you'll see in those documents, article five, section four of the Garnet Bend charter states that a single woman or widow is not entitled to own land outright."

Horror rang through me. "What?"

"I know." Wayne shrugged. "It's a terrible old law. But it's there. It hasn't been changed in all this time. And, Your Honor, the law is the law. Since I had an easement with Charles Townsend, I'm here to ask to be given first rights to buy the property once the state assumes control."

"You can't be serious," I said. I felt like I was drowning. That couldn't be real, could it?

"What's your name?" the judge asked.

"Wayne Gleason."

"Mr. Gleason, in what way would you say this doesn't directly contradict the Montana constitution? Particularly in terms of inalienable rights and individual dignity?"

It was as if I were watching all of this from far away. I'd known that he would try something, but this was so far outside of what I expected I couldn't form a coherent thought.

"Property ownership is not a civil or political right. And she is free to pursue property ownership in a city that abides by a general charter. I'm not denying her protection under the law, and I am not preventing her from voting, getting an education, accessing government services, or entering public facilities. But she cannot prove that she's the rightful owner of the land, and even if she could, Garnet Bend would have the freedom to remove her at will." He shrugged again. "I'm simply a law-abiding citizen taking an opportunity."

This couldn't be happening. This couldn't be real. "Your Honor," I said, my voice rasping. "That law is clearly antiquated—"

"I agree," Wayne interrupted. "But it is the law. You're free to try to change it."

I saw the look on the judge's face, and my stomach sank. "I agree that it is an antiquated law. But Mr. Gleason is right that it is on the books, and it can be enforced until it is changed. Unfortunately, there's nothing I can do in a jurisdiction with a home charter."

No.

"That said, if you can secure the required documents, I'll see what I can do with regard to the municipal side."

I blew out a shaky breath. "Thank you."

"Given that Mr. Gleason seems particularly...motivated to buy your property—" the look of disgust on his face gave me a certain gratification "—and will no doubt pursue the legal action he needs to in Garnet Bend, I can only give you one week."

Piece by piece, the world fell out from underneath me. Somehow, I managed to nod and acknowledge what he said. The sickeningly happy smile on Wayne's face would haunt me. I knew that. I went through the motions of gathering the papers for the next hearing, and eventually, I made it to my car.

With the haze of horror and panic surrounding me, I barely remembered the drive home.

## Chapter 7

*Grace*

This couldn't be happening. Those were the only words on repeat in my head all the way back to Garnet Bend and home.

Of course, Wayne would have found something like this. He'd made it clear he wanted Ruby Round, and today's events made it painfully obvious that he would do anything in his power to take it.

Including pulling up some bullshit law. Of course, I was going to double- and triple-check that it was an actual law. There wasn't anyone in Garnet Bend who would actually uphold that, right? Would they have a choice? The judge seemed to think it was a done deal and that a week was all the time I had. If he couldn't do anything, what would anyone in a local municipality be able to do?

I wouldn't stop trying, but I wasn't hopeful.

Harlan's truck wasn't in the driveway when I got home,

thank goodness. Seeing him after all of this would have been overwhelming for me. And God, I *wanted* to see him. But it was better this way. Everything was too tangled, too much to handle while all the rest of this was happening.

I sat in the truck. It felt as if all the energy had drained out of my body on the drive back. I wanted to melt into the seat. But I couldn't stay here all night. Especially since I kept wondering if Wayne had already made the drive back from Helena. What would he think when he saw I was home? Would he feel victorious?

The asshole was probably out drinking. Celebrating the way he had utterly and completely played me. Why hadn't I seen it coming? I'd known he would try something. I should have thought harder and been more creative. I should have *looked* deeper. It would have been much more difficult for him to have any kind of footing if I'd had the appropriate proof.

Or at least I hoped. Maybe I was screwed either way.

I practically ripped myself out of the truck and forced myself into the house. My house. For now.

My stomach grumbled, but I couldn't bear the thought of food. With all the acid climbing up my throat, I doubted I would be able to keep anything down anyway.

I kicked my shoes off at the door. I was cold and I ached. Physically, emotionally, and psychologically. Every piece of me hurt, and I wanted nothing more than to go to sleep. The big, empty house seemed to swallow me whole. The loneliness I could usually fight off enveloped me like a midsummer thunderhead.

With the last of my strength, I trudged up the stairs and headed for my bedroom. In the corner, I saw the easel and paints Charles had bought me before he died. It had been an unusual expense for him, given how close to breaking even Ruby Round usually was. The items were an odd gift because I hadn't painted in years, but they were all a part of the strange happiness that had come over him. He'd sworn things were about to change and that everything was going to be different.

And then he was gone, leaving me to fend for myself.

I was so tired of holding it all together, and right now, my tank was empty. I didn't have anything left. I turned away from the easel, burrowed myself under the blankets fully dressed, and cried myself to sleep.

The next morning, my head pounded and my eyes were half-swollen shut from crying, but I felt clearer. I brewed coffee and did my best not to think about Harlan and that space on the counter where he'd kissed me. I had work to do, and for that, I needed a plan that didn't include obsessing over Harlan Young kissing the life out of me.

But what kind of a plan? I was going to scour every room in this house. The floors. The walls. Everything. Just in case I'd missed something.

I wouldn't put it past Charles to have a hidden safe. He was an old-school Montana man who'd rather keep money in a safe than in a bank. And if he'd found something good, maybe he'd installed additional security measures without me knowing.

But it would take time. This was a big house, and it had been in his family for generations. There were definitely secrets in here that I didn't know about.

I started on the second floor, moving from room to room and checking every place I could think of. Under every loose floorboard and behind every painting. The walls of the house were ancient logs, and I looked closely for new seams—the beams were definitely thick enough to contain something.

I ignored my phone when I heard it ring throughout

the day. I didn't want sympathy, and I didn't want to talk to anyone. The way I was tearing through the house might seem like paranoia, and I couldn't bear for my friends to think I'd gone off the deep end. I would talk to them. Eventually.

It took me the full day to make my way through most of the house. By the time I called it quits and crawled into bed, I had only the living room left to search. I'd finish in the morning after I checked the texts and messages I had been ignoring all day. Exhausted, I slipped into a dreamless sleep and slept too late the next morning.

I barely stopped to shower before searching the living room. My hope was fading, but I had to finish. I hadn't found anything out of the ordinary. The next step after this was to go through all the documents in Charles's office again, hoping to find something I had missed the first time around. It didn't matter how long it took; I would look at every single piece of paper.

There was no way those things had disappeared. I'd seen them myself. They existed. It wasn't like Charles would burn our marriage certificate.

I was running my fingers along the floorboards when the pounding on the door started. "Gracie, are you in there?"

That was Harlan's voice. I ignored it. Maybe he'd think I was out back with the horses or something.

"People are wondering if you're okay. And I know you're not out on the property. So, please answer the door. I'm going to wait here until you do."

Of course he would check first. Harlan was nothing if not thorough. I stood up and went to the door. The second I pulled it open, Harlan looked me up and down like he thought I might be hurt. His face was grim. "You look like hell."

"Wow, Harlan. You really know how to make a girl feel good." I retreated from the door, and he followed.

"You understand that you going on a road trip—no matter how short—and then not answering your phone does to the people who care about you, right?"

My stomach dropped for a second, and I looked at him.

"No one has seen you or heard from you. No one knew if you were back. Or if—"

"I get it." I cut him off. "Sorry. I've been a little preoc-cupied. As you can see, I'm fine."

He crossed his arms. "I do see that."

"If you were so concerned about me, why didn't you come by yesterday?"

"Because my so-called brothers, who I would die for, practically had my ass nailed to the floor," he said, jaw hard. "Otherwise, I would have been."

I shook my head. "I'm fine. You can go."

"We're back to that? I told you I would be here for whatever you needed, and I plan to back that up. You say you're fine, but you don't look fine. What happened in Helena?"

I knelt on the floor, to examine the seams. I didn't care if it looked strange. "Nothing happened in Helena."

"Bullshit."

I knew he was trying to help, but my crippling terror about what might happen was too close to the surface, and I was barely hanging on to my composure.

"As your friend, Gracie, I want to know if you're about to be homeless."

"Don't call me that."

He waited in silence. It was an effective tactic, and I absolutely hated it.

"What happened?"

I lost my grip on my panic. "I got crushed. That's what happened. Wayne was there, and he pulled out this bullshit law that Garnet Bend still has on the books that says a single or widowed woman can't own property. So I have one week to find the proof that this place is mine, and even if I do find it, there might be nothing that I can do.

"So, congratulations. You got me. I'm not fucking fine."

"Grace—"

"Yeah," I cut him off. "I'm going to be homeless because I didn't pay attention, and I don't know where my husband kept his will."

He took a step closer to me. "We won't let that happen."

I shook my head. "You don't have anything to do with it. No one does."

He strode across the room and grabbed my arms. I hadn't realized that I'd been gesturing so wildly that I'd almost hit him. "Of course we do. You have friends, Grace. We're not going to let you be homeless. You don't have to do this all by yourself. You know that, right?"

I said nothing.

Maybe he was right, but it didn't feel that way. This was my problem. My issue to deal with. Everyone else had already been through so much...Evelyn and Lena...Lucas. They didn't need to be dragged into my troubles. And what would Wayne do if he knew that other people were helping me? Would he retaliate against them? The last thing I wanted was that bastard near any of my friends.

"Why didn't you tell me?" Harlan asked. "Tell anyone?"

"You disappeared once without a word. What's stopping you from doing it again? Especially now that you know how much trouble I'm in." The words flew out of my mouth. I regretted them immediately, but I couldn't seem to stop myself.

I tried to pull away from his hands on my arms, but Harlan didn't let me go. His strength was gentle but firm as he pulled me against him. Nothing more than embracing me.

I pushed against him once, and the fight went out of me completely. The way I melted into him was so instinctual, it suddenly felt like I could breathe again.

"I know you believe that," he said quietly. "And I know it will take longer than a day to see otherwise. But please, Grace, let me help you. Whatever you need, I'll do it. I'll be by your side. You don't have to go through this by yourself."

I rested my head on his chest, savoring the sparks his fingers caused as he caressed my spine.

"Let me help."

I shuddered. "Okay."

Harlan tightened his arms around me, and we didn't move for a very long time.

A week was a painfully short amount of time. I didn't have enough hours in a day, and the ones I had moved way too fast.

Harlan kept his word and helped however he could. We made quiet inquiries around town about the law and seeing how quickly it could be changed. Quiet, because we didn't want Wayne to know what we were doing.

But there was no way to change the law within the time frame I had. Though the response was overwhelmingly positive for getting rid of it eventually, that didn't help me now.

I went to the county seat to verify the legitimacy of Wayne's claim about the home charter and the law itself, and to see if they had copies of the ownership records for the ranch.

The law was real, but the news got worse. The ranch had been in Charles's family for so many generations and had changed names so many times that the records the county clerk had weren't helpful. Not because they weren't up-to-date, but because there weren't any records of Ruby Round at all. The clerk seemed shocked by the revelation, but I wasn't.

It was Wayne. It had to be. That was certainly something he would do.

Harlan and I spent hours in Charles's office, looking at all the documents. My eyes got blurry from looking at records of feed purchases and bank statements. Taxes. Every record that he'd ever made or kept. But nothing was what we were looking for or held a hint of where he might have put them.

We went through the bookshelves too. Charles wasn't one for journaling, but every notebook I could find was filled with useless information. I'd called our bank and our insurance company but came up empty. I felt as if I'd washed up on an island of nothing but sand.

With only two days left to the hearing, I'd given up hope. I called the girls, and we ended up in Resting Warrior lodge, drinking. And this time, I drank the way I wished I could have at the family dinner. Evelyn had already promised me her couch so I wouldn't have to drive.

"Wayne seems like a real piece of work," Evelyn said.

Lena shoved her glass into the air. "Can confirm."

I raised an eyebrow. "Really?"

"Oh, hell yeah. You know that thing where, like…hair stylists and bartenders know everything about everybody? They should really extend that to small-town baristas. You wouldn't *believe* the shit people say in front of me because they kind of forget that I'm there."

"Aww," I said. "That's not cool."

Lena laughed. "I mean, I know I'm a little different. Most people know me and treat me well. But I don't know everyone in town personally. However, even people I don't know need coffee and cookies. And Wayne Gleason is cold and rude on the best days."

"He cozied up to the judge. I would have sworn they were best friends the way that Wayne smiled at him."

Evelyn shuddered. "Nathan was like that. It was part of the reason that it was so hard to get away. He could make anyone like him. Smiles go a long way."

I took a long sip of my drink and shook my head. What Nathan, her ex-fiancé, had gotten away with still blew my mind. I'd seen Evelyn in the hospital, and I would never forget the angry red lines burned into her skin. I would also never forget sitting at Lena's side, wondering if she would ever wake up from the forced drug overdose Nathan gave her.

And they would probably never forget worrying about me and thinking I'd died the same way that Charles had. "I'm sorry I didn't answer my phone the other day. I really wasn't thinking about what it would look like." I sighed. "I was so desperate to find something, and I didn't want you to look at me with pity or as if I was crazy."

"Girl, you don't have to worry about that. We've all been a little bit crazy, and in this case, it's completely warranted. But if you make me think you're dead again, I *will* have to come over and kick your ass."

That was Lena's go-to threat. That she was going to

come over and kick my ass. I smiled into my glass. She would never be able to, but I let her think that she could.

"So," Evelyn said. "Do you want to drunkenly plan Wayne's demise? Or do you want to completely forget about him?"

"Honestly? I want to drink so much that I don't remember my own name."

"That's something we can do," she said and drained her wineglass. "Hell, I'm already drunk."

Lena leaned forward on the table. "Are you going to get mad if I ask you how it went with Harlan staying over?"

I blushed. Part of me knew I wouldn't be able to dodge these questions forever. Especially the way he'd been helping me. And he *was* helping. He'd been quiet since I yelled at him, but when I looked at him, I saw pure determination. He wanted to fix this as much as I did.

"Why are you blushing?" Evelyn asked.

"No reason."

Lena rolled her eyes. "You're a bad liar, Grace."

I paused. "It's…really complicated."

"Yeah, no kidding. We got that. But I'm pretty sure we can keep up."

I looked back and forth between them with a sigh. They were *not* going to let this go. "We grew up in the same town. Not Garnet Bend, a little farther south and east. We were together in high school. I thought we were going to get married. And then one day, Harlan disappeared. He didn't say goodbye, and he didn't come back. Until he showed up on behalf of Resting Warrior to look at this property. It was a complete coincidence he saw me in town." I shrugged. "That's pretty much it."

"That doesn't seem complicated," Evelyn said.

I snorted. "It's a very watered-down version. I skipped

the years of heartbreak and trust issues. And…other things I don't particularly want to talk about."

Lena nodded. "So, what about now? He wants you back?"

"He wants to fix what's broken. I don't know if it can be, and I don't know if he wants more than that."

Evelyn laughed. "She's right, you're a terrible liar. He kissed you, and despite *the slap*, it's clear as day that he wants you."

I couldn't deny Harlan wanted me. I'd known that before we were pressed together in my kitchen and I'd felt exactly how much he still wanted me.

But did I want him?

My body did. And if it weren't for the guilt and pain, the rest of me would want him too.

"So," Lena prompted. "He stayed the night. Anything happen?"

I took a sip. "Not much."

Shrieking and shouts filled the kitchen, demanding I tell them absolutely everything. After feigning innocence and letting them cajole me a bit, I finally told them a very condensed version of the kiss I was still reeling from. But I glossed over the other stuff: what he'd said and the argument we'd had.

"So, he didn't get slapped." I pointed at Evelyn. "Don't tell Lucas. I can't promise there isn't one in his future."

"I won't," she said with a laugh. "It's kind of fun watching them in suspense. They would fight and die for one another, but that doesn't mean there isn't a good pinch of frat boy mixed in there."

I lifted the wine bottle; it was empty. "Damn."

"We could crack open another one," Evelyn said.

"Yeah, but I'm getting sleepy," I admitted. "I hate that it's true, but it is. I'm so not twenty-one anymore."

My friends' distorted laughter filtered through an alcoholic haze. I grabbed the edge of the table to steady myself as I stood, but I still wobbled. Images around me swam in and out of focus. I couldn't remember the last time I'd been this drunk.

Holding on to each other for support, Evelyn and I stumbled toward her house. Was I hallucinating, or were Lucas, Harlan, and Jude chatting outside the lodge?

"Were you spying on us?" Evelyn asked, practically flinging herself into Lucas's arms.

I swayed again but managed to stay upright.

Lucas grinned. "Of course not. We would never intrude on female bonding time."

"We have faced death multiple times and survived. Something tells me we wouldn't this time," Harlan said with a small smile.

"Good," Evelyn said. "We're ready to take the party back to our place."

"We weren't spying," Lucas said. "But we are here to break up the slumber party."

"Why?"

Lucas leaned down and whispered in Evelyn's ear, and in the dim light thrown from the lodge, I saw her turn pink. She curled her fingers into Lucas's shirt. I fought down the stab of longing in my chest. They were so perfect for each other, it made it hard to breathe.

"That's okay," I said. "I'm sure I'll sleep better in my own bed anyway."

"Right," Lena added. "That's probably right." Jude reached out to steady her, and they had a frozen moment where they touched before he pulled back and simply gestured to his car. Lena followed him without comment.

Lucas swept Evelyn up into his arms and walked away

with her. Which left me alone with Harlan. This was dangerous. The alcohol had lowered my normally sky-high walls.

"I can crash on the couch in the lodge," I said.

Harlan offered me his elbow. "Not happening. Come on, let's get you home."

I eyed his elbow. I could make it to his truck myself, but the way my luck had been running, I'd fall and break something. I didn't need that complication, so I reluctantly accepted his offer. "I don't normally drink like this. I promise."

"This week?" He threw the truck into reverse. "I really don't blame you."

Montana had earned the nickname Big Sky Country, and as impressive as the sky could be during the day, I'd always loved Montana nights best. I leaned against the window and enjoyed the twinkling of hundreds of stars as we drove in silence. It was a comfortable silence. I couldn't remember the last time silence had been comfortable with him.

We pulled into my drive too soon. "You know," Harlan said. "I've been thinking about everything."

I snorted ruefully. "I can't stop thinking about it."

He hopped out of the truck and came around to open the door for me and help me down. "Well, I haven't been able to stop thinking about it either, and I have a solution. One that will fix everything."

"What's that?" I snorted again. "The end of this joke better be hilarious."

Harlan walked me to the door, and I leaned against it while he took my keys and unlocked it. "It's not a joke."

"I don't understand. There's nothing that we can do."

"Actually, there is," he said, suddenly stepping into my

space and looking down at me. He was so close and so warm that I wanted to lean into him. The delicious scent of campfire smoke and cedar wood pulled me in. Hypnotizing me.

"Tell me," I said.

"I can marry you."

## Chapter 8

*Harlan*

If I lived to be a hundred, I would never forget the look on Grace's face. Utter shock combined with her alcohol-clouded brain left her looking like a puppy that couldn't understand why they couldn't find the snowball you'd just thrown into a snowbank. It took every bit of discipline I'd learned as a SEAL to fight the urge to smile. Because if I smiled, she would think I was joking, and this was the furthest thing from a joke.

Marrying Grace was all I'd ever wanted, and even though this wouldn't be a union entered into out of love—at least not on her part—I still wanted it.

"Marry you?"

"Yes."

She stared at me again, slowly sagging until she leaned against the front of her house. "*Marry* you."

Now I did smile. "Gracie, no matter how many times

you say the words, they'll be the same. Yes, I want to marry you."

"Don't call me that," she mumbled.

I'd been trying to stop, but to me, she would always be Gracie. The woman-child who had snuck away from the world with me and given me everything.

And I'd thrown it away, but not because I'd wanted to. My heart carried the same pain as hers. Maybe it was my imagination or wishful thinking, but it seemed as if she'd started to trust me a little over the past week, and I wanted to nurture that trust.

Offering to marry her out of the blue might not be the best idea. Kind of like big, strong Tarzan rushing in to rescue a seemingly helpless Jane, but another thing the Navy had taught me was how to work the problem. How to use the given framework and whatever else was available to come up with a solution that, while it might not be brilliant, it would overcome whatever obstacle needed overcoming.

Right now, one of Gracie's obstacles was not being married. I could fix that. It was better than her being homeless. It was absolutely ridiculous that she was about to lose her home because she was a woman. When Grace was safe and this was past us, I would work on getting the town to change that law. All of us at Resting Warrior would.

Grace shook her head. "I can't marry you."

I'd figured she'd say that. "Why not?"

"Because…" Her mouth worked like she was searching for the words. "Because I *can't.*"

Tempting her wrath, I stepped a little closer so she could see my face under her porch light and focus only on me. "It fixes everything, doesn't it?"

"I'm too drunk for this." Grace put her hand on her forehead and leaned harder against the wall.

"If you're not single, you don't need to prove anything. The judge can give you time to find the documents without Gleason beating down your door. All you need is a little breathing room to get him off your back. I can do that for you."

I watched her try to process my words and knew that it might take time. Not only had it not occurred to her, it was the last thing she wanted. Because I was the source of her pain. She looked at me and saw the person who had fucked up our relationship, and she wasn't wrong.

She was aware now that there was more to the story, but she had no idea how hearing it would affect her understanding of our past. I knew she would ask when she was ready for me to tell it. A lot of time had passed, but that wouldn't make it any easier to hear. Knowing the kind of danger she had been in because of me still made me sick to my stomach.

But I couldn't change that now. All I could do was be there for her, and marriage was the only way at the moment.

"I need water," she said, pushing through the open door and into the living room.

"I'll get it. You sit."

The fact that she went to the couch and sat without argument made me wonder how much alcohol she'd drunk. Or how much I'd shocked her with my offer. Or both.

I got a glass of ice water, but I also put more water in her kettle and set it to boil. She'd sober up at some point, and when she did, she might want tea.

Grace liked coffee in the mornings and tea in the evenings. She wasn't a morning person, and if she had to choose, she always opted for comfort. I *knew* her. There were plenty of things that I needed to catch up on, but Grace was still the woman I'd fallen in love with.

She was the only person I had ever loved or ever would love. Over the years, plenty of people had told me otherwise, but I knew better. Grace was it for me. She was imprinted on my soul in a way that would never go away. And if she never wanted me again, I would live with the pain of her absence, knowing that I hadn't had a choice.

That I'd saved her life by leaving her.

I handed her the glass of water.

"Thank you."

"Do you want to change your clothes?"

She looked up at me. "Is there something wrong with what I'm wearing?"

"Not at all. But I have a feeling you're tired and probably drunk enough to fall asleep on the couch. I thought you'd be more comfortable."

"I hate it when you're right," she muttered, drinking about half the water. "Fine. I'll be right back."

I hid my smile and sat down to wait. Every instinct told me to help her, but this was delicate. She was already vulnerable from my surprise proposal. I knew her well enough to know that I could only push one boundary at a time.

She reappeared in a camisole and sweatpants that didn't have any right to make her look that good. I could see the swell of her breasts and the roundness of her hips. A strip of skin where the cami rode up. I focused on her face. The last thing I needed was a hard-on while I was trying to convince her to marry me.

At the very least, she looked steadier, more sober. A little.

"Okay." She sat and drained the rest of the water. "Explain to me how this will work."

I shrugged. "It's a little clichéd, but Vegas."

"Seriously?" She looked half panicked and half in disbelief. "Eloping? Aren't they going to see through that?"

"There's nothing in that law about how long someone has to be married. And it doesn't say that I have to be the one who officially owns the property. All it says is that single or widowed women can't own property. As soon as you're no longer single, your immediate problems will be solved."

Grace scrubbed a hand over her face. "Okay, and why can't we just go see a judge here?"

"Montana requires a blood test, and we don't have time for that."

"Right." She cursed under her breath. "I forgot about that."

"It's all pretty simple. Head to Vegas and get married. Get the license and a couple of rings, and I'll come with you to Helena on Monday. You know Gleason will be there, and once we show the court the license, his argument will be blown out of the water."

For a moment, I saw grief on Grace's face. Such impossible sadness that it reverberated in my own chest. The kind of emotion that was so raw you couldn't fight it when it came. But somehow, she did. With a shudder, she wiped the despair from her face, and I wondered if she was aware that I could see it. Maybe not. Hopefully not.

The kettle's whistle from the kitchen broke the silence. Grace jumped. "Oh my God."

"Sorry. I thought you might want some tea." She stared at me as if I was an alien. "What?"

"You did that for me?"

I blinked. "Put on water for tea?"

She nodded, and tears suddenly appeared in her eyes.

"It's just tea, Grace. It doesn't have to be anything else."

I went back to the kitchen to fix her tea and give her a few minutes to compose herself.

By the time I got back to the living room with her tea, Grace was sitting cross-legged on the couch, holding a pillow to her chest. I set the cup on the end table.

"Why are you being nice to me?"

The misery in her voice cut me. "Why wouldn't I be nice to you?"

"Because I'm horrible to you," she said into the pillow. "I'm always horrible to you."

I sat down on the couch a safe distance away. "I've earned that."

"Anyone else would have told me to fuck off and never wanted to see me again, but you keep trying. Why?"

Her wide, glassy eyes broadcast her vulnerability. Grace was still far too drunk. Would she remember my proposal come morning? I had a minefield to navigate, but it wouldn't be the first time. "Grace, I'm not going to answer questions you already know the answer to. But trust me when I say I've faced far worse than your anger."

She blew on her tea before taking a sip. "You got my tea right."

As if I could forget anything about her. "Good to know."

"I drank too much tonight."

"Maybe," I said. "But it's nice to let go sometimes."

Grace shook her head. "I can't do that. I can't afford to do that."

Her tone held a hint of resignation, maybe even desperation. Like the day I'd found her on the floor, frantically looking for the hidden secret that would solve her problems. Grace's default setting was to assume she was alone. On her own with no one to help her.

Of course, she knew she had friends. But that kind of instinct ran deep, and she'd lived with it far too long. Now that Charles was gone and her home was under attack, it made sense she would feel vulnerable.

"But you can. You can afford to let go. You're not alone, Grace."

"I don't want to be alone." But I saw in her eyes she still thought she was. "I don't really have another option but to marry you, do I?"

Not the enthusiastic *Yes!* a part of me had hoped for, but I'd take it. "I don't think so."

"Yeah…"

Grace went silent for so long, I worried she'd fallen asleep. Or passed out. She stared into her tea and occasionally rubbed her thumb up and down the handle. Finally, she took a long sip and put the mug back on the end table. "All right."

"All right?"

"I'll marry you."

Relief flowed through me. She was going to let me help her. I stretched out my hand, and she took it. And even more than I expected, she let me pull her into my arms. "I'll take care of everything."

Grace relaxed against me. "Thank you."

I needed to book a flight for the morning. Tell the RWR guys what was happening. Double-check the requirements in Las Vegas to make sure we didn't miss anything. But for as long as Grace would let me, I was going to hold her.

Déjà vu sucked me under. One night when we were in high school, we'd snuck out to see each other. It was one of the first times we'd truly been together. And afterward, I'd held her across my chest just like this. We'd looked up at the Montana stars together and planned our future.

I didn't think either of us imagined it quite like this.

Grace's body eased, and her breathing smoothed out. She was completely asleep. I would sit with her in my arms all night if I could. But I needed to make sure things were ready.

Slowly, I eased her backward and moved her so I could lift her without waking her. She didn't stir. I knew where her bedroom was from helping her search for the missing documents, so that was where I took her.

I covered her with the throw blanket from the foot of her bed. As I tucked the blanket around her, she caught my arm. "Harlan."

Her voice was drowsy. Dazed.

"Grace."

"I shouldn't want you," she murmured.

My heart stopped. Grace sighed back into sleep, curling into the blanket and snuggling down. She was back asleep so quickly, I wasn't sure she knew she'd said it.

But I sure as hell wouldn't forget.

# Chapter 9

*Grace*

Not everything that happened in Vegas stayed in Vegas. Especially not marriages. Why was I doing this again? Oh yeah, to save my ranch.

This morning, I'd awoken at that ranch with a pounding headache and severe cottonmouth. It felt as if someone had attacked my temples with bricks. Exactly why I shouldn't drink that much anymore.

But there was something else. The fuzzy memory of Harlan's proposal and my acceptance.

I was going to *marry* Harlan.

I could see the caution in his eyes when he'd knocked on my bedroom door this morning. He'd been worried I wouldn't remember. But I did. It didn't fix everything, but he was right. This marriage would buy me time.

Now the sun was setting, and I stood in the bridal room of a Las Vegas wedding chapel. It had been shockingly easy to get the license and the appointment, and now I was minutes away from marrying the man whom I had sworn to hate forever because he'd broken my heart.

This afternoon while Harlan had been taking care of some of the marriage license stuff, I'd gone shopping. My rational brain knew this wasn't a real marriage, but I felt strange getting married in jeans.

I'd found a green dress. I'd always liked the way the color looked on me. In no small part due to the fact that Harlan had loved the color on me when we were young, and I still felt beautiful when I wore it. He had been the first person to call me beautiful. I blushed at the memory.

Last night, I'd ended up in bed, though I didn't remember getting there. He'd carried me there. It would be so easy to lean into his familiarity and his kindness. I struggled to remind myself why I couldn't, but it was getting harder to resist with every day that passed.

There was a small knock on the door. "Grace?"

"Yeah."

"It's time."

Harlan stood in the doorway, and I lost my breath entirely. In his dark suit and crisp white shirt, he looked more suited to being on the red carpet in Hollywood than here with me. It was easy to forget how built Harlan was when he wore ranch clothes.

The truth was that Harlan always looked good, and I'd made a hobby out of ignoring it. Because when I looked at him, *really* looked at him, longing sparked in my stomach, and I remembered the things he'd said about why he'd left. And it was so much harder to hold on to the anger I'd survived on for years.

But we were getting married. I couldn't not look at him. And right now, he was all I could think about.

"Wow."

It took me a moment to realize that he was looking at

me the exact same way I was looking at him. His eyes consumed me from head to toe, hand frozen on the doorknob. He cleared his throat. "You look beautiful."

The echo of those words from our past hit me in the gut. "Thank you. You clean up pretty good yourself."

"Couldn't get married in dusty jeans. My daddy raised me better than that." He put on a slightly twangy accent, and I laughed. "Are you ready?"

My stomach clenched. "I guess I have to be."

Harlan reached out and took my hand. "Then let's do this."

My mouth went dry. I was really doing this. I was marrying Harlan Young. There was a time when this was all I dreamed of, but not like this.

The chapel was nothing special. Simple and plain by Vegas standards. A few pews on either side of a short aisle. Boring beige walls. No neon. No beyond-ugly carpet. Pretty tinkling piano music flowed through hidden speakers instead of the constant chirping from the slot machines. The only people in the room were the officiant, the witness, and us.

Harlan squeezed my hand as we walked down the aisle. Another memory slammed into me out of the blue. The two of us walking hand in hand, anywhere and everywhere. He would squeeze my hand. A silent reminder that he was there, and that we were together.

"You ready to get started?" the officiant asked.

"Yes," we said together.

"Is there anything you'd like in particular? Or just the basics?"

Harlan looked at me and then back to the man. "Just the basics, I think."

He nodded. "All right. I need to ask if you're both here

of your own free will and are of sound mind, free of any doubts."

"Yes," Harlan said immediately.

"Yes." My voice felt like it was disappearing.

The officiant turned to me. "Repeat these vows after me."

He spoke the words, and I followed. And as soon as I started to speak, all I could see was Harlan. "I, Grace, take you, Harlan, to be my wedded husband. To have and to hold from this day forward, for better, for worse, for richer, for poorer, in sickness and in health, to love and to cherish, till death do us part."

Emotion swelled in my chest, and I had to look away from the matching emotion in Harlan's eyes. This wasn't supposed to be real. Why did it feel so damn real?

He turned to Harlan. "And now you repeat the same."

Harlan's eyes locked on to mine, and now I couldn't look away if I tried. There was such raw emotion in his words and his voice that I knew he meant every single syllable.

"In sickness and in health, until death do us part."

"Do you have rings?"

I shook my head. "No—"

"Yes."

"What?" I blinked at him.

He pulled two rings from his pocket, and by looking at them, I knew they weren't rings from the claw machine at the mall. "Harlan."

"You're my wife," he said softly. "You need to look the part."

If the officiant thought that was a weird thing to say, he didn't mention it as he guided us through exchanging rings. Then he looked at Harlan. "You may now kiss your bride."

Harlan looked at me. I could say no—I knew that. If I stopped him, he wouldn't insist.

I didn't stop him.

He slipped his hand around my neck, fingers tangling in my hair as he lifted my mouth to his. This kiss was different. It wasn't desperate; it was deliberate. The exact kind of kiss I'd always imagined he would give me on our wedding day.

Heat and longing bloomed in my gut. I closed my eyes and decided that for this moment, nothing else mattered. I kissed him back. Harlan's arm came around me, and he drew me in closer. There was no hesitation or feeling of uncertainty. There never was with him.

When he pulled away, it felt as if the earth was no longer stable. Everything had shifted.

"I've got your license here," the officiant said, breaking the spell. "Just a couple more things and we're finished."

We signed the license together, and then the officiant and witness. "By the power vested in me by the state of Nevada, I pronounce you husband and wife."

Husband and wife. We were married.

Married.

Even after the vows and that kiss, it didn't feel real. I felt myself slipping into a fantasy world. It would be too easy to get carried away. Harlan had the ability to make me lose my senses, and that couldn't happen. This was a means to save Ruby Round. Nothing more.

"That wasn't so bad," he said as the next couple on the list walked past us into the chapel. "Right?"

"Right." I cleared my throat. "Listen, Harlan, I need to say a couple things."

"Okay."

"You know that I'm thankful you're doing this for me. Helping."

Harlan raised an eyebrow. "But?"

"But I want to make sure that you know it's not a real marriage. I don't want you living at Ruby Round, and there won't be any other…benefits."

"I know, Grace," he said with a sad smile. "I didn't imagine you'd forgiven me that much."

His eyes flared with a heat I couldn't ignore. No more than I could ignore the pang of sadness in my gut. I'd already had one marriage that was in name only. I'd always thought if I got married again, it would be real. And happy. And full of love.

Then again, nothing about my life had turned out the way I'd thought it would. Why would this be any different?

The cab ride back to the hotel was quiet.

"We have an early flight," he said. "If you want to meet in the lobby tomorrow morning around six."

"Yeah." I swallowed. "That sounds good."

"If you want to get food or see the city a little, let me know. I'll be in my room."

"Thanks. Goodnight, Harlan."

I felt his eyes on me all the way to the elevator. Every part of me wanted to turn around and go to him. Have him sweep me off my feet and take me out on the town. Instead, I held my breath until the elevator doors closed, and he was gone.

"This is…unexpected, Mrs. Townsend." The judge looked over his glasses at me. He held our newly minted marriage license. But we hadn't changed our names. That took too much time.

Harlan stood beside me, completely at ease despite Wayne Gleason glaring at him from across the courtroom like he wished lasers could come out of his eyes. I'd nearly laughed this morning when Harlan had shown up wearing a shirt that was clearly at least one size too small. It showed off every muscle he had and made it a lot harder to ignore the way being close to him made me feel, but the look on Wayne's face was well worth it.

"Mr. Young," the judge asked. "Are you receiving any compensation for this marriage?"

"No, Your Honor."

"Were you coerced in any way?"

He smiled. "No, sir. In fact, it was my idea."

I saw the judge cover a smile. "Well, the statute says that an unmarried woman may not own property, not that the husband has to be the primary owner. As far as I'm concerned, this fulfills the requirement."

"Thank you." My voice was raw with relief, even though I could feel Wayne focused on me.

"Now—" The judge cleared his throat. "As far as the original matter is concerned, I can give you a little more time. Thirty days from today, I'd like to reconvene and have a progress report. We'll reevaluate then."

"Your Honor," Wayne said.

"Mr. Gleason. Do you have another obscure and anti-quated law to bring into my courtroom?"

"Not today, no. But I would like to protest the length of time. Mrs. Townsend has already had six months to locate the necessary documents and has not. There are financial implications for me and anyone else interested in the property."

The judge narrowed his eyes. "Mr. Gleason, you've already interrupted what should be relatively mundane procedures multiple times. If you can show me detailed specifics about your finances that could impact my decision, you can send them to my office and I will consider them. In the meantime, Mrs. Townsend, thirty days."

The gavel sounded through the room, and my shoulders released their tension.

I opened my mouth; Harlan put a hand on my shoulder. "Don't say anything." His voice was quiet. "Not while he's still watching."

He meant Wayne. I nodded and followed him out of the courtroom. But that didn't get rid of our shadow. He was behind us, watching, until we got into my truck. At least he couldn't hear us anymore. I leaned back against the seat.

"Thirty days. That's a relief. So why do I feel like there's still a two-ton weight on my shoulders?"

He hooked a thumb over his shoulder out the back window to where Wayne stood. "Because that's about how much Gleason's stare weighs. Let's get out of here."

That was number one on my to-do list. "Thirty days isn't going to help much. I've looked everywhere I can think of. Called everyone."

Harlan reached for my hand then pulled back. "We'll think of something. At least there's a little less time pressure."

"Yeah." But I bit my lip, chewing on it since my hands were on the wheel. I needed something to get the nerves out. Because they were still there. At the very least, the marriage had worked.

I glanced down at the ring on my finger. It caught the light and shone in the afternoon sun. There's no way this was a cheap ring, but I hadn't worked up the courage to ask Harlan where he got it. I had a feeling the answer would make my stomach flip and drag me further down the road I'd already taken too many steps on—the road to forgiving him.

And as childish as it seemed, I wasn't sure I was ready for that.

After the trip to Vegas and the stress of the hearing, all I really wanted to do was rest. But I had things at the ranch I needed to take care of.

"You okay to stop at Deja Brew?" I asked Harlan as we pulled into the south side of Garnet Bend.

"Hell yes. I could use some coffee." Out of the corner of my eye, I watched him scrub a hand over his face. He was tired too. I'd been too hungover and then too preoccupied to think about it, but he had to be exhausted. Arranging everything for the wedding and the license, traveling the same time and distance.

I pulled up to the curb in front of Deja Brew. "Before we go in there," I said, "I'm sorry for anything they might say about the whole marriage thing."

Harlan had told the others at Resting Warrior because he couldn't disappear for a few days without letting them know. Telling his brother SEALs was the same as my telling Evelyn and Lena. I hadn't called them or texted them on purpose because I couldn't begin to imagine the teasing I was about to endure.

"You think they're going to be upset?" He was suddenly concerned. "Because I can take care of that."

I laughed. "No. It's more that I think they're going to be over the moon."

"Why?" he asked, seeming a little shocked.

Crap. I shouldn't have said anything. I turned off the truck and glanced at him. "They—Evelyn and Lena—know we have a past, though I haven't told them a lot about it. And they don't understand why we're not together."

More like they didn't understand why I wasn't jumping Harlan and dragging him to bed when any number of women in Garnet Bend would do almost anything to roll around in the sheets with him.

Harlan made an inelegant sound that wasn't quite a snort and wasn't quite a laugh. "They're not the only ones who know we have history."

"Yeah." I guess anyone not knowing about that had gone out the window when I'd slapped him. "Sorry about the bet, by the way. And for slapping you. I—"

"You don't have to apologize for that, Grace. I was out of line."

The words were on the tip of my tongue to tell him he hadn't been—that it had all been okay and something that I wanted before the guilt and grief came slamming down on me. But Harlan pushed open his side of the truck and took the opportunity to say anything away with him.

Lena was helping a few customers in line with coffee when I walked in behind Harlan, but she saw me immediately. She smiled and gave me a signal to wait a minute. It was amazing to watch Lena in action. She rarely forgot a customer's name, and once she knew them, she also knew their favorite order.

No matter how she felt, she always provided a smile for people. I envied that about her. Everything she'd gone through with Evelyn and the struggles that she'd faced— the nightmares and health effects—would have taken me a lot longer to overcome.

Sure, there was more to those obstacles than met the eye, and I knew she was still dealing with them. But she didn't let what had happened to her steal her joy. I should try to do the same.

My eyes darted to Harlan waiting in line. Did my mind already associate him with joy and comfort?

The last of the customers left with their coffees, and

Lena nailed me with a sharp gaze. "Do you have good news, or do I have to kick someone's ass?"

"Thirty-day reprieve."

Her eyes locked on my hand and the ring. "So it worked? Getting married?"

I swallowed. "Yes."

The teasing I'd been afraid of lurked behind her grin, but she didn't say anything. Yet. I knew it would come at some point. Instead, she looked at Harlan. "I know you guys have some shit to work out and this was mostly for the ranch, but you hurt her, and I'll hurt you. No, scratch that. I'm not that stupid. Hurt her, and no more coffee or cookies for you."

Harlan held up his hands in surrender. "I know you're serious about that. All I want is for Grace to keep her home. I don't plan on hurting her."

His words hit a spot deep in my gut.

"Good," Lena said. "You guys want coffee?"

"Please."

"Regular or fancy?"

I smiled. "Fancy."

When she'd first opened the shop, Lena had tested drinks on me and found a concoction I was only mildly obsessed with. No matter how many times I tried to make it at home, it never tasted the same. And a drink that was purely sugar and caffeine sounded really good right about now.

"Harlan?"

"Just regular coffee for me."

Lena rolled her eyes. "You men. Always the regular coffee. There's nothing wrong with enjoying fancy coffee, and I swear to you I'm going to have you all addicted sooner or later."

"Okay," he laughed. "I'll try it. If only to prove to you that I'm taking your threat seriously."

She grinned. "Perfect."

A few minutes later, she set the two cups of coffee on the counter along with a box of cookies. "Here you go. You still okay to help me bake this week?"

I nodded. "Sure thing. And you don't have to give me cookies."

"Yes, I absolutely do."

Harlan swiped the sweet treats off the counter. "I'll make sure they end up in her kitchen."

"Thank you." The chime over the door tinkled, and she waved to us. "See y'all later."

Harlan chuckled when we got into the truck. "She's a force of nature."

"Truly."

Harlan took the lid off his cup and sniffed. "Be honest. Is this going to kill me?"

"Only if you're allergic to sugar. It's a latte with cinnamon and vanilla and a few more spices she refuses to divulge because she loves having a secret recipe. It's my favorite drink on the menu."

He took a sip. "Holy shit, this is good."

"I know, right?"

He took another sip. "God, she's too good at this. And she probably will make converts out of all of us."

I hid a smirk. She undoubtedly would. She was unstoppable when she was on a mission.

At Ruby Round, I pulled in next to Harlan's truck. "Thank you for today. I think Wayne is terrified of you."

"That wasn't my intent." I gave him a look, and he cracked a smile. "Fine, it wasn't my *only* intent."

"What was the other?"

That familiar heat filled his eyes, and an echoing

warmth stirred in my stomach. He didn't have to speak to tell me what he was thinking, but he did anyway. "I wanted to look good for my wife."

I couldn't control the blush that raced up my cheeks. "Well, as I said, thank you. If I think of a new place to look for things, I'll call you."

Harlan looked at me for a long moment. "You can call me any time, Grace."

I waited in the truck until he'd pulled away then I went into the house. It was nice to sit in my living room and know that, at least for the next thirty days, I wasn't in danger of losing this place.

As if I'd flipped a switch, the exhaustion of the past week caught up with me all at once, and even the double shot of espresso in Lena's delicious concoction was no match for it. I'd been clinging to everything so tightly for so long that I didn't realize how much I'd been running on fumes. With today's business behind me, there was no reason for me to stay up, so I was in bed before the sun had fully set.

Right before I fell asleep, I realized I hadn't taken off the wedding ring.

Sound jerked me awake, and I bolted straight upright in bed. What time was it? What *day* was it? The clock told me it was three in the morning. So what had woken me?

There. The sound of my cattle. They should be sleeping. So why were they making so much noise? Nerves gripped me. I'd gone to bed so quickly, did I remember to lock the doors?

Without turning on the lights, I crept down the stairs and checked them. They were locked. Okay. Good. I leaned against the wall by the back door and breathed, hand on my chest. The adrenaline was still racing through me. But I was fine. I was fine.

Outside, I heard the crunch of gravel. Rhythmic. Like someone was walking on the path between the barn and the stable. Soft, but distinct in the night.

Terror froze me like prey, and a brand-new wave of adrenaline hit me. That was a person. Every instinct screamed at me that it wasn't an animal or one of the cattle that had gotten loose. *Danger*. That's what that sound said.

I forced myself to move, keeping quiet as I went back upstairs to my room and my phone. Now I was glad I hadn't turned on the lights.

Maybe it was nothing. Maybe I was spooked from waking up at a strange hour and hearing the cattle. They could be disturbed by anything. Even the wind.

But barely a week ago, someone had been in my house, and right now in the dark, that was all I could think about. This wasn't the time to be a hero. And he'd said that I could call him any time. I hoped this counted.

I grabbed my phone and called Harlan.

## Chapter 10

*Harlan*

I started throwing on clothes as soon as I saw her name on my phone. "Grace, what's wrong?"

The pure fear in her voice sent panic shivering through me. Grace was one of the strongest, proudest people I knew. If she was calling me in the middle of the night, she was scared, and the thought of Grace being scared made me see red. I didn't know if there was anyone on her property, but I was going to find out.

Grace was pale when she answered the door, and she immediately locked the door behind me. She led me back to the kitchen, where a shotgun rested on the table. "Loaded?"

"Yes."

"Good."

Grace didn't like violence, but I was glad she was armed.

"Any more noise?"

She shook her head. "No. It was probably nothing and I'm imagining things."

"Maybe it was nothing," I said. "But don't ever ignore your instincts. Mine have kept me alive more than once. I'm going to check around the house."

I slipped out the back, and she locked the door behind me. Thankfully, the bright moon and clear sky made it easy to see. Everything looked peaceful, but I checked anyway. I didn't go all the way out onto the property, but I circled the house. I didn't see any footprints or signs that anyone was still close. That was fine. For now.

Grace let me in when I knocked softly. "Clear for now."

"Okay."

"Are you all right?"

She stretched, and I was momentarily distracted by the way her shirt rode up. "I think so. I feel a little silly that I called you over here for nothing."

"You don't know it's nothing. Remember, someone has already broken in to your house. I'll have a look around in the daylight."

Grace shuddered. "Yeah. That's all I could think about. I went to bed early. Guess that's a good thing because I'm awake now."

"Should I make tea?"

She gave me a tired smile. "Seems like we keep ending up here, don't we?"

I filled the kettle and got two mugs out of the cupboard. Sleep probably wasn't in the cards for me either. I wanted to make sure that she was okay and safe, and protect her against any other intrusions for the rest of the night.

Grace cleared her throat. "I think I'm ready."

"For what?"

"To hear why you really left."

I turned back to her so I could see her face in the dim light of the small lamp that was on. "Are you sure?"

She took a deep, shaky breath. "Yes."

I pulled out the chair across from her at the table. I'd imagined this conversation a hundred times. A thousand. Because this wasn't something anyone wanted to hear.

Grace's father was an abusive asshole. For as long as I'd known her when we were younger, she'd been bound to his whims to prevent him from taking out more of his anger on her than he already had. Her mother was gone, and it was only him.

I'd begged her to run away with me, but she couldn't. Not while we were underage. Too many laws were in place for him to drag her back if we were caught, and it would be so much worse after that.

She hid the bruises he left on her, and as much as possible, I tried to give her a place of safety and peace. She snuck out and came over to my house at night. And my own father looked the other way. When we started sleeping together, we'd go outside and make love under the stars. Grace always told me that those were her happiest moments, and we made plans for after graduation.

Her father was a drunk and an addict with a lot of friends in the police department, and he possessed an uncanny ability to appear normal when it came to keeping his parental rights. But there were things neither of us had known.

"Harlan?"

I'd been sitting in silence for too long.

"Sorry. I'm trying to figure out the way to tell you this."

"It's that bad?"

The kettle sounded, and I jumped up to turn it off. I

didn't answer her as I made our tea. The only way to get it out was just to say it.

"Do you remember the last time I saw you? Before I left?"

Grace winced. "Of course I do."

It was one of my favorite memories. Right after graduation, and both of us finally adults. The night had been cool and beautiful, a light wind out of the mountains. We'd gotten lost in each other. That was the night we'd promised each other forever. In my soul, I'd known Grace was the only person for me. We had plans we were going to put into action soon.

Then everything changed.

I blew out a breath and set our cups on the table. "Your father followed you."

She blinked up at me. "What?"

"He figured out that you were sneaking out, and he followed you. The next day, he came to the shop after hours when no one was around." I'd worked at my father's garage when I was younger. "And he confronted me about it."

She pushed her cup away from her. "Maybe I should have chosen something stronger than tea."

I sure as hell wished I had. "Maybe."

Her lips pressed together. "What did he say?"

The words that Mason Cunningham had screamed at me that day were ones I would never forget. And ones I would never, ever repeat. "In short? He accused me of stealing you from him. And taking what was his by sleeping with you." I shook my head. "He was on something."

Her voice got small. "Dad was always on something. You're not telling me all he said."

"The actual words he used aren't important. He was pissed. He wanted me gone."

She shuddered again. Grace was well aware of what her father was capable of. When I'd found out he was dead, I'd nearly danced a jig, and I didn't care if that meant I was going to hell.

She studied me for a long minute. "Him confronting you about that wouldn't have been enough to make you leave."

"No." I walked back over to the counter. There was no way I could sit. I tried to force down the anger that still burned red-hot every time I remembered that day. First at Cunningham for the shit he'd said, but afterward at myself. "He threatened me. Told me that if I ever touched you again, he'd break every bone in my body and make sure I'd never walk again. That was, if he decided to let me live."

"Oh." She slowly wrapped her arms around herself. "Well, then it makes sense that you left."

"No." I crouched down beside her. "Hell no, Grace. I didn't give a shit what he did to me. He could've tried if he wanted to."

I would've taken anything Cunningham wanted to dish out. He could've put me in the fucking hospital and it wouldn't have mattered. I wasn't going to leave Grace.

"But you left."

Her voice was so small it broke my heart. She was always full of such fire, standing toe to toe with me about every little thing. To see her wrapped so protectively around herself now—shutting me out—shattered me into pieces.

I stood and walked back over to the counter. Adrenaline was buzzing through my system like I was about to go into battle. Fury at young Harlan for not handling the past better, even though he'd just been a scared teenage kid.

Hindsight was 20/20. If Cunningham had made his threats after I'd had my SEAL training, I would've known how to handle it. Would've known a dozen different ways to neutralize the menace.

Including taking Cunningham out completely.

After my training, I would've known that leaving was the worst thing I could do, even if it was with the best of intentions.

SEALs never left a man behind.

I'd left Grace behind, and I could never undo that. Could never forgive myself. All I could do was try to explain it to her now. Pray it would somehow be enough.

"When threatening me didn't work, he threatened you."

She stared at her tea. "Not exactly a surprise. He did that all the time."

"Not like this. He told me that if you were going to be with anyone, he would be the one to choose. And that he'd gotten plenty of offers for you."

"*What?*" Blood drained from her face as her gaze jerked up to mine.

"Offers to trade you for enough drugs to last him for years. Enough drugs that he probably would have over-dosed and killed himself." I folded my hands into fists and held my body perfectly still. "He showed me the messages proving it—his buddies offering to take you off his hands on a temporary or permanent basis."

The details in those messages still burned like acid in my gut even today. I would never tell her the sick details of what Cunningham's friends had offered to do to her.

I wished I had the messages in front of me again right now. I would hunt down every single one of those bastards that were mentioned by name, nickname, or even initials. I would make sure they paid for the things they'd wanted to do to teenage Grace if her own father would trade her.

As her father, he should have been sickened by those messages. They sure as hell had sickened me.

I'd been too young and without any resources to stop them. All I could do was protect Gracie the best way I knew how.

"Harlan—"

"He told me that if I came near you again, he would do it. He would make sure he traded you to one of the men who would make you disappear so that I would never see you again. Because you were his, not mine, and he could do whatever he wanted with you."

I forced myself to keep eye contact with her. "I told him that I would call the police. I'd seen the names, and those people would be arrested within hours. That's when he showed me the message from a dirty cop who wanted you. Police weren't an option."

Her green eyes were huge as she stared at me wordlessly.

I would give half my life if I could go back as the man I was now and handle this. Mason Cunningham would not have left that building alive. Even if it had cost me my own life.

Or, Jesus, if I could just go back and whisper one sentence to my younger self. To tell myself to take Grace and run. To literally go get her right that minute and get the fuck away.

"I was eighteen," I continued. "So young and stupid. I believed him and thought my only option was to get away from you so he wouldn't make your life hell to get back at me. So I took off. Keeping you safe was all that mattered. Then—and now."

A tear rolled down her cheek. "I didn't know. I can't…"

I went over and crouched down by her again. "That is a shit ton to take in about your father. I'm sorry."

She grabbed my hand and clutched it to her. "No, I mean, I didn't know you were protecting me. I didn't understand at all. All the things I've said to you—"

I put a finger over her lips. "Are completely understandable. You thought you'd been abandoned." My chest was heavy as lead. "You *were* abandoned."

She turned toward me and grabbed both my wrists. "You were protecting me the best way you knew how."

For all the fucking good that had done either of us.

I shook my head. "I asked my father to watch out for you and begged my family to keep you safe any way they could. They wanted me to stay and find a different way, but I wasn't going to risk that. I called my uncle too, and asked him to find a way to help you because your father didn't know him. Even if you weren't taken, you weren't safe."

"Your uncle?"

I kept my eyes locked with hers. "Ethan."

"Oh. *Oh*."

She sat in silence for long minutes. She was putting things together. Ethan and Charles had been friends. They'd managed to get her away from her father, but I hadn't seen her marriage to Charles coming.

There was more to this story, but that would have to come later. What I'd shared so far was more than enough for her to process. If I were on the other side of this conversation, I didn't know how I'd react.

I sat back down beside her and pushed her tea gently toward her. I wasn't going to let her descend into a spiral if I could help it. "Why does Gleason want this place?"

Her eyes snapped to mine, and she blinked, coming back from whatever dark thoughts she'd been having about her father. "I'm not sure." She took a sip of her tea, eyes still a little unfocused. "We have a water easement. I'm assuming he wants to expand it and have easier access to the spring. Or because he's a misogynistic asshole who can't stand the thought of a woman running a ranch. Who knows?"

Montana had a long, rich history of ranchers going to war over water and an even longer history of misogynistic assholes, but Gleason's attack seemed extreme even by Montana's standards. Something else was at play, and I made a mental note to keep a sharp eye out when I checked the property in the morning.

That led me to another thought. I wanted Grace to be happy, and I wanted her to have a home, but running a ranch had never been her goal. When we'd been together, she'd dreamed of being an artist. I'd seen the untouched easel in her bedroom. What had happened to those dreams, and why was she holding on to Ruby Round so tightly?

If she wanted to be here, I would fight however I could to make sure she stayed here. But if it was out of some kind of guilt, maybe I could help her gently let it go. But that was a conversation for another night. She'd been through enough for right now.

"Either way, we're not going to let him get it if you don't want to let it go."

She nodded vaguely, staring into her cup. I sat in silence. She needed time to process whatever was going on in her mind.

"Why didn't you tell me?" she finally asked. "All this time, you let me think the worst of you."

"When I saw you again, you were married," I said gently. "You wanted nothing to do with me. Then Charles died suddenly and violently. The time never seemed right, and the story isn't the kind of thing that you show up, say hello, and spit out."

"I know. I…" She rubbed her temples as she trailed off. "You carried this alone all this time. I thought I was justified in how I treated you. Thought you'd done me so wrong, when you'd really saved my life."

Her guilt was the last thing I wanted. "I would do anything to protect you, Grace. Then or now. I just wish I'd been better at it back then."

We sat in silence, both of us lost in our own regrets.

"I should feel something about what my father did," she finally said. "Maybe cry. But it's all so much that I feel…nothing."

I nodded. "Your mind is protecting itself. That's okay, good even. Processing all of this is going to take time."

She stood with her arms still wrapped around her stomach. Her wedding ring—my ring—was still on her finger. I loved seeing it there, no matter that it didn't mean what I wanted it to. "Thank you for coming to my rescue. When we were kids and again tonight."

"Always, Grace." I'm not sure she understood the true extent of those words, but she didn't have to.

I would safeguard and shield this woman for the rest of my life. From near or far, whatever she would allow.

"I'm going to try to get more sleep." Her voice was still small as she stood. I wanted to do more.

"I'll be down here."

"I could make up the guest room for you," she offered.

"No thanks. I'd rather be right here." Between her and the door. To protect her from anything that might come to hurt her.

To protect her the way I should have protected her all those years ago.

"Okay. Thank you. Good night, Harlan."

"Good night, Gracie."

She paused for a moment but didn't correct me. I watched her disappear upstairs before settling into the now-familiar couch. But tonight, there was no more chance of sleep.

## Chapter 11

*Grace*

When I woke up, I felt more refreshed than I had in years. Decades.

When I'd asked Harlan to tell me what had happened, I had never dreamed the truth would be so sordid. I had always known my father was a piece of shit, so Harlan's words weren't a surprise, but that didn't make them any less shocking. It would take me a long time to process and accept what I'd learned.

All this time, I'd been furious with Harlan. Livid that he'd changed his mind and disappeared because he didn't love me. Or he was afraid of the commitment we'd made to each other.

Mostly, I'd just plain been hurting and it was his fault, so I didn't stop to think about why. Every day, I'd passed places Harlan and I had been. His father's shop. Our high school. Hidden spots where we'd made love. The memories had been too much, so when an opportunity arose to move away and work on a ranch, I'd jumped at it, hoping a fresh start would help me heal. It didn't.

My father had come after me the way I knew he would, but there was no way in hell I was going back with him, so I did the only thing I could to stay out of his clutches—I married Charles.

I stared at the ceiling. There were so many threads to our story, I didn't know if I could untangle them all. Especially the one winding itself around me hard and fast: the sense of loss. Loss of the life Harlan and I could have built. The happiness we would have shared. The children we might have created. All lost because of my father.

If I'd known, would I have done something? Would I have run away with Harlan? Yes, we were young and it would have been difficult, but the rewards vastly outweighed the risks. The gaping maw of so much lost time, so much lost love, crushed me as if an elephant were sitting on my chest.

Rehashing the should-haves and could-haves and would-haves over and over again was only going to drive me crazy, so I got up. I'd spent too much time and energy trying to find the documents I needed, getting married, and going to court that I'd entirely ignored the ranch's administrative needs. Not that I loved doing it, but it came with the territory and had to be done.

I dressed quickly and headed downstairs. Harlan wasn't there, but he'd made a pot of coffee and set out a mug for me. The little things he did now had a different connotation. Telling me why he'd left had changed everything.

His truck was still out front, so I knew that he hadn't gone back to Resting Warrior. He was somewhere on the property, probably checking it over the way he'd told me he would. I felt a certain comfort at that—knowing he had my back, no matter what.

Cradling my coffee, I went into the office to spend some time wading through the paperwork that had built up.

Before Charles had died, the ranch had done well enough to get by but not much more. He'd made it clear the financial ins and outs of Ruby Round were not my concern. I'd done other things to help out on the ranch: cooking, cleaning, gardening, but he'd never let me get involved with the money. I didn't think it was because he didn't trust me. It was just something he viewed as his job.

The man's job.

But now, that attitude was biting me in the ass because I had no idea what to do. I was learning as I went, but the ranch was taking on water faster than I was able to bail it out. In the end, it might not matter if I could find the documents to prove Ruby Round was mine because I wouldn't be able to afford to keep it.

But I would be damned if I sold it to Wayne Gleason. Charles still had enough friends in the area; I could find someone to take the ranch off my hands.

With my coffee finished and the most urgent bills paid, I went out to help Dana and Rachel, the two ranch hands who helped me with the animals in the mornings and early afternoons. They were almost finished with the chores and waved me off when I tried to help.

As I was walking out of the barn, Harlan rode up on Big Red, our oldest stallion. The man was made to ride a horse. Just looking at him, I saw the power in his body and the bond he had formed with my favorite chestnut stallion. They made such a striking sight, I couldn't look away.

After last night, a million and one things swirled around inside my head. Harlan's revelation had changed my whole perspective on our past, but I still didn't know how to act around him. Hearing the truth hadn't fully erased my guilt over Charles or the years of anger toward Harlan's apparent desertion that I had allowed to fester. But if he hadn't done what he did, would I have lived to feel those things?

Wait. Had I just thought of Harlan as my husband?

A few days ago, this was all fake. But suddenly, there was more between us than saving a piece of property. So much more. Would we come out the other side of this healed? Or would it all backfire, leaving us irrevocably broken?

Harlan dismounted, loosened Big Red's cinch, and walked the last few feet toward me. "Morning," he said.

"Afternoon," I replied.

He pushed his hat back farther and wiped the sweat from his brow. "I stand corrected."

"Does everything look okay?"

He jerked his head toward the barn, and I followed him and Big Red inside. "Yeah. Everything looks good, and I didn't see any damage." Harlan handed Big Red off to Dana. "There are signs of some kind of disturbance, but whoever was out there did a good job hiding it, so I can't draw any solid conclusions."

I stared at the ground, kicking at the dirt.

"Look at me, Grace."

A week ago, I would have told him to go to hell. Again. But today, I did as he asked.

"I know who you think it was, and the second I can prove it was Gleason, you'll be the first to know."

"Yeah." My voice stuck in my throat. I wanted it to be Wayne because it seemed the easiest. But maybe my mind was too clouded. Maybe I was jumping to conclusions and it hadn't been him at all.

The elephant that had threatened to crush me earlier danced between us. We had things to discuss, but not in front of my employees. They were discreet and I trusted them, but all of a sudden, I felt vulnerable. Fragile. And I didn't want them to see me like that. I turned and headed back to the house.

Harlan's footsteps crunched in the dirt behind me. He caught up to me on the back porch. "Grace."

I stopped but didn't turn. I didn't want to see the look I knew would be on his face. Completely understanding and full of what I had refused to admit was longing and love. There was no way to unsee it now, and I wasn't sure if I was ready.

"Are you okay?"

"Yes," I said. "No. I honestly don't know."

He huffed a soft laugh that held no humor. "Yeah, that seems about right."

"I haven't processed all of it. It's going to take time."

"I know," he said softly. "But are you going to look at me in the meantime?"

I covered my face with my hands. "I just looked at you in the barn."

He took a step closer; I felt his heat behind me. "You know that's not what I meant."

Finally, I turned to him. He was so close, I almost bumped into him.

"Grace, I know you already know this. We've been tiptoeing around it long enough. Getting married helped you. And if that had been the only reason, I still would have done it. But it's more than that for me."

I dared to look up at him, and I saw exactly what I'd expected. The blistering heat and intensity that were always there. The blistering heat and intensity that I'd managed to ignore when I'd thought he'd abandoned me and ripped out my heart on purpose. The blistering heat and intensity that were so close and so real that a growing part of me wanted to drown in it.

But I still wasn't ready. "I don't know if I can give you more."

The faintest smile crossed his face. "I know. But that doesn't mean I don't want to make love with you again." Tension sizzled in the few inches between us. "I've waited for you for a long time. I can wait as long as you need me to."

Harlan took a step back, breaking that magnetic force pulling us together and starting to walk around the house. Away. I couldn't let him go yet.

"Why didn't you come back?"

He stopped.

"You walked away to save me. Left everything. But if you've been waiting for me all this time, why didn't you come back?"

When he turned to look at me, his expression was broken and thunderous. "I did come back."

"What?" The words hit me in the chest. "When?"

"A few years after I'd left. I'd gotten through BUD/S and was active when I got word my father was sick. I was on a mission and didn't get the message soon enough. When I got home, he was already gone."

"Harlan—"

He stalked toward me now, the graceful and lethal warrior those years had made him on full display. "So I took care of things. And when I looked for you…" He paused. "You were already married."

Little cracks formed in my heart. He'd been here. He'd known. And he hadn't told me. "You didn't think I'd want to see you?"

"Of course I did." He stepped into my space, closer than he'd been before. I couldn't ignore his closeness now.

The need to touch him was nearly overwhelming. "But I couldn't."

"Why?"

Harlan shook his head. "It would have done nothing but hurt you more."

"I—"

"You were safe," he said. "And you were happy enough. Your father was still alive. It was better for you to hate me than to see me and know that we still couldn't be together." Harlan's voice dropped to nearly a whisper. "I didn't want to break your heart any more than I already had. My bereavement leave was over, and I had to get back to my team."

The sadness in his eyes told me that wasn't the whole story, but I shook my head. "So you let me go on hating you? I might have understood, Harlan. I know now that you did it to protect me, but you didn't let me choose. And I don't know if thinking the worst of you for so long was better than being broken."

"Yeah." He started to reach for me but pulled back. "I know. If I could do it over again, I don't think I'd make the same choice. It's not an excuse, but I knew I was already out of my mind with grief and loss. And the thought of hurting you again—" He looked away. "I couldn't do it."

Silence hung between us, thick and alive. There was so much to untangle, it was overwhelming.

He turned back to me and leaned in close. "But I won't stop trying to get back what we lost."

We came together, sinking into each other as if it was the only way we could be. His lips brushed mine, but he didn't kiss me. We were caught in limbo, and he was strong enough to let me be the one to make the choice.

I wanted it. Him. And everything that came with him. He was the person I'd always wanted him to be and the person that I'd grieved. I was terrified to fall into him again, but the feelings between us were too powerful to ignore.

"Thank you," I whispered. "For checking everything."

"Of course."

I let out a shaky breath when he pulled away. Hell, my whole body shook.

"You can call me any time, Grace."

I knew full well he meant it. And not only if it was something to do with the ranch or Wayne Gleason. He would take my call for any reason.

Harlan walked around the house and out of sight, and as soon as he disappeared, it hit me—I could rely on Harlan Young.

## Chapter 12

*Grace*

There was something deeply therapeutic about working with dough. Whenever I helped Lena with her orders, I always felt better after.

Right now, dividing up dough into pieces and rolling them into balls was incredibly soothing. I was up to my elbows in flour, sitting at one of the giant tables in the kitchen across from Evelyn, while Lena flitted around the kitchen and occasionally ran out to serve customers.

"How are things going?" I asked Evelyn.

She blushed and looked down at the cookie she was decorating. "Good. We're figuring things out as we go and not putting too much pressure on anything. It hasn't been that long."

With everything going on at my ranch, I hadn't been around much and had only seen Lucas and Evelyn in passing.

"You're good for him," I told her. "I'm shocked that he hasn't proposed to you yet."

Evelyn's head stayed down over the cookies as if she was avoiding looking at me. "Like I said, we're taking our time."

"But it will happen," Lena said, sweeping in from the front. "Sooner or later. I've never seen a man so smitten with someone." She paused after pulling another tray of cookies out of the oven. "Well, that's not true. Harlan is absolutely smitten with you."

I said nothing.

"How's married life?" Evelyn asked.

I placed the last two balls on a tray and passed it to Lena. "About the same as the first time around."

"Aw, come on," Lena whined. "Give us some juicy details."

I grabbed another piece of dough and started shaping it into a ball. Somehow, this time, it wasn't as soothing as before. "There are no juicy details. Harlan only married me to save Ruby Round. There's nothing more to it."

Evelyn rolled her eyes. "Give us a little more credit than that. Even not knowing the whole story, I think Lena and I can figure out the man didn't *only* marry you to save Ruby Round."

"It's complicated." I smashed the ball I'd been working on with enough violence for both women to turn and look at me.

"Are you okay?" Lena asked. "I know we're giving you a hard time, but for real?"

I squished the ball of dough even harder. "There's so much I didn't know about Harlan's and my history. I've spent the past ten years so hurt and mad that I couldn't breathe when I thought of him. And then I found that I didn't know the whole story at all. But it's hard to change your thinking when it's been a part of you for so long. I'm struggling."

All the words came out in a rush, leaving my chest hollow.

Lena eased the ruined dough out of my hand. "Our teasing you about it probably doesn't help."

I knocked her hip with mine. "No. But then again, me teasing you about Jude probably doesn't help either."

Lena's face turned the fiery red it always did when anyone mentioned Jude's name. "I don't know what you're talking about."

"He drove you home the night we got drunk. How did that go?" God bless Evelyn for changing the subject and getting it off me.

"It was fine."

I raised an eyebrow. "Fine?"

"Yes," Lena said stiffly. "It was fine. I was so drunk, I almost fell asleep on the way home. And when I got out of the car, I pretty much fell on my face. Exactly the humiliation I needed. No need to tease me anymore about it."

"Why not?"

The door chimed, and she disappeared to take care of the customer. But when Lena stepped back into the kitchen seconds later, she was pale. "Grace, it's for you."

"Who?"

She shook her head.

I quickly washed the flour off my hands and went to the front. My stomach dropped. Charlie, fully dressed in his police uniform, stood there. This couldn't be good. "Charlie?"

He sighed and looked resigned. "I got a call about an incident out at the ranch. You need to come with me. I already have other officers en route."

"Who made the call?"

I could tell he didn't want to tell me, and he wasn't exactly happy about it. "Wayne Gleason."

"Shit." I cursed under my breath. "Let me grab my stuff. I'll follow you." Charlie nodded. "I'm sorry, I have to go," I said as I slid into the kitchen. "Something happened at the ranch."

"Do you need help?" Evelyn asked.

"I don't think so, but I'll call you."

I wished I didn't have to leave in the middle of our conversation, but this was my life right now. Following Charlie's cruiser out of town, I realized this was what my life was going to be as long as the situation with Wayne remained unresolved. Wayne wanted Ruby Round, and he was going to do whatever he could to disrupt my life as often as possible. From disturbing my sleep and messing with my cattle to whatever I was about to walk into.

It wasn't going to stop. He wasn't going to stop.

Deep inside, I knew that now that he'd set his sights on what he wanted, he wouldn't rest until he forced me to give in. The stubborn part of me wanted to believe I could stand up to whatever he threw at me. But I also knew that I was tired.

As Charlie had said, a police car was already in the driveway when we pulled up.

Dread pooled in my stomach as we walked around the house and back into the fields. A cluster of people gathered in the distance, and a horse was lying on the ground. That much, I could see.

My stomach dropped further. Was it one of mine? It didn't matter because I didn't want any animal injured on my property. Adrenaline spiked in my veins, and I ran the rest of the way. The closer I got to them, the more I could see.

Wayne stood next to the horse, looking thunderous. It

wasn't mine. I saw Cori's turquoise-streaked blond hair as she knelt over the horse. She must have already been out in this direction for her to beat us here from town.

Charlie's deputy stood there too.

I was out of breath by the time I reached them. "What happened?"

The horse seemed calm enough where it was on the ground, but Cori looked furious. The firm line she'd pressed her lips into told me she was struggling against the urge to lash out at my neighbor.

"Your property nearly killed my horse and me," Wayne said. "That's what happened."

"That seems like a bit of a stretch." Charlie's voice came from behind me. "Why don't you give us a few more details and explain why you called and asked for me to come out here personally."

Charlie hadn't mentioned that earlier, but I appreciated him trying to give me a heads-up now.

Wayne sneered at me, and anger rose in my chest. He spread his arms wide and gestured around. "Look at the ground around here. Completely neglected and full of holes. It's an accident waiting to happen. My horse slipped in one of the holes. Fucked up his leg and threw me. I'm lucky I didn't hit my head on one of those rocks." He pointed to a smattering of stones that hadn't been there earlier.

We stood near the spring that was on the property. It was outside the bounds of the fields that we used for cattle, so it stayed pure. And while we didn't closely maintain it, it hadn't looked like this the last time I'd seen it. I noticed more holes in the ground than before, and those rocks scattered around were clearly not the same kind of rock visible under the spring.

I looked to my right, toward his property, and my heart

skipped a beat. The fence between our properties was down. Mangled. The ground looked as if someone had taken a pickax to it.

Not something that Harlan would have missed when he rode the property yesterday. Which meant that first night had been a test. Nothing had really happened, so he'd come back *again* and sabotaged the fence. Dug holes and scattered rocks. But I didn't have proof. Or a reason why.

"That doesn't explain why you were trespassing," I said evenly. My body was tight from holding my ground the way it had been at the courthouse. I refused to let this man intimidate me.

Anger sparked in his eyes. "It's not trespassing when you have an easement."

"You have an easement for water from the spring. That doesn't entitle you to come on to my land whenever you please."

"It does when you're not taking care of it." His voice was low and deadly, then he shifted his gaze to Charlie. "See the fence? Something has clearly been over here, maybe messing with the spring. Who knows? And she hasn't fixed it. Now I have an animal that might be lame."

I looked down at Cori. "How is he?"

"He might be all right," she said. "I'd like to do X-rays on the leg to be sure there are no hairline fractures."

"Right," Wayne said. "You'll take him in and charge me out the ass for X-rays, only to tell me that it's fine or it's not fine. I'll be able to tell that in a couple of days anyway."

Her face darkened. "If it is broken, that will cause him unnecessary pain."

"I want *Mrs. Townsend*—or is it Mrs. Young now?—to

be charged with negligent endangerment for not taking care of her property." He ignored Cori entirely.

I crossed my arms and stared him down. "Funny, because my husband surveyed the entire property yesterday, and he didn't find any broken fences."

Charlie looked at me with a raised eyebrow. By now, I was sure news of my marriage to Harlan had made the rounds.

I knew Charlie would take Harlan's word that he hadn't seen anything wrong, and also, I knew Harlan was thorough enough that he wouldn't have missed something like this.

There was a long, full silence. The horse whiskered quietly, and Cori murmured comforting words to it.

"I intend to press charges, Chief," Wayne said.

Charlie cleared his throat. "That's not the way this works, Mr. Gleason. Grace is right. You're on her land. A water rights easement doesn't give you the right to be here. If you want to try a civil liability suit, that's your business. But I'm thinking that won't go well for you either."

"Because of her negligence, I was almost injured, and now I'm going to have fucking *vet* bills."

I barely recognized my voice when I spoke. "I'm not negligent, Wayne. The fence will be fixed by this evening. And if you ever see anything wrong with my property while you're busy continually monitoring it, feel free to come to me directly instead of calling the police. But make sure you do it from your side of the property line."

"I'll be sure to do that. And you'll be hearing from my lawyer."

"I'm sure I will."

He looked down at Cori. "Get the horse up."

A shiver of rage went through the petite vet. But Charlie, the deputy, and I helped her get the horse on its feet while Wayne did nothing but watch. Thankfully, the horse didn't seem as if it was in too much pain, and it walked fine. Otherwise, I didn't think Cori would have been able to contain herself.

Wayne tipped his hat at us like he was the consummate gentleman and led the horse away.

Cori waited until he was out of earshot before she turned, vibrating with rage. "That was a perfectly preventable injury. All he had to do was be careful. And that could easily be a fracture."

"Yeah." I nodded. "I'm sorry."

"I—" Her shoulders drooped, and she sighed. "Any of your animals need anything before I head home?"

I placed a hand on her shoulder. "No. We're all good here. I'll call you if we need anything, though."

"Okay."

"If you have time," I said. "I left Lena in the middle of making an absolutely huge number of cookies. She could use the extra hands."

She gave me a wan smile. "Maybe I'll stop by. Thanks."

I didn't like watching her walk away. Cori had a reputation for being a bit of an oddball, but she was sweet and well-liked around town. She had a soft heart that made her good at her job, and that meant things like this could hurt. I hoped she would stop by Deja Brew. Lena could make anyone feel better.

"You can take off, Edgar," Charlie said to the deputy. "I can take it from here."

We waited until he was gone too before Charlie spoke again. "You all right, Grace?"

All I could do was shrug. "As good as I can be, I suppose. I don't have a lot of options right now."

"Yeah." His voice was quiet. "I'm sorry about this. If

there's anything I can do to help, let me know. Charles would have wanted me to look after you."

"Thanks." I felt a squirming sensation in my belly. It was a nice sentiment, but it also felt strange now.

Something moved behind Charlie. Harlan strode across the field toward us. His face was grim and determined as he surveyed the damaged fence.

He stopped a few feet away. "Charlie."

"Harlan."

"Everything okay?" He looked at me. The tension in his body was visible, but he was doing his best to keep it at bay.

I gave him a smile to make it seem like no big deal, but it didn't work. "Well, I've got a broken fence and a whole bunch of rocks that need to be hauled away now."

"I'll take care of the fence."

Charlie turned to me. "I'd like to help with that, if you're all right with it."

"In your uniform?"

"I've done worse," he said with a chuckle.

Nodding, I started toward the barn. "I'll work on the rocks."

I grabbed the wheelbarrow and picked up the offending rocks Wayne had clearly scattered, while Harlan and Charlie worked on repairing the fence. I dumped the rocks in a pile next to the barn, just in case there were fingerprints or fibers or anything on them. It was a long shot, but I still hoped.

I watched Harlan and Charlie work on the fence from a distance, trying not to hover. But from my spot, I saw what they didn't.

Wayne was still there and still watching. The horse was gone, but he stood near a tree, observing the process of rebuilding the fence. Somehow, I doubted seeing the police chief help fix my fence would do anything to endear me to him.

Who was I kidding? There wasn't anything that would endear me to that man.

I watched until Harlan and Charlie finished, and then I stepped inside the house while Harlan walked Charlie back to his patrol car.

Once Charlie was gone, I had no doubt Harlan would head straight back to me to see if I was okay.

And for the first time in years, that thought was pure, welcome relief.

## Chapter 13

*Harlan*

As soon as Charlie's cruiser disappeared around the bend, I damn near ran inside to find Grace. Anger sizzled low in my veins. I'd had enough of this Gleason bastard.

He'd come back last night. While Grace had been alone in the house. He'd come back and fucked with her property. He could have chosen to mess with the house, and I wouldn't have been there to protect her. I didn't know what he wanted or how far he would go, but the idea that he could get anywhere near her—had already gotten near her—drove me insane.

Grace was waiting for me in the kitchen. I went straight to her and enfolded her in my arms. Instead of pulling away, she relaxed. Barely. A tiny fraction, but it was there.

"It wasn't like that yesterday," I said.

She nodded into my shirt. "I know. I told him that to

his face. And Charlie is smart enough to know that you wouldn't lie. How did you know about it?"

"Lena called me." I held her tighter, grateful to be so close to her. She didn't realize the magnitude of what I felt for her. Not yet, at least. "I should have been here."

Grace let out a humorless laugh. "Don't go there. It was probably in the middle of the night. You wouldn't have known."

"Maybe I would have heard something."

"Maybe." Grace stiffened and pulled away. "He was watching you and Charlie fix the fence. He's probably not too happy about Charlie helping you."

"No, I'd imagine not."

She paced. "I hate this. I hate that he can keep doing things I can't prove and skulk off back to his property like nothing happened. And I *hate* feeling powerless, but I don't know what to do."

"I'm not entirely sure what we can do for concrete proof," I said, leaning against the counter. "But I know where to start."

"Where?"

"The basics. Cameras. We can head over and pick some up from Jude right now."

Grace wrapped her arms around herself, and it was all I could do not to reach out and hold her again. "That would be good. But I'll stay here."

"No."

"Harlan—"

I shook my head. "After that? I'm not leaving you here alone on the property." Holding up a hand, I stopped the protest I knew was coming. "I'm not saying that you can't handle yourself, but he's already pissed off at you. If he's watching, I don't want him to think it's a good idea to move fast."

Grace's shoulders drooped. I hated how defeated she looked. Whether she considered this marriage real or not, I did. She was my wife, and I wasn't going to let Gleason make her miserable anymore.

"You don't have to see anyone or answer any questions," I said. "You can stay in the truck. But let's go now. A storm is coming in, and it would be good to get the cameras up before it starts."

Finally, she nodded. I made quick work out of locking up and took her hand. She didn't fight. I walked her to the truck and helped her in. It felt like the most natural thing in the world.

Grace leaned her head back on the seat. "I should let him have it."

"Why would you say that?"

"Because Wayne Gleason is almost as stubborn as you. Cameras aren't going to stop him."

I smiled. "If he's stubborn, then we're evenly matched."

"It's not just that," she said with a sigh. "Ruby Round isn't doing well. I may have to sell it even if I can prove to the state that I own it."

Unease settled in my chest. Grace had no reason to tell me about the ranch's finances. It wasn't my business. But I didn't like that she had extra stress. She'd been through enough. "I'm sorry."

Out of the corner of my eye, I saw her shoulders lift in a shrug. "It is what it is. But it can be dealt with. It's not as if I have a stalker trying to kill me."

We pulled into Resting Warrior. "Is that what you're comparing this to? The piece of human garbage who came after Evelyn?"

She shook her head. "No one in their right mind thinks someone breaking my fence is on par with getting stalked, kidnapped, and tortured. I have it good by comparison."

I slammed on the brakes and threw the truck into park. "If you're comparing it like that, yeah. But you shouldn't."

"It's the truth."

"Gleason has violated your home, your property, and your peace of mind, and he's promised to do it until you give in. That is stalking. It's intimidation. It's trauma. Just because he's less likely to burn you with a red-hot ring and bury you alive doesn't mean that he's not impacting you."

"Yeah."

I saw in her eyes that she didn't believe it. "Do you want to come inside?"

She shook her head.

"Okay. I'll be right back."

The wind whipped around me as I jogged inside. The storm was coming in fast and would give Gleason the cover he needed to cause more trouble, and I didn't want to miss the chance to get proof.

Jude usually took care of security at Resting Warrior, but Grant sat at Jude's desk, viciously attacking his laptop the way I'd seen him attack an objective during a mission. Intense. Focused. I knew better than to interrupt whatever drama was unfolding on the seventeen-inch monitor that held his attention, so I pulled out my phone and punched in Jude's number. He answered on the first ring. Most of us did now in case of an emergency. "Harlan?"

"You have a stash of cameras I can raid, right?"

"What kind do you need?"

Grant looked up at me with interest. "Wireless and waterproof," I answered.

Jude laughed. "Is there any other kind? Locker three in the back. Anything for one of my brothers."

Brothers. That, we certainly were. I would fight and die

for my Resting Warrior brothers. When I didn't want to kill them myself. But wasn't that the way with biological brothers? Only siblings could truly get under your skin one minute and stand ready to help you battle your way out of trouble the next. It was the passion that deepened the bond. "Thanks."

Grant shut the file he'd been working on. "What's going on?"

I caught him up on some of the details of Gleason's antics. Today, especially. Grant's face was grim. "And how are you holding up with all of it?"

The surprise registered on my face before I managed to catch it. If Grant was asking me how I was, then I must not be covering things as well as I thought. But I brushed it aside. Grace was all that mattered right now. I could handle my shit later.

"I'm working through some stuff. I've talked to Rayne a few times. Nothing I can't handle."

Grant raised his right arm, the fingers in his famous "Hook 'em Horns" sign, then brought his left arm up to meet it while wiggling the fingers of his left hand. American Sign Language for bullshit.

I didn't much like being called out that way, but it was something only people who had gone through hell together could get away with. And I loved Grant all the more for it.

Not that I would ever blurt out those exact words. Brotherhood had rules.

"I want to catch this guy in the act. Grace feeling helpless isn't helping anything. Plus, if we catch him doing something as simple as purposely injuring another animal, that's something."

Grant's eyes narrowed. "An animal?"

Charlie had told me what Gleason had done while we fixed the fence. I had no tolerance for a man who would hurt a woman or an animal. One more example of how Gleason was a piece of shit. As if I'd needed more convincing.

"Was Cori there?" Grant asked. I looked at him for a moment, trying to decipher the look on his face. He caught me looking. "What? She's my next-door neighbor, that's all," he said quickly.

"Yeah," I said. "She was there. She wasn't happy about leaving the horse with Gleason. Grace told her to stop by Deja Brew so Lena could cheer her up, but I don't know if she went."

He stood. "I'll go see if she's okay."

I stared at him again, unable to keep the grin off my face.

"She has a boyfriend, Harlan. This is nothing more than neighborly kindness."

"Sure thing."

"Fuck off," he muttered, heading out the door. I went to the back of the lodge where we kept the tactical supplies locked up and got the cameras I needed. We didn't have nearly enough to cover Ruby Round as thoroughly as I wanted, but I could get a decent view of some critical points.

I turned up my jacket collar against the dropping temperatures. A quick glance at the mountains told me the storm was rolling in sooner than expected. I had to hustle if I was going to get the cameras installed before all hell broke loose.

I stashed the cameras in the toolbox in my truck bed and hopped into the driver's seat. Thank God I'd left the heater running full blast for Grace because the short walk from the lodge to the truck damn near froze the blood in my veins.

"Are cameras going to work in this?" she asked.

"Jude says they're made for this weather."

I wasn't sure she believed me until I heard her half whimper, "All right."

We made the short drive back to Ruby Round in silence. By the time we pulled into Grace's driveway, I had a firm plan in place for *Operation Catch Gleason Red-Handed.*

"Do you need help?"

I shook my head. "I'm all right. No need for you to get soaked too."

"Okay." Grace smiled, and my breath caught in my chest.

I cherished every smile she gifted me. And I would never take one for granted. It was my personal mission to restore the happiness her father had stolen from us.

"Grab the shotgun while I'm out there."

Her brows knit. "Really? Why?"

"I don't want to take any chances with you."

"But he knows you're here."

"Please—" I took a breath. "My gut says to be careful."

She studied me for a long moment. "All right."

I grabbed the cameras. "I'll be fast."

Fat, lazy raindrops splattered on the ground. Not enough to connect the dots yet, but enough to warn of the fury to come. I jogged around the house and out into the field.

## Chapter 14

*Grace*

The rain didn't seem to bother Harlan in the least as he made his way toward the back of the property. I'd set the shotgun on the kitchen table the way he'd asked. The Resting Warrior men had instincts that were completely unrivaled. When Harlan's gut said to be careful, I listened.

The rain was hard enough now that it was difficult to see Harlan. My nerves ratcheted up to a painful level. He was out there, cold and wet and possibly in danger, to keep me safe. Instinctively, I filled the kettle and set it to boil. It was still early for nightly tea, but I needed something to do with my hands. Besides, I wasn't going anywhere.

I jumped at a mighty crack like thunder. I nearly spilled my tea. And then it came again. And again. Holy shit, it wasn't thunder. Someone was pounding on the front door. Chills covered my skin, hair rising off the back of my neck as if I'd seen a ghost.

Harlan's gut had been right.

I knew who was at the door. There was only one person it could be. No one who knew me or Harlan would pound on the door like that. Hell, anyone who knew us would probably walk right in.

With shotgun in hand, I walked to the door and looked through the peephole. Sure enough, Wayne leaned on the doorframe with one hand and stared directly at the peephole as if he knew I was already there.

Terror skittered down my spine.

He banged on the door again. There wasn't time to get Harlan, so I had to handle this myself. Wayne needed to know I was dangerous on my own.

"What do you want, Wayne?" I yelled through the door.

"I want to talk."

I swallowed. "I can hear you perfectly fine."

In the same way Harlan had known I would need the shotgun, I knew I shouldn't open the door. Wayne was at least twice my size. I wasn't helpless, but it wouldn't be a fair fight.

More chills raced down my spine as Wayne's low laugh filtered through the air. "You want to hide behind a piece of wood? That's fine. We'll be face-to-face soon enough."

I kept my breath steady and soft. Let him say what he'd come to say so he could leave.

"You've been making my life difficult, Grace Townsend. It's time for that to stop."

"I could say the same of you."

"You don't know what the fuck you're doing, girl." His voice was nearly a growl. "Your husband—or should I say, your first husband—always meant to sell this ranch to me. Did you know that?"

Steel encircled my spine, and strength I didn't know I had surfaced. "The hell he did, Wayne. Ruby Round was

Charles's pride and joy. He would never sell it to someone like you. And I'm not going to give it up. You need to get used to that idea."

"You can try to hold on to it as hard as you want, Grace. But I've got plans on plans on plans, and your little ranch is at the center of all of them. Do you really think you can outlast me? When you're here all alone?"

"She's not alone."

I jumped at the sound but soothed as Harlan laid his hand on my shoulder. He was soaked through and dripping on the floor. And it was all I could do to keep my eyes from roaming all over him and taking in the way the rain had plastered his clothes to his skin and revealed all of his delicious muscles. I wanted to taste each and every one of them. And I wanted Wayne to be far away so I could have a very different conversation with Harlan. One that I was suddenly very ready for.

Harlan strode to me and opened the door. Wayne was taller and heavier than Harlan, but I knew my husband could take down Wayne in a second. The relief that knowledge brought was palpable. The feeling solidified when Harlan reached over and placed his hand on the small of my back. I was still holding the shotgun, so he couldn't hold my hand.

"Right," Wayne sneered. His eyes traveled from Harlan's rain-slicked hair to his soggy boots. Was he gauging his chances in a fight? "The new husband. Sooner or later, there won't be anything or anyone standing in front of you, Grace."

"Are you threatening my wife?" Harlan asked. His voice was so quiet I barely heard it over the rain. But the lethal steel in it wasn't up for debate.

Wayne had to be able to feel Harlan's fury, but he didn't back down. He straightened and made himself bigger. "This was me giving you a chance." He stared straight at me, ignoring Harlan completely. "An easy way out. Sell me the ranch by the end of the week."

"Or what?"

His smile made my stomach swim. "Or I'll take it from you. Piece by piece, if I have to. Until you have nothing left."

He turned and stalked off the porch to his truck. Neither of us moved until he was gone, standing as a united front until he was completely out of sight.

Then Harlan started moving. He shut the door and locked it. "I need to get a better lock for this door. Maybe a bar. For the back, too. We can do it for you." He meant the Resting Warrior crew. "The cameras are up. All I have to do is connect them to my laptop."

I put the shotgun back in the closet on its rack then watched as Harlan strode through the room, checking the windows and the back door. "I don't think he'll make the mistake of coming back, though. At least not right away."

I couldn't look away from Harlan. It was as if my eyes were glued to his powerful body and the confident way he moved.

Desire coiled inside me like a living, breathing thing. I couldn't ignore the fact that everything had changed between us. He had given up everything for me. *Everything.* And standing here in the doorway with him had felt easy and right.

I didn't want to be alone.

Not right now. This house was so brutally empty all the time. It was too much. So many emotions swirled in me, I couldn't process them all. But I knew one thing: I was done pushing Harlan away.

I wanted him.

No matter how much I pretended I didn't. No matter

what had happened in either of our pasts. No matter that this marriage wasn't supposed to be real. I wanted him, and I was done waiting.

In the time it took for the thoughts to run through my head, Harlan had stopped moving. He stared at me because I'd frozen in the middle of the room.

"Grace?"

No more hesitation. I didn't question myself when I crossed the space and jumped into him. I knew he would catch me.

Surprise splashed across his face as I closed in to kiss him. After the shock wore off, he returned my kiss. This kiss was different from any of the other kisses we'd had. Those kisses had been passionate, but they'd been desperate, and deep down, we'd known they wouldn't go anywhere.

But this kiss would go everywhere.

Harlan's hands held me easily. I was so taken with his lips I barely registered that we were moving. Climbing the stairs. All the time we'd spent searching this house, Harlan knew exactly where he was going.

The water from his clothes and skin soaked into mine, but I didn't care. It wouldn't matter if he carried me out into the rain right now and laid me down in the grass. This had been coming for far too long.

We tumbled onto my bed together, and Harlan broke away from my lips, staring down at me. "Are you sure?"

"Yes."

He searched my face as if he couldn't believe this was happening. "Is this because of Gleason?"

I shook my head. "No. Yes. But not in the way you think."

I ran my hands up his shirt. I caressed his face. I combed my fingers through his hair. I let myself *look* at him. Now that those clouds were gone, I could absorb the details I'd been ignoring for so long.

Warm brown eyes that reminded me of chocolate and brownies and all the sweet, gooey things that gave me comfort. Slightly crooked nose—that was something new. Probably a story there I hadn't heard. Yet. I wanted to hear all the stories now.

Harlan leaned his forehead against mine, water dripping from his hair onto my skin. "You know how much I want this. *You*. But only if you're sure. Because there is no going back for me," he said quietly. "You've always been everything. And I won't pretend this never happened."

I pushed down the tears of joy that threatened to hijack this perfect moment. "I can't go back either. I don't want to go back."

"Thank God." The words were a prayer before his lips claimed mine again. His kisses had always left me breathless, but I hadn't realized how much Harlan had been holding back.

He didn't hesitate. He pulled back enough to yank the wet shirt over his head and toss it aside.

I'd seen him from a distance, but up close, his adult body was overwhelming. His skin glistened in the dim light, shadows lining the cut of his muscles and his hardness. Everything about him was beautiful, and everything about him was about to become mine.

"You don't know how long I've been wanting this and trying not to take it," he said. "God, I've missed you."

Harlan dropped his mouth directly to my skin, leaving a trail of fiery heat down my jaw and throat to the edge of my shirt.

My gasp stopped him short, and he moved, fitting himself over me so I could feel how hard he was through his jeans. He moved his lips at my ear, his voice low and raw. But there was no mistaking the power there. The same intensity he'd shown Wayne, but a different side of that strength. Unyielding and dominant.

"This won't take long," he breathed. "I think we both need it hard and fast. And when that's finished, I am going to *worship* you. Explore you until I relearn every piece of you that I've missed. And then I'll do it all over again."

An uncontrollable shudder ran through me, followed by heat. The kind of heat I hadn't let myself feel in years. More years than he could know about. "Yes."

"Good."

He kissed me, only breaking the connection when we needed to get rid of inconvenient clothes. For a brief moment, I lamented not having chosen prettier underwear this morning, but one look at the way his eyes darkened as they ran over my body put that thought to rest. He simply didn't care about my underwear. At this point, it was merely an obstacle, and my handsome SEAL was on a mission.

He might have said we'd go fast, but he took his time removing my bra and pressed kisses on each new piece of skin he exposed.

It was a little like déjà vu. The first time we'd done this, he had been the same. Absolutely enamored, and I had never felt more adored. I felt the same way now.

Harlan backed off the bed. I already missed his heat, his delicious weight. He stripped off his jeans and underwear then retrieved his wallet from his pants. But I barely noticed because I couldn't take my eyes off him.

He was bigger now in every conceivable way. He was nothing short of magnificent. Harlan could have been a model for any art class in the country. Museums could cast him as a mold for statues. Why had I resisted this for so long?

Another shiver of heat ran through me. "Wow."

He smirked at me. "That better be a good wow, because let me tell you, that feeds a man's ego like nothing else."

"Definitely a good wow."

The smirk deepened as he rolled on the condom from his wallet.

"You've been carrying condoms around?"

"Always be prepared, right?"

I raised an eyebrow. "Prepared for who?"

He came to me slowly, bearing me back onto the bed and unbuttoning my jeans without looking away. "Only for you," he said quietly.

"So you've been hoping that I'd fall prey to your charms and you needed to have a condom ready so you could ravish me?"

"Exactly." He laughed as he pulled my pants down my legs. "Or I could tell you all the ways condoms have saved my ass in the past—and I'm not talking about sex. But I think I'll save those stories for later."

I wiggled the panties off my hips and tossed them aside. Harlan went entirely still. "Definitely later."

We came together like an explosion. A tangle of limbs and mouths and tongues. His skin was hot on mine, and everything that we'd been holding back disappeared. He was right. We needed hard and fast to get it out of our system.

In one breath, he parted my legs. He leaned his forehead against mine again, and we shared a breath, both groaning as he pressed in. "Oh…"

He kissed the moan away, easing his way into my body. It was a mix of pleasure and pain and something so much deeper I couldn't fathom all of it. "Damn, Grace," Harlan murmured. "You're so tight."

I could feel every inch of him. So full I could barely breathe. It seemed like he went on forever, and I had another moment of déjà vu—those breathless moments when we had been together our first time. The irreversible realization that we would never be the same. That I would never be the same.

I wrapped my arms around his shoulders and held on, waiting until he was seated in me so deep that it felt like he was a part of me. We were on the brink. The burning fuse on the stick of dynamite.

My body eased, accepting him, and suddenly, reality faded away, taking us with it. We moved together, unleashed.

A flood of pleasure crashed over on me like a wave. We were a blend of paradoxes. So familiar and so new. Too full and not full enough. Too hard and not hard enough. Harlan drove himself into me again and again, and all I could do was hold on to him and *feel*. And I was feeling everything. Every delicious inch of friction that drove me higher and faster and into a golden cloud.

Molten heat spiraled from a point so deep in me I was sure he would be the only man who ever reached it. All of this was because of him. And only him. The wave caught up with itself too quickly, pushing me over into a free fall of pleasure that blinded me. I shook and pulled and arched as if riding a wild stallion.

More. I wanted more of this. If I'd known—

No. The connection between us was now. The power that drove all this ecstasy was because of what we'd gone through. If we'd done it sooner, it wouldn't have been the same.

Harlan's breath was hot on my neck between desperate kisses and whispered groans. The rhythm he needed faltered. Slowed. He thrust harder. Every deliberate movement made us shake. Aftershocks and sparks ran along my nerves, teasing me while he found his own release. His hips pressed into mine and pinned me as his climax overtook him with a groan.

For a while, there was only the sound of the rain and our heartbeats. Harlan was still deep inside me, and I didn't want him to move. After so long, the idea of being anything other than connected was unacceptable.

"Grace," he whispered. Nothing more than my name.

He moved, and I made a sound in protest that brought a smile to his face. "I'm not going anywhere. But I did make a promise."

In the heat of the moment, I barely remembered it. He said that he was going to worship me. And I was about to find out what he meant.

He traced my jaw with his lips, brushing down the line of my throat and lower. Across my chest and down, until his mouth ghosted over my nipple. They were already hard, but the gentle hint of his breath made them harder than the stone of the mountains around us.

I arched into him as his tongue made first contact. Gentle teasing and circling, there wasn't any destination in the way he touched me. This was his exploration. I already knew that I would be wrecked by the end of it.

Harlan closed his lips over me, swirling his tongue around until I squirmed underneath him. I had nowhere to go and no desire to go there. This was the only place I wanted to be.

I gasped as his teeth grazed my skin and soared as his low laugh vibrated along my flesh. Slowly, he wove the fingers of our hands together and pinned mine to the bed. "This is amazing."

All I could do was moan.

He barely took a breath before moving to my other

nipple and doing it all over again. This time, I swore he did it slower. "Harlan." His name was a whine and a prayer and a request all in one.

"Yes?" Slow, lazy circles with his tongue.

"I don't know."

"Mmm."

I pressed my thighs together when he finished with me, but he wasn't really finished at all. He slid his mouth all the way down my body without it leaving my skin. Fingers traced my ribs, and he memorized inches of me that I'd forgotten existed.

Harlan eased my legs apart, and a furious blush rose across my face and neck. He wanted to see me—really see me—but I couldn't. "If you do that, I might die."

One side of that infernal mouth rose in a sinister grin. "Accurate. The French do call orgasms *la petite mort*, the little death."

This was something we'd never done before. The sex had always been good, but looking back, it had also been a little awkward and bumbling. A mess of fingers and hands and things passing too quickly. "I—"

"I don't think you understand how long I've wanted to taste you, Grace. I want to make you come on my tongue. Every time you see my lips, I want you to think about how loud I've made you scream with them."

The blush grew hotter, and I didn't have a chance to say anything. Harlan's mouth was on me, and I dissolved into nothing.

His lips covered me, and his tongue moved back and forth. He began with the same swirling motion that he'd used on my nipples, then transitioned into curling strokes up underneath the swollen bundle of nerves. This was ecstasy.

Harlan scraped his teeth across my skin again, and I

arched off the bed so far, I felt like a rainbow. Then I melted back into the mattress as the intense pleasure morphed into luxurious bliss. With long, slow strokes, he used his tongue to make me wetter than I'd ever been, and I unleashed my voice. Screaming his name.

"There it is," he murmured.

He'd been playing. Looking for the spot that made me lose my mind.

His eyes locked on mine as he thrust his tongue deeper, and new waves of fire licked up my body. And he didn't stop. First I gasped, then I moaned, and when I reached for him to pull him closer, I begged.

He grabbed my hands again, holding them against the bed while he ravished me with his tongue. I was lost in the feeling of his mouth and the euphoria of being on the brink without going over.

He never wavered or slowed, just sealed his mouth over me and sucked. Licked. Devoured.

Until I couldn't endure another moment of pleasure. I didn't fall over a cliff; I was pulled down into a tidal wave of silvery pleasure. Drowned and revived and drowned again. I didn't know the moment I'd started to come, but I also couldn't tell if I stopped. My orgasm never seemed to end. My whole body shook, and I flooded brand-new wetness into his mouth.

Harlan drank me deep and kept going, working me through one orgasm and the next until I was so spent I was limp on the bed. His lips glowed with my *la petite mort*.

"You taste better than I ever imagined."

The rush of an embarrassed blush sped across my body. And yet, I wasn't truly embarrassed. I reveled in the fact that he liked the way I tasted. It made me hungry for him.

"I think I wore you out," he said with a chuckle.

"No," I breathed.

"No?"

I shook my head and smiled. "Oh, no."

He kissed me once then lowered us back to the bed. Sated. Spent. And forever changed.

I missed his warmth and strength when he pulled away. He disappeared for a moment before returning. He covered us with the blankets and wrapped me in his arms.

This felt right.

I always knew it would, but it had seemed impossible. Regret niggled at the back of my brain. Regret that we'd missed so much time. But I wasn't going to waste any more of it. I refused to let regret steal my joy. With one last contented sigh, I snuggled into Harlan's arms and fell asleep.

## Chapter 15

*Harlan*

I woke before the sun rose. The sky was still a pearly gray, and Grace was in my arms.

For the first time in years, I hadn't woken to fear or panic or nightmares. I simply...woke up. Came to consciousness knowing that she was here and she was with me. Safe.

Looking down where her head was tucked into my shoulder, I couldn't see all of her face, but that didn't matter. I could see the bridge of her nose and her plump cheek. The way her chest rose and fell. Her fingers curled up against her chest.

This had been so long coming that it felt as if it was inevitable. But I wasn't ever going to take our connection for granted. Not when I'd spent years wanting and anticipating.

Part of me couldn't believe it was real. I worried I would wake up in my own bed in my own house and *this* would have been the nightmare. That I'd had her and lost her once again. My arms tightened instinctively around her, and she stirred, snuggling closer into me.

We'd only ever spent one full night together—that last night. Under the stars where we'd stayed tangled together until dawn. It had felt as if the whole world was laid out in front of us and everything was brand-new and anything was possible.

Until it wasn't.

The sky lightened, and I breathed in the wind and wild-flower scent of her hair until she woke. She stretched against me, arching deeply and making me painfully aware of her body. I was already hard partly because it was morning and partly because I could barely control myself in her proximity. Feeling her stretch and hearing her contented groan was unbearable in the best way.

"Good morning," I whispered into her ear.

A smile blossomed on her face. "Morning."

For a moment, we soaked in the nearness. Then I touched my lips to her forehead. "I like this."

Grace closed her eyes and breathed in slowly. We'd been gradually breaking down the barriers between us, but I knew this was still a lot. She wasn't where I was yet.

But she slipped a hand around my ribs, pressing us together.

"Is it still raining?" Her voice was quiet. Sleepy.

I shook my head. "No. All clear."

"Good."

Shifting, I laid her back so I could see her face better in the morning light. "Why?"

"Footprints. If he did anything."

My thoughts darkened. Last night when I saw him in the doorway, I'd needed to lock myself down. The urge to *attack* and *protect* was there, but I wouldn't make Grace look weak. At the same time, the bastard needed to know that she was *mine*. Unequivocally. And if he touched her, he would bear the consequences.

"You were right," Grace said.

"Yes, probably," I said with a grin so she knew I was kidding. "But about what this time?"

She shook her head, eyes focused on a point beyond me. "There's no way this is about water. It can't be. Not with what he said."

"I agree."

But I didn't know what he wanted. His determination didn't exactly make sense. Then again, it didn't have to. Until we figured it out, I only cared about her safety.

My wife's safety.

Connected to her like this, the word struck a chord so deep in me I didn't think I would ever be the same. Whether this was real or not.

"Charles didn't really talk to me about ranch business, but I would have known if he was going to sell it. Especially to Wayne. Charles didn't like him. I might not have been involved with the details, but he always told me about the big decisions."

"He didn't say anything about selling to Gleason?"

Grace's brow furrowed. "The only thing is…he was *happy* before he died. Not in the normal, day-to-day way. He was lit up like a firework—came to me and said that everything was going to be different and better. He was going to take me to Missoula to celebrate. We never got there."

I leaned down and touched my forehead to hers. "I'm sorry."

"Don't be." She blushed. "I mean—not that—" Grace's flush deepened, and she dropped her hands away to cover her face. "I'm so bad at this."

"Hey." I pulled her hands away from her face one by one. "What's going on?"

"Our marriage—Charles's and mine," she clarified. "It wasn't like that."

I shook my head. "Like what?"

Grace's lips parted, and her eyes flickered over my face. Down to my chest and back. "It wasn't like this. He married me to save me, not to love me."

Shock rolled through me. "So you—"

"We were never together."

They'd had such an age difference, I'd assumed it wasn't a normal marriage between them. Especially being in and out of this house for the past couple of weeks and seeing they had separate bedrooms. But I'd never imagined it wasn't a real marriage at some point.

"But people don't know," she said. "And I always feel guilty because I'm not grieving the way I should. Of course, I'm sad. I loved him, but not romantically. And you're here, and all I wanted was you. What kind of person does that make me when my husband just died?"

I leaned down and kissed her. Not softly. I plundered her lips as if they were a goddamn gold mine. Her tongue was hesitant, waiting for my lead, and I was happy to give it to her. We would dance.

Every part of me ached for her. This woman who had always been my everything. "You are nothing short of an amazing person who was dealt a shitty hand, Grace. And I'm not just saying this for me, but do what you want, regardless of what anyone thinks of you. They don't know your relationship. They don't know your heart or what's happened to you."

Grace shuddered. "I wish it wasn't so complicated. When Charles died…it was awful, but I thought I could survive. Get past it. Who knows what will happen to me if Wayne gets his way."

"Nothing is going to happen to you, Grace. I won't let it," I said, barely recognizing my own voice. "He's not going to touch you."

The silent promise hung between us. I meant it and the deeper things it promised. Even if Grace wasn't ready to hear them yet.

But if I was going to protect her, I couldn't do it from afar.

"Grace," I said quietly. "I need to stay here."

The light in her eyes came back, and she grinned. "One night and you're already moving in? Bold of you."

"We can talk about that later." Because I sure as hell planned to talk her into that. "But with Gleason so close and so motivated, I don't want you here alone. And I don't want to leave the property unattended either."

"Yeah, I know. But I can handle myself." Her eyes lit with resistance, but they were shadowed with panic.

Kissing my way along her jaw. "I know you can. I thought you were going to clock him over the head with that shotgun last night when he mentioned selling the ranch to him."

I eased back so I could look her in the eyes. I didn't want to scare her, but she needed to know the truth. "Gleason has already told you that he's not going to stop, especially now that he's put a clock on you. Resting Warrior is close, but it's not close enough to get to you if something happens—when it matters. And I need to be here when it matters."

I'd prefer it to be in her bed, but if not, I'd be sleeping in my truck. Either way, I wasn't leaving her alone when she needed me.

Never again.

She nodded. "Okay, you can stay."

I rolled over her with a predatory grin, savoring the small gasp she let out. I covered her lips with mine—a much slower kiss than before. Grace traced her fingers up my arms, finally locking them around my neck. I loved the desperation that leaked through her fingers as much as I wanted to banish it.

Now that I'd tasted her again, I was addicted. I moved my lips to her neck. She arched it, leaning away from me to expose more of herself. That movement told me everything I needed to know; she trusted me, and that meant absolutely everything to me.

I followed the same path I'd traced last night. Down her chest until I reached her breasts, and I had the same echoing déjà vu. A younger us, fumbling and trying new things. Laughing as if we were the only two people in the world.

Her nipples hardened under my tongue and lips and teeth. I'd dreamed about her like this—no matter how hard I'd tried not to—but the reality was so much better than anything I'd ever imagined. I could spend all day in this bed with her, memorizing the curves that I should have gotten to know a long time ago.

"Talk to me," I murmured into her skin.

"What?" Her voice was flustered and breathy.

Brushing my mouth over her skin, I watched it rise into goose bumps from my breath alone. It was the sexiest thing I'd ever seen. "It's been a long time since I've touched you, and now we have all the time in the world. I want to know what you like."

"You did pretty good last night."

"Pretty good isn't enough," I growled. "Every time I touch you, I want everything, Grace." I drew my tongue over her pebbled nipple. "Do you like that?"

Her moan sent what little blood was left in my brain straight to my cock. I didn't think I'd ever been harder in my life. "Yes."

With aching slowness, I covered that diamond peak with my mouth and sucked. Gently at first, then harder. I rolled my tongue around the tip, tracing the shape. I barely let go of her to speak. "And that?"

"Oh yes."

I drew a line down her skin toward her belly button and glanced upward. "You're going to tell me yes or no, Grace. Every time I move my mouth, until you can't speak anymore."

Grace grabbed a handful of my hair and tugged hard enough to pull a sound from my lips. Hard enough to drive me crazy. I dipped my tongue into her belly button, and she squirmed under my body. I paused, waiting. Not moving until she spoke. "No. Yes. I don't know."

"Mmm." I painted her with kisses and licks, sucking down across her skin to the quiet, desperate chorus of *yes* and *yes* and *yes*.

I settled between her legs, guiding her thighs apart so she was spread in front of me like a feast. Her face was flushed, glistening with sweat, hair tangled across the pillow from trying to keep still and not being able to.

"I like being here."

She flushed deeper. "I—"

Moving my lips over her, I used the smallest of touches, and her voice disappeared entirely.

Last night, I was a man starving, and right now was no different. She was sweet and wet, and my intent to go slow disappeared. I sealed my mouth over her and sucked hard, holding her hips down when they tried to arch off the bed.

I loved hearing her find her voice and call my name.

She was soaking wet, delicious, and all mine. I closed

my eyes and savored her, licking deep and slow. Grace writhed under me, grabbing the comforter and fighting for more.

"Harlan, I need you."

I raised an eyebrow. "Come first."

"Please," she begged. "Please, I want it with you."

A shudder ran through me. Her body was heaven, and her begging completely undid me. I barely got the condom on. Grace pulled me down to her and guided me inside. One smooth stroke and I was buried in tight heat and pure ecstasy.

Pressing my lips to her neck again, I gathered her to me. I needed her fully in my arms. She was here and real, and I planned to silence any part of me that still didn't believe it.

"Harlan," she whispered. "I need to tell you... I tried... He would have let me, but I couldn't."

It was nearly impossible to focus on her words when all I could feel was her tight heat surrounding me. "What?"

Those perfect green eyes stared up at me, and I saw such heartbreaking vulnerability there, I froze. "It's only you. I've only ever been with you."

For the second time that morning, shock consumed me. "Grace..."

Deep, possessive satisfaction rolled through me. Knowing that I was the only man who had ever touched her—been inside her. And yet, all this time, she'd been alone.

My mouth crashed down on hers. She wrapped herself around me, and we moved together. Drunk on each other and everything that was between us—good and bad. I drove myself into her and never wanted to pull away. I burned with the need to imprint myself on her so deeply she'd never forget this moment. Neither one of us would ever forget this moment.

I ground my hips down into hers, making sure to rub against her where she wanted it most with every thrust. Until she was gasping under my lips. Until she was squeezing me so hard that I was blind with barely contained pleasure. Until her voice filled the air with my name and she shuddered in my arms.

My orgasm chased hers in seconds. I moved slow, hard, deep…drawing out both of our pleasure as long as possible. The aftershocks were visible all over her body in the way she shook. She was so damned sexy like this, breathless from what we'd done together.

I was the only one.

I didn't even know how to process that.

Slowly, I kissed her, lowering my weight so she was cradled under me. "You're beautiful."

"You're only saying that because you know it embarrasses me."

I shook my head. "You have absolutely nothing to be embarrassed about. Not about that. Not with me. Not ever."

Her cheeks tinged pink anyway, but she didn't protest. "So you're moving in?"

"I am."

She nodded slowly, running her hands over my shoulders and down my chest. "Why am I nervous?"

"Because it's new. And everything that happened is still there. It's not going away."

Grace nodded.

"I need to go get my things."

"Yeah."

I grinned. "But I don't want to move."

Her fingers grazed my ribs, pulling me down against

her, leaving no space between our bodies. "I don't want you to either."

I kissed her one more time before pulling away. "I can't leave you here. Not right now."

Grace smiled, stretching as she sat up. "I'm going to Deja Brew. I feel bad about having to leave so suddenly yesterday, and I think Lena's still working on that giant cookie order."

"Okay." That, I could live with. Not only was Deja Brew public, but it was pretty much known as Resting Warrior territory. If anything happened, Charlie would be close enough to get there fast.

The thought of having Grace out of my sight, even for a little while, was uncomfortable. Especially now that *this* had happened.

We took our time getting dressed. I didn't hide the fact that I was watching her, and she snuck glances at me as well. Suddenly, I wanted to leave as quickly as possible because the sooner I left, the sooner I could get back to her.

I made sure she was safely buckled into her truck, and I took the time to press her into the seat and kiss her hard before I shut the door. "A reminder, for later."

"You really think I'd forget?"

"Just making sure."

She bit her lip. "Okay."

I watched until she disappeared around the bend before getting into my own truck. I had already made a mental list of everything I needed to get. And once I pulled up to my house on Resting Warrior, it didn't take me long to get everything together and into the truck.

I packed more than I would normally take on a trip. I didn't know how long I would be staying. A small voice in the back of my head whispered the hope I wouldn't be coming back here at all. I loved my house on the ranch, but given the choice of living here alone or living with Grace at Ruby Round, I'd already be a trail of dust between the two ranches, with no plans to ever look back.

Jude sat in his usual spot in front of the security monitors when I walked into his office.

He nodded at me. "Hey."

"Hey. I didn't get a chance to check the cameras last night after it started raining. Can you pull them up?"

Jude raised an eyebrow.

"What?"

"You didn't get a chance?"

I shrugged. "No."

A smirk crawled across his face, and I resisted the urge to punch it off him. Just like a real brother. Begging for help one minute, and itching to beat the shit out of him the next. We'd usually saved our battles for our missions, but we had tussled a time or two. This couldn't be one of them. "Sure. I'll pull them up."

When he connected to the cameras that I'd placed, we saw nothing but static.

"You're sure you put them online?"

"Yeah. I took pictures if you need them."

"No…" He trailed off and typed quickly. A line of code popped back into the terminal. "They were online. Now, they're not. I'm not getting a ping of power off them."

I cursed under my breath. "Any chance the rain got to them?"

"Those cameras? Not likely."

"Then Gleason took them. Fucking hell. This guy is starting to get on my nerves. And by my nerves, I mean I'd love the opportunity to pound him into the ground." And not in a brotherly way.

Jude crossed his arms and leaned back in the chair. "What's going on?"

I filled him in about Gleason's visit last night and the stunt with the horse. "I need to do some research before I get back because there's no way this has anything to do with water."

"Definitely agree with that." Jude stood and waved to his chair. "Have at it."

The computers in the security suite had access to plenty of databases and resources that might not be available to the average person. And if Gleason wanted the land, then there was something that we didn't know about it.

That was where I started.

When Grace and I had looked for records of ownership for Ruby Round, we hadn't been concerned about what was actually *on* the ranch. I should have thought about that earlier, given the way this guy was coming after her. I'd been so consumed with wanting her to be safe, that anything other than the obvious had slipped by.

My brothers were right—there was no way I was objective about any of this, but it was too late now.

Unlike the deed and the other documents Grace needed, the records of the ranch itself were easy to find. Grainy scans of the property documents loaded up on the computer, outlining the edges of the land. And for all the world, it looked exactly like every other record that I'd seen.

Hell, it looked a lot like Resting Warrior's records—though those intentionally left out the significant technological improvements we'd made, like all the security, the fence, and the state-of-the-art gym facility we built behind the lodge.

Ruby Round looked like a large, slightly wobbly

rectangle. The spring was marked, and a couple arbitrary blocks across the fields. The start of the mountains were labeled on the edge past the property line, and it all matched up with what I'd seen when I'd ridden along the fences the other day.

Nothing we could use here.

Then in the corner I spotted a notation with the date that this record had been updated—only a year ago. Which didn't make sense for a ranch like Ruby Round. Property lines on plots like these were rarely changed because the places stayed in families for generations, and a lot of rural ranchers were territorial on the best day and mistrusted the government *every* day.

I wasn't as good at all the computer stuff as Jude or Grant, but I could hold my own. Over the years, I'd learned a few things from them, so I decided to follow the path of the records myself.

It looked as if the new record had been submitted voluntarily. But where some of the other records in the area had names attached to them, this one didn't. Only "anonymous."

Anonymous, my ass. I didn't know Charles Townsend well, but I'd encountered him enough in the short time I'd been here to know he wouldn't bother being anonymous on paperwork related to his own land. The previous record was there too, though not where I expected it to be.

I stilled. Enough that Jude noticed from whatever he was doing messing around on his phone. "You found something?"

"Maybe."

This older property record looked different—larger. The older record showed the Ruby Round as line as extending into the foothills of the mountains at least another mile. In the new, *anonymously* updated record, that mile was not included in the Ruby Round land.

"People don't cut the edges of their land short unless someone makes them, right?"

Jude snorted. "I wouldn't think so."

So there was a mile missing from Grace's property. A mile I guessed that Gleason didn't want her to notice. And a mile that he wanted access to without anyone getting in the way.

"What are you thinking?"

I stood and headed for the door. "I need to check it out, but I think I've found what Gleason wanted to keep to himself."

## Chapter 16

*Harlan*

"Hello?" Grace's voice was filled with laughter when she answered the phone.

"Just checking in. Everything okay over there?"

I could practically hear her eyes roll through the phone. "Is this what we are now, husband dear? A couple who calls just to check in?"

Husband.

The way she said the word so casually slugged me in the gut so hard I lost my breath. I wanted her to call me that every damned day for the rest of my life. "When you have someone who's threatening you? Yes."

"Yeah, I know." She sighed a little, and everything in my body went hard. Especially below the belt as I remembered the way she'd made that exact same sound in my ear last night. And this morning. We'd made the perfect kind of progress, and I would make sure she didn't pull away again.

Grace was mine.

It was an indisputable fact carved into my DNA. I knew it the way I knew which way was north.

"I'm heading back to Ruby," I said. "To drop some stuff off and check something out."

"Did you find something?"

"I don't know," I said, not wanting to get her hopes up before we actually knew anything. "Maybe. I need to look first."

"Okay. I'll be back before too long. I need to do some more admin work."

I could see her face in my head, scrunching up her features in distaste, and I laughed. "Well, I'll be there."

"See you soon."

The line went dead, and I took a deep breath. See you soon. It was almost impossible to look at the past month with anything but awe. A month ago, Grace couldn't look me in the eye. Now we were married, moving in together, and she might actually be happy to see me.

And it wasn't something I was ever going to take for granted.

I grabbed Big Red from the stables as soon as I made it back to the ranch. I nodded to Dana, who was in the barn feeding the other horses. "Let's go, boy." I patted the horse's neck. "Let's see if we can find an answer to all this mess."

I headed toward the west property line, knowing there was a good chance Gleason was watching. He already knew too much, and if he was behind this, I wanted to investigate without his getting wind of it. If it was possible.

I headed north once I hit the fence line, straight to the back fence at the fictional end of the property. I hadn't thought anything of it, but looking at things, it made sense to build the fence here. Beyond it, the ground grew rocky and more treacherous. For a cattle ranch, constructing a fence any farther back would be more trouble than it was worth.

But still, owning a piece of the mountain was valuable. Why keep it and not protect it? Why not sell it off instead of simply erasing it from the records?

There was a gate at the back, and I dismounted to lead Big Red through it. It was beautiful back here, the mountains so close you had to tilt your head back to see the top of them. Pure blue Montana sky stretched overhead. Big Sky.

I'd missed this place when I'd left. The Navy had sent me all over the world to some beautiful—and not so beautiful—places, but none of them compared to this. To home. I hadn't just been born in Montana; it had been born in me. I was addicted to the wide-open sky and the air's sweet scent. I missed the sight of mountains on the horizon when they weren't there.

But as beautiful as it was, I didn't see anything that made me think this was worth all the trouble Gleason was going to for it. Not yet, at least. I got back into Big Red's saddle and turned west again. I would walk the edges.

I probably passed the strict line that the second record had placed, but that was fine. Better to be thorough in this case than anything else. So far, there was nothing but rocks.

The shade of the mountain was cool, and a stiff breeze flowed down off the top of it. Big Red tossed his head, suddenly nervous as we ascended the shallow hills that led to the higher cliffs. "What is it, boy?"

It wasn't the wind. Wind didn't cause this kind of anxiety. Big Red continued to shy away from the place I was trying to lead him: east over the hill. Never discount an animal's instincts.

I got down, grabbed the reins, and led him on foot. The big horse nudged my shoulder and neighed in my ear. He didn't want to be here.

Easing over the hill, I saw it. It would be simple to miss it if you weren't actively looking for it. Deeper in the shadows of a crevice between two hills, beams of wood framed a hole in the stone.

A mine.

Holy shit.

Okay, depending on what could be in there, it might be worth all the trouble Gleason had gone to, but from the looks of the entrance, it had been abandoned for years. Maybe decades. Were there other entrances?

"I got you," I said to Big Red, jumping back up into the saddle. Maybe he felt the ground wasn't stable if there were tunnels underneath us. That was definitely something different, and now I wanted to move quickly. Before Gleason ever knew I was here.

I retreated from the entrance until Big Red stopped trying to toss his head and pull away, and I rode east toward Dominion. There weren't any other entrances to the mystery mine that I could see, but I could see a hole.

One massive hole on the edge of Grace's property. If I estimated right, it was exactly on the line that divided Ruby Round and Dominion, Gleason's ranch. And the hole opened into more of that mine. I saw the support beams of the tunnel at least two stories down. Not only was it a mine, it was also one that sprawled.

Relief and determination settled in my chest. Finally, this was information I could work with.

I pulled out my cell and called Grant. "What's up, Harlan?"

"You still have the name of that guy who came out and

did the mineral rights assessment on the Resting Warrior property?"

"Not off the top of my head, but I'm sure it's in the office. You need it?"

"Yeah," I said. "I'm hoping I can get him out here today. I think I found something."

～

A short man got out of the truck with a huff and looked me over. "Yeah, I remember you now."

I kept my expression mild. "I hope that's a good thing."

His own expression told me it probably wasn't. "I had to cancel three clients this afternoon to come out here for you. This better be worth it, Harlan."

When he opened the bed of his truck to grab a pack full of equipment, I rolled my eyes. "I'm sure what I offered is more than worth it."

Grant told me what we'd paid the guy last time, and I'd offered him triple when I called him. Nelson Barnes. One of the top mineral inspectors in the county—and in all of Montana. Prickly guy with an attitude, but he was here. He knew his stuff and could tell me what was in the mine and if it was anything someone would kill over.

Obviously, I hadn't mentioned that when I'd asked him to come here. He tossed me a hard hat. "You'll need that. And that." A second pack, smaller than the one he carried, that contained a small canister of oxygen and a breathing mask. "In case the air is bad."

"And if it is and the canister blows?"

The way he looked at me told me exactly what he thought of me and who I was. "The only way that happens is if your steroid-soaked military brain goes Rambo and shoots the canister point-blank."

"Rambo was Army. I'm Navy. A SEAL, to be exact. I know at least a dozen ways to take someone down without a gun." I didn't wait for whatever smartass comment he was ready to assault me with. I led him over to Big Red and Dove, one of the other ranch horses. But I could hear him muttering behind me. For an hour, I could handle the attitude.

"So, how'd you find this thing?"

"By accident." There was no reason he needed to know I'd gone digging into the property records, or why. As far as I was concerned, Wayne Gleason was a loose cannon, and the fewer people on his radar, the better. "I was out beyond the fence giving Big Red here a little more room to stretch his legs, and I saw it in the hills."

"Lucky."

I looked over my shoulder and smiled at the man. "You could say that."

If I'd run into him anywhere, I would never have guessed this man was a born and bred Montana native. He looked about as at home on a horse as if he were balancing on a tightrope. Given his occupation, I would have thought he'd learned some things.

I shook my head. As long as we got in and out fast, I didn't care about the rest.

As we rode out to the fence, I kept glancing east. If Gleason was watching, he would probably be smart enough to keep out of sight, but I kept a sharp eye out anyway. It was as if I could feel his eyes on the back of my neck. A tingling awareness that something else was out there.

I took Nelson to the sinkhole first. "This is the entrance?" He looked at me skeptically.

"No, but I wanted to show you this so you could see how far it spreads. This isn't something small."

For a moment, he looked troubled. "If it's anything valuable, you're right. It's strange no one noticed."

"That's what I thought."

It looked as if the idea of me being right caused him pain. I tried not to laugh.

Grace hadn't been home when Nelson had arrived, but I was sure she would be soon. I had yet to decide whether I wanted to be right or wrong about the mine. If I was right, it explained Gleason's actions. But if I was wrong, she was going to have a hell of a lot of questions I didn't have answers for. Such as, did her late husband know about this?

Big Red did the same thing he'd done before when we'd gotten too close to the mine entrance. He tossed his head with enough force that I couldn't control him. I dismounted and attached his reins to a nearby tree. I gestured for Nelson to do the same. "I think he's spooked by tunnels below us. He won't go any farther."

Nelson eyed Big Red with wariness and handed me Dove's reins.

"Put on your mask," he said as we approached the dark hole in the mountain. "We've got no idea what's in there, and there's no point in taking chances."

I strapped the clear mask over my face and took a hit of oxygen. Nelson handed me a flashlight and took the lead. Here, he was clearly in his element. He ran his flashlight along the edges of the mine, checking the ceiling for safety before we stepped inside.

From the looks of it, no one had set foot in this mine in years. Maybe a decade. Cobwebs were thick in the corners, and the stone itself sported a layer of dust. "It looks abandoned."

"Probably," Nelson said. As he flashed his light down along on the ground, I caught sight of a footprint that was darker and obviously more recent than anything else.

"Shit."

We followed the mine's main hallway as it angled down and continued north, farther and farther, until it felt like the mountain's weight pressed down on us from above. There wasn't anything in the walls that looked valuable, but Nelson said nothing, so I kept following.

Suddenly, we came into a larger room. "Well, okay then," Nelson said.

There was no doubt people had been here. Assembled mining equipment stood in front of the beginning of a new tunnel. An upside-down hard hat waited off to the left for its owner's return. But even with the equipment, it felt as if no one had been here in a while.

Nelson went to the new tunnel and examined the wall. I glanced down the other tunnels. Most of them faded into the darkness. No telling how far into the mountain this mine went or how long it had been here.

I heard footsteps, and Nelson muttered something as he went down a different tunnel. "What is it?"

He shook his head and looked at me. "Well, you were right. This mine is…valuable."

"What's here?"

Nelson took the flashlight and pointed it at a dark, shiny stone in the wall. Dirty and unpolished, but unlike the rest. "Sapphires," he said. "The whole damn place is lined with sapphires."

## Chapter 17

*Grace*

No matter how I did the numbers, they didn't add up. We didn't have the income we needed to stay afloat. I hated to admit that the idea of selling the ranch was becoming more appealing, but it was. At least then it would be over.

But no.

This was Charles's legacy. I couldn't let it die because running a ranch hadn't been my first choice. I needed to do something to fix it. I had the option of cutting back the ranch hand hours. I didn't want to, but I could take up some of the slack myself.

I could sell some of the cattle. Maybe in a few years, I could start to grow the herd again, but all of it made my head hurt.

I kicked myself for not being more involved when Charles had been alive. He had been so insistent about me staying out of it, and I was happy to. But now, I wish I'd pushed back. Maybe he'd been doing it as a favor to me because he'd thought I wasn't interested. Would he have changed his mind if I'd been more forceful?

I would never know now.

Heavy footsteps on the stairs startled me. "Grace?"

Harlan's voice. I blew out the breath that had frozen in my chest. For one second, I'd thought it was someone else.

I shook my head. If that was my first reaction, Harlan moving in was a good thing. "I'm in the office."

He appeared in the doorway, and his smile was mesmerizing. "Come with me."

"Where are we going?"

"It's a surprise."

I sighed. "I really need to work on this. The finances are a mess, and—"

Harlan rounded the desk, pulled me out of the chair, and against his chest. Suddenly, we were face-to-face, close enough to kiss, and the breath in my chest froze for an entirely different reason.

His kiss slanted across my lips, reminding my body what he could do with those lips. And how much I liked it. "I promise you—it will be worth it."

He took my hand, pulled me down the stairs, and out the back door. Big Red and Dove were already there and saddled. "A ride?"

He grinned again. "You're going to like this."

I raised one eyebrow in question, but he had my curiosity piqued now. We rode to the back property's eastern side and to the back gate. "Going past the property line?"

"That's the thing," he said. "I did a little digging. This isn't the end of the property."

I followed him through the gate and to a tree in the foothills, where he dismounted. "On foot from here."

"If you're dragging me out here to kill me, tell me now."

Harlan grinned. "Believe me, I'm not." He took my hand again. This time, he pulled me toward the mountains until we stood in their shadow.

"Harlan, seriously," I said. "Where are we—" I saw it. The dark gash in the rock directly in front of us. "Oh."

"Yeah." His voice was full of unbridled excitement, and he pulled me along faster. He picked up a couple of flashlights by the door and handed one to me.

"I had no idea that this was here," I said, looking into the darkness in front of me.

"I don't think many people did," he said. "Come on."

"It's safe?"

"It's all been checked out already. We're fine."

I stepped into the mountain and paused. I was not a huge fan of small, dark spaces. But I took a long, slow breath. "How in the hell did you find this?"

He told me while we walked in the dark. The replaced documents and the way he'd checked to see if anything was there. And the guy he'd brought out this afternoon. He finished telling me as we walked into the big room he'd told me was coming.

"And?"

Turning to me, he took my face in his hands. The flashlights provided enough light for me to see the way he was looking at me. His eyes were full of hope and satisfaction. "It's sapphires."

I blinked. "What did you say?"

"This is a sapphire mine. This place is *full* of them."

Holy shit. Holy *shit*. My mind raced. Montana sapphires were a huge treasure. The color and quality. There was a mine here. Oh my God.

"This is why he wants it," I said. "He wants the mine."

"I'd bet money on it."

I pulled away from him and looked around the room and the tunnels branching off in multiple directions. If this mine was full of sapphires, it was worth more than I could wrap my head around. "Charles bought the mineral rights to the property too," I said. "He told me once."

"And those transfer in a sale," Harlan said.

The threats made so much more sense now. If Wayne had unrestricted access to this mine, he would make a shit ton of money.

"But we didn't know it was here. Why not just keep doing this?" I gestured to the equipment.

"Eventually, someone would have noticed. You can't quite see it from the fence, but at some point, there would have been too many people coming in and out to ignore. Gleason doesn't strike me as the kind of guy to bide his time."

"No kidding," I muttered.

It hit me like a lightning bolt. Was *this* what Charles had planned to tell me before he died? He'd been so alive and happy in a way I'd never seen before. He'd said he was going to take care of some things and then take me on a night out on the town…

This explained everything. It was exactly what he'd needed to solve the ranch's financial problems. Why he'd said that things were going to be different.

"He knew."

"I was going to ask."

I looked over at Harlan. "This has to be what he was going to tell me before he got in the accident."

An arm snaked around my waist, and he pulled me back against his chest. "I'm sorry. He was probably excited to tell you about it."

"It would have solved a lot of problems." I sighed and leaned back into him.

"It still could."

Shit. Yeah, it could. Depending on how much was in here? This was the solution to the headache of the paperwork in the office. "I need to have the mine assessed."

"The guy this afternoon—Nelson Barnes—I scheduled him to come back day after tomorrow to do that. He didn't have everything he needed on him because today was so short notice."

"Nelson Barnes…" The name was familiar. "He knew Charles. I'm pretty sure."

"Really? He didn't say anything."

I gently pulled away from Harlan and turned. "I've heard the name over the years. Could be a coincidence, I guess. But I would think he'd say something."

"Maybe he didn't realize since I was the one who called him?"

"Maybe," I nodded. "Let's go. I need to go back to the house and look through all those files again. I had only been scanning for the deed—I didn't read the contents more than to see that they *weren't* what I was looking for. If Charles had anything about the mines or sapphires, it would be there."

Harlan made a sound. "If that paperwork is not with the things we're missing."

I stared at him. "You think he has them? That he stole them?"

"Gleason?" Harlan sighed. "Maybe. I wouldn't put anything past him. Especially now that we know he has proper motivation. But if he had the documents, I would imagine he would have found a way to use them against you by now."

We walked back up the mine's hallway. When we were

within sight of the open sky, I stopped. "How does this help us? Sure, I'll have the money. I can save Ruby Round. But Wayne is still coming. This doesn't stop him from coming after me the way he promised he would."

Harlan's eyes went dark. "I already told you, he's not going to touch you."

I shivered. The power and possession in Harlan's tone rocked me down to my toes. There wasn't a sliver of doubt in my mind; Harlan meant what he said. "I know. But this doesn't solve anything with him. He's still going to try for it."

Harlan pulled me against his body and walked with me until my back hit the wall. "He can try all he wants, but he's not getting to you. It's not going to happen. But now that we've found one piece of what Charles was dealing with, maybe we'll find something else that will tell us where the deed is."

My body was wedged between Harlan and pure rock. And judging from what I felt in his pants, there was pure rock in front of me, too. "Here?" I smirked at him. "You're hard here?"

Harlan dipped his mouth to my neck and kissed a line up to my ear. "Anywhere you are. It doesn't matter where. I get within three feet of you, and I'm ready."

Air shot out of my lungs. Tingling warmth and want spread out from my core to consume all of me. "That must be uncomfortable for you."

His voice was more rumble than speech at this point. "You have no idea."

This felt *good*. This felt real. And I was right where I wanted to be. With Harlan. Now that we'd started, I wanted all of him. We had a decade of lost time to make up for. "We should do something about that discomfort, shouldn't we?"

A groan filled my ear. "Let's get back to the house. Because if I start this now, I'm not going to stop. So unless you want to spend tonight in the dirt…"

Smiling, I placed my hands on his chest and pushed him away from me. "Give me a five-minute head start."

"Why?"

I had a few things I'd never had an opportunity to wear that were buried in my closet. More than anything, I wanted to see the look on his face when I wore them for him. "You had a surprise for me, and now I have one for you."

His brows rose into his hairline. "I like surprises."

Going up on my toes, I brushed my lips across his, a barely there breath of a kiss. "If you want a better one, give me a ten-minute head start."

"What do I get if I give you fifteen?"

"Can you last fifteen?" I asked with a laugh.

Harlan stood back and adjusted himself in his jeans. "They better make me a fucking saint after, but I can make it."

"See you there." I swung my hips a little more as I walked away from him, and I heard the curse he let out. Laughing, I practically skipped my way to Dove, and I realized that I was smiling like a fool.

Happy.

That's what I was.

Harlan Young made me happy.

## Chapter 18

*Harlan*

I looked up at the ceiling, trying in vain to catch my breath. There was no stopping the smile on my face. I'd taken my sweet time bringing Big Red back to the house. And I had been well rewarded with an outfit that was black, lacy, and the last thing I ever thought I'd see on Grace.

Grace wasn't shy, but this was a side of her I hadn't seen before. And the sex…

To say we were making up for lost time was an understatement. Every time I touched her, kissed her, made love with her, it got better. And right now, there was no end in sight.

"That was definitely worth the wait." My voice was so raspy I hardly recognized it.

I felt more than saw Grace's head turn toward mine. "Better have been. You know how hard it is to get all those straps in the right places?"

Turning on my side, I let my gaze slide down her body to the straps that were still there…and in very different places than they'd started in. "And it was so easy to move them out of place."

Grace fought a smile. "I think you enjoyed that too much."

"Not possible." I reached around her and slowly undid the hooks that kept everything where it belonged. "The only thing that's better is getting you out of it completely."

Her breathy sigh sent blood straight to my cock. I could easily take her again right now. She helped me wiggle her out of the barely there piece of lingerie, and I tossed it aside. "Is it too early to just stay in bed?"

She laughed. "Yes."

I tried to keep her with me, but she slipped away and out of bed. "I want to look through the office again. And as for the other thing…" She looked over her shoulder with enough heat to make me groan. "We still have tonight."

Grace picked up the shirt I'd had on earlier and had discarded in our frenzy. I didn't think she could get sexier than she already was. Then I saw her in my clothes. Long, bare legs peeking out from underneath the shirt that was hardly long enough to cover her ass. I had a vision of picking her up and slipping into her.

"You're going to drive me crazy," I said.

She grinned. "That may or may not be the point."

When she disappeared from the room, I grabbed a pair of sweats out of my suitcase before I followed. If she was going to be half naked, two could play at that game. I knew the way she looked at me, and I fucking loved it.

Grace stood in the doorway of the office, arms wrapped around herself. Her entire energy was different. I wrapped my arms around her, matching her own. "You okay?"

"Yeah." She nodded. "It's…weird. Sometimes when I walk in here, it really hits me. This was Charles's place, more than anywhere else in the house. He spent a lot of time here, and I never did. So, coming in here still feels a bit wrong."

"I get that."

Sighing, she pulled away from me and crossed to one of the giant filing cabinets. She sat on the floor and pulled out the lowest drawer before grabbing a bunch of folders. "I still worry about what they think of me," she said quietly.

"Who?" I pulled out a different stack of files. The process was familiar, but at least our search had a singular focus this time.

"Everyone. Lena and Evelyn. The other Resting Warrior guys. It's only been six months, and now I'm married to you."

I flipped through what looked like receipts for feed from a couple of years ago. "They know why you did it."

"Yeah…"

My stomach clenched at her hesitation. Was there any chance she wanted more than sex and connection—perhaps a real marriage? The air was thick with it. But now wasn't the time to ask.

Instead, I cleared my throat and deflected. "Tell me about him."

Grace looked up at me. "You want to hear that?"

"Why wouldn't I?"

"I don't know…seems as if my current husband wouldn't want to hear about my dead one."

I pinned her with a stare. "Grace, Charles was a huge

part of your life that I wasn't there for. I want to know everything about your life."

"It won't be weird for you?"

"No." I took a long breath, looking for the words. "He's gone. You were married, and it's natural to miss him. Ignoring the fact that for a long time you lived with him— and *loved* him—would be foolish."

She shook her head. "I didn't love him like that."

"I know, but you're still grieving. Just because it's not the way that everyone expects you to grieve doesn't mean it's not valid."

Grace put the files in her lap and ran her fingers through her hair. "I know. It's so hard. You're the only one who really knows everything. It wasn't something we talked about, you know? 'Hi, this is my wife, Grace. Our marriage is completely platonic because I married her to save her from her asshole of a father and gave up any dreams that I had of having a real family.'"

I watched her as she flipped her hair over her shoulder and went back to opening files and scanning the contents. "You feel guilty?"

"I already said I did."

"Not about that." I shook my head. "You feel guilty that he married you?"

She paled. "A little."

"It was his choice," I said gently. "If he hadn't wanted to, he could have found another way."

Grace shook her head and chewed on her lip. This wasn't something I could help her with. She had to move through her grief and guilt in her own way, and me trying to tell her how she should or shouldn't feel wasn't going to help her.

"Tell me something about him." I repeated my request.

Silence reigned over the office for a few minutes—

nothing but the subtle sound of paper on paper. "He was a foodie."

I blinked. "Really?"

"Yeah." She smiled. "He wasn't really that picky. It's not like we ate truffles every night or recreated gastropub food. But if we went to a place that had food like that? He *loved* it." A small laugh. "In that way, he was a lot more adventurous than me."

"I never would have imagined that."

Grace shook her head. "Yeah, he didn't look the part. But he was. A couple years ago, I bought him a meat smoker. Whenever he got on a tear about food, he would bring up this smoked pulled pork sandwich that he'd had when we went on a trip to Seattle. He never shut up about it."

She stared into the distance and smiled at the memory. I was glad she had good memories, even if I wasn't in them. "So I figured if he had a way to make his own smoked meat and experiment, maybe he would find a way to make that sandwich."

"Did he like it?"

"He did. He was a fiend with that thing." She shook her head, still smiling. "It's still out by the barn."

I hadn't noticed, but then again, I hadn't been looking for a smoker. "I'm glad he liked it."

"Yeah." Grace sighed. "I think part of the guilt— whether it makes sense or not—is because it was so sudden. He was there, and then he wasn't. It wasn't like he was sick or we knew it was coming. Now there's the big black hole of no closure."

I stayed silent, sensing there was more.

"I didn't really know how to handle it. I still don't. When they handed me that bag with his things, I kind of shut down about it."

"Can't say I blame you," I said, putting back the files that I had and retrieving more.

"You have to tell me about your life too, you know," she said. "I bet your life is way, way more interesting than mine."

I leafed through the next file. More receipts. This time for repairs that had been done on the ranch over the years. Nothing to repair a sinkhole or anything to do with a mine. "Sure," I said. "I have lots of stories. I'll tell you any ones I'm allowed."

Grace's eyebrows rose into her hairline. "How many are you not allowed to?"

"I'd tell you, but then I'd have to kill you," I said with a grin. "And I have a vested interest in keeping you alive."

I loved the pink blush on her cheeks. She exchanged her stack of files for a new one. "Anything interesting?"

"I wish. Just tax paperwork. I'm looking through the assets and stuff, but nothing about a mine."

"It'll be here somewhere."

She smiled, but it looked forced. "I hope so."

I finished looking through the papers I had in my hands and put them back into the filing cabinet. "This is going to take a while."

Grace sighed and leaned back against her cabinet. "Yeah. I wish Charles had trusted me more. Then maybe we wouldn't be here."

Something about the way she said it kicked my instincts into overdrive. Grace had said Charles was happy just before he died. They were going to dinner, and he'd told her things would be better. If he was planning on telling her that night, maybe he'd had what we were looking for with him.

She'd said they'd given her a bag of his things, but I

hadn't seen it when we'd gone through the house. Unless she'd put it away. "Grace."

"Yeah?" She looked up from scouring a piece of paper.

"Charles's effects. From the hospital."

I hated the way she looked nauseated, but I needed to know. "What about them?"

"Where are they?" Grace hesitated, fingers fidgeting like she had something to hide. "What did you do with them?"

"I never opened them. I was...so blindsided that I didn't want to look at the stupid bag. It's in my closet."

I took a breath. I didn't want to get her hopes up, but a prickling feeling in my gut told me this was something. "Where?"

"The shelf on top. In the back."

"Can I get it?"

She nodded but didn't move. I went back to her room —which I was quickly starting to think of as ours—and opened the closet. The item wasn't hard to find. I'd seen enough of those clear bags in my time.

I took it back to the office. "Is this okay?"

"What are you thinking?"

"I don't know," I told her honestly. "But we didn't check. And if he was planning on telling you…"

Understanding lit her eyes. "Yeah."

"Do you want to be the one to open it?"

"No," she said quickly. "No, I don't."

I nodded and sat back on the floor, closer to her this time. "Okay."

Slowly, I broke the seal on the bag. The faint scent of hospital wafted out. Grace sat apart from me, leaning away unconsciously. The bag was jammed full. I removed his jeans, a shirt, shoes, socks, underwear, and a folded leather jacket. A set of keys that I assumed were to his car and the ranch.

As I searched the clothes, I tried to be as methodical as possible. The shoes and socks were empty. Nothing in the pockets of the jeans or the shirt.

Maybe I was wrong. Maybe there wasn't anything here.

"He loved that jacket," Grace said quietly when I picked it up. I reached out and held her hand for a moment. She didn't look or sound upset, but this had to be strange for her.

I pulled an envelope out of the jacket's inner pocket. Grace gasped. "What is that?"

I turned it over. Her name was written on the front of it. "Whatever it is, it's meant for you."

Grace gingerly took the envelope from me and opened it, and I finished looking through the rest of the jacket pockets.

Suddenly, she sat up. "Harlan. Holy shit!"

"What?" My fingers closed around metal in one of the outside pockets as she showed me the papers.

"It's a receipt. For the sale of a *sapphire*."

My instincts settled. It wasn't much, but it was something. Maybe we could uncover more of what happened. Or how Wayne Gleason was involved.

"There's something else," I said. A key had been in the jacket pocket. Small, silver, and nondescript.

Grace took it out of my palm. "How will we ever know what it goes to?"

"If we're lucky," I said, playing a hunch, "it will open a safe-deposit box."

## Chapter 19

*Harlan*

The next morning, I finished setting up the new cameras and motion detectors around the house. My instincts told me that it was a bad idea to leave the property unattended, but it wasn't realistic for either Grace or me to be here at all times. So, new cameras. This time, I made sure they were well hidden. Especially the ones I put near the entrance to the mine.

Hiding them was a risky proposition. With the weather and the wind, there was a chance the tree branches would get in the way. But it was better than letting Gleason hunt them down one by one.

After finding the key last night, we'd made a list of banks in the area. The ones she knew Charles had accounts with and some he didn't. That was where she was right now, going to a few of the closer banks to see if she could find the safe-deposit box the key fit into.

I didn't like her going alone, but I'd driven down the

road and made sure Gleason's car was still in his driveway. Unless he'd bugged the house—which didn't seem to be his style—he would have no idea where she would be.

I wanted to be with her. For moral support. For protection. For a possible celebration, but it seemed more likely a grieving widow would be granted access if she was alone than with her new husband shadowing her every step.

I pulled out my phone and checked the camera feeds. These cameras had higher resolution and more functions than the previous ones, and they would send me a notification any time they captured movement in the area.

Perfect.

This morning, I'd started out early so there was less of a chance that Gleason would be watching me place the cameras. The bastard had to have a telescope over there. Or maybe it was my imagination that I always felt as if he was watching.

I shook my head. No. He was watching. I'd bet money on it. As I walked into the house, I texted Jude, asking him to double-check the feeds to confirm the cameras were performing as expected.

Since I'd gotten such an early start, I'd skipped the shower. Now, though, I had the time.

It felt both strange and perfectly normal to be showering in Grace's house while she wasn't here. There was an odd intimacy to it because it made the house feel more like mine. Of course, that was what I wanted. And I needed to talk to Grace about it. Eventually.

Now that she was speaking to me, and I was in her bed, I was going to make one thing crystal clear to her—for me, this was forever.

If she didn't already know, she would.

After showering quickly, I stepped back into the bedroom. Our bed was messy from the night before, and the closet still stood open from when I retrieved the bag of Charles's personal effects from the hospital. This time, something else caught my eye.

This was the one room we hadn't thoroughly searched because Grace obviously knew that the documents we'd been looking for weren't in here. But now I spotted something in the closet I hadn't noticed yesterday.

Canvases.

Grace was a talented artist. When we'd been younger, she'd painted whenever she had the chance. But these canvases looked old.

I pushed the closet door open fully. Holy shit. I recognized the painting at the front of the stack. The mountains near the town where we'd grown up. I remembered watching her paint it.

Slowly, I flipped through the stacked paintings. I'd seen all of them before. The only things that were new here were the easel in the opposite corner that still smelled of fresh-cut wood and a set of unopened paints next to one of the legs. Just the basic colors, but it seemed clear Grace hadn't painted in a long time.

How long?

I smiled. The one thing she didn't have right now was a selection of blank canvases. I could take care of that.

My phone chimed with a text—Jude confirming that the cameras were up and running. Perfect. This would be a good test run to see if I got any notifications while I was out. We still had two days until Gleason's ominous deadline, but I knew men like him. He was chomping at the bit, waiting for us to give in.

We never would.

I grabbed my keys and headed to my truck, mentally daring the man next door to come and get me.

~

Grace still wasn't home when I got back, and I didn't see any sign of a disturbance. Good. I wanted to set this up just so.

The ranch house was big, and the main floor was a huge open space. The kitchen took up part of the back, but there were also several large windows that looked out toward the mountains. Perfect.

I brought the easel down from the closet and put one of the new canvases on it, stacking the rest of the canvases against the wall. I set up a little table I'd bought, and I arranged the paints Charles had given her on it. And the paints I couldn't resist getting while I was at the little art store in town.

Gravel crunched outside. Perfect timing. I opened the door and leaned against the frame, watching her get out of the truck. Her shoulders drooped as she slowly made her way to the house, exhaustion clear in her features.

"That bad?"

She didn't answer me at first, just let me pull her close, and leaned against my chest. "Not bad, I guess, but tiring. And no luck."

"I'm sorry."

"Not your fault," she sighed. "Obviously."

I laughed quietly. "Well, I have a surprise for you."

Grace lifted her head and looked at me. The afternoon sun caught her hair, and I drank in her face wreathed in flame. Perfect green eyes and pink lips…I traced every inch of her face with my eyes. She was so damned beautiful, it took my breath away.

"You do?"

"I do." I lowered my head to hers and kissed her. The

way she melted underneath me—I would cherish it until the day I died.

She smiled when I pulled away. "Was that the surprise?"

"No. But first, Nelson confirmed our appointment for tomorrow. He'll be here around noon."

"I'm sure that will be interesting," she said. "And maybe worthless if I can't figure out what Charles wanted to do with it."

"It won't be worthless. No matter what, it's yours. You can do whatever you want with it."

Grace snorted. "If Wayne doesn't take it away from me first."

I stopped. "Are you worried about it? I put up the new cameras. He won't find them this time."

"Of course I'm worried. I believe you when you say you won't let anything happen, but I've lived next door to the man for years. He's a bastard. He has always been a bastard. If he doesn't know about the mine and he finds out about it, then everything gets worse. If he already knows, and it's worth something real, I don't think there's anything he won't do to get his hands on it."

I hated that she was right. But I wasn't going to scare her with the way my gut clenched at the thought of that man. Or the way he made my instincts explode. If I had my way, I'd get her away from him completely. "Well, let's wait and see what Nelson says before we worry about that." Gently, I moved us both through the door and into the house. "And the kiss wasn't your surprise. That is."

I felt it when she saw. Her whole body went still. "What?"

"I took a shower, and the closet was still open. I saw your old paintings. I remembered how much you loved to paint, and I didn't see any canvases or any new paintings. So, I got some. I hope you don't mind."

Grace let me go and approached the easel hesitantly. Was she afraid of it? She reached out and brushed her fingers across the wood as if she didn't fully believe it was real. "Is it okay?"

"Yeah." She looked back at me and glanced away quickly. But not quickly enough for me to miss the way that her eyes shone. "Yes. It's amazing. Thank you."

"You okay?" I caught her from behind and pulled her against me. "I didn't mean to make you cry."

"I'm not crying," she said, the tears obvious in her voice.

I laughed softly. "No?"

"Fine. But they're not bad tears."

"That's good."

Grace leaned her head back against my shoulder. "Why here?"

"Good view of the mountains. When it's nice, you can take everything out on the back porch."

She didn't say anything, so I leaned in and kissed the skin below her ear. "I'm sorry you didn't find the bank. But now the list is smaller, and I will do whatever I can to help you."

"I know you will."

"Then why do you sound like I ran over a puppy?"

A laugh burst out of her, and she turned in my arms. "I do not."

"Do too." Her whole face scrunched up, and I grinned. "But what's wrong?"

"I promise, there's nothing wrong, Harlan. It's—"

I waited for her to find the words she wanted.

Grace shook her head. "I know I keep talking about Charles, and that can't be fun for you. But—"

"Grace," I said. "You spent ten years with him. And he did what I couldn't. He saved your life. I don't mind that you talk about him."

A blush spread across her cheeks. And I suddenly needed to focus because the blush conjured images of her underneath me in her bed and how desperately I wanted that right now. I was insatiable around her.

"It's another thing I'll have to…accept or get used to. I know Charles loved me in his own way. But we were nothing more than roommates. He didn't really *do* things for me, if that makes sense. And of course, he didn't need to. But he gave me the easel and paints right before he died. It was the biggest, most personal thing he'd ever bought me. And that was after ten years."

She stared into the distance over my shoulder. "And?"

"And you did this after, like…three days. It hit me harder than I thought it would."

"More making up for lost time," I said, pressing my forehead to hers. "Three days, my ass. If anything, I'm very, very late getting you presents. I plan to give you a gift for every occasion I missed."

Her hands tightened on my shoulders. "You bought me this." She held up her hand with the wedding ring.

I swallowed. "I did."

"You never told me where you got them."

"I didn't think you'd want to know," I admitted with a laugh. "The wedding was full of enough tension as it was."

The tears faded from her eyes. "Did you *steal* the rings?"

"No, I didn't steal them."

"Then where—"

"I already had them." I pulled away from her quickly and crossed the room. She would find out eventually, but admitting the truth would lay my soul bare to her.

I glanced back at Grace and watched her swallow. "What does that mean?"

"It means that I've had them since I left. I knew I wanted to marry you. We'd basically promised each other forever. I had the rings in my pocket that night."

"Seriously?"

"Seriously."

She shook her head. "Holy shit." Then she laughed. "I'm amazed they still fit."

"I got lucky."

"Wait a second." She focused an intrigued glare on me and lifted her hand. "This is a wedding ring. Did you buy an engagement ring?"

"I did."

"Where is it?"

I told the truth. "It's at my house. At Resting Warrior."

"Are you going to give it to me?"

My heart stopped. For three beats, there was nothing in my chest before the world came rushing back in. "Do you want it?"

The words hung in the air, and I let her think about the implications. I wanted nothing more than to put that ring on her finger. But that would make it real. If I ever gave Grace that ring, it would mean forever.

If I put it on her hand, it was never coming off.

"Oh." Her breath was soft as if she'd read every emotion on my face and more.

She crossed the space I'd put between us. "I'm not saying no."

I smiled. "That's a start."

"But do you know what I am saying yes to?"

"Spending the rest of the day in bed with me?"

She rose on her tiptoes and wrapped her arms around

my neck before pressing her lips to my ear. "That's what I'm thinking. As a thank-you. For the gift."

"I didn't buy it for you so you'd sleep with me." I lifted her off the floor as I said it, however. She wrapped her legs around my hips as we walked toward the stairs.

"I know you didn't. And maybe I'm using it as an excuse. Because I need you. Right now."

She would get no argument from me.

## Chapter 20

*Grace*

Harlan's heart beat under my ear. My body still felt drugged from last night. Too much pleasure and exertion —could there really be such a thing? If there was, I wasn't used to it, but I was sure I could get used to it quickly. I snuggled closer to him.

I was drowsy and wanted to go back to sleep in this perfect warmth, but Nelson Barnes was coming to see the mine, and I needed to be awake and ready for possible battle. Still, I took a long breath and listened to Harlan's heart. It was a calm, slow rhythm. Steady.

I stiffened without being able to help it. The last time I'd felt that steady beat under my head had been ten years ago. I'd thought nothing could take him away from me.

But he'd left, even if he had good reason. My whole life burned to the ground.

Then I'd finally gotten my life back together, even if it

had been in a way I'd never planned, and it had burned down around me once more.

Was it just a matter of time before it happened again? Was this heartbeat fate's way of laughing at me before I lost everything for the third time?

Damn, there went all my calm and peace. My nerves were back, and with them, the instinct to move. The only reason I stayed put was because Harlan was still asleep, and that was rare. When I was awake, he was awake, and I didn't want to disturb him. But I couldn't stop the slow movements of my fingers and toes, subtly trying to take the edge off my energy.

"What's going on?" Harlan asked. His voice was rough with disuse and sex, but it definitely wasn't sleepy.

I sat up. "How long have you been awake?"

His mouth curved into a smile, though he didn't open his eyes. "A while."

"And you didn't say anything?"

"I like feeling you next to me. Lie back down."

My insides clenched at that sexy, authoritative tone. And I liked feeling him next to me too. Too much.

I didn't want to tell him what was going on in my head. I needed to move. Work it off. I'd go to the stables and get an early jump on the work before Dana and Rachel got here.

But using that lightning SEAL speed, he pulled me closer and rolled me underneath him, effectively trapping me. Damn him. Because I loved being trapped this way, and no matter what was going on in my head, my body decidedly preferred the position it was in.

"Hey." His hips pressed against mine. "What's going on? You were fine and soft and relaxed against me then that suddenly changed."

I let out a small sigh. "I don't know. I guess I'm just nervous about Nelson Barnes coming."

Harlan knew it was more than that and wanted to press. I could see it in his eyes. But he didn't.

"Okay," he finally said. "Then I want to ask another question that's been on my mind."

Anything was better than the current topic. "Sure."

"Why don't you paint anymore?"

I'd been wrong. This was even worse. This was a topic I wasn't ready to talk about at all.

Especially not since he'd surprised me with that beautiful gift. After his gift, for the first time in forever, I felt as if I might actually be able to create again. Every time I'd thought about picking up a paintbrush over the past ten years had been like taking a knife to my own heart. So I hadn't even tried.

"When I saw those paintings yesterday," Harlan said softly, searching my face, "I noticed there weren't any new ones. They're all ones I recognized from years ago. Have you not painted in ten years?"

I looked away, which was hard with him so close and big over me. "No, I haven't."

"Why?"

"I don't want to talk about it." I pushed at him, and he let me slide out from under him and slip off the bed.

"Grace." His voice was firm. I could hear the military in it. "You need to tell me."

I didn't look back at him as I pulled on my clothes. "Talking about it isn't going to do any good."

"You're basically turning into a ball of stress over it, so maybe talking would actually do some good." I looked over my shoulder. He'd swung his long legs over the side of the bed, the sheet wrapped around his hips as he studied me.

"It won't change anything."

"It's because of me, isn't it?"

"After you left, I couldn't," I whispered. "It *hurt* to pick up a brush because all I could think about was you. So after a while, I stopped trying. Charles tried to encourage me, but that part of me died when you left."

His eyes were bleak. "You shouldn't have let me stop you from doing something you loved."

Something snapped in my chest, like the final tether on what had been holding back this storm inside me.

"Losing you broke me. Do you understand that? I realize it was for a good reason, but that doesn't mean the pain didn't happen and that all my pieces are magically glued back together."

I took a breath, trying to calm myself down, but it wasn't helping. "I survived without you. And part of that survival was not picking up a paintbrush since all it did was cause me pain."

Looking at him, I realized I wasn't just mad at him. I was mad at myself because I'd thrown away such a vital piece of myself for a decade.

I needed air. I needed out of this house. I spun for the door.

"Grace." He called from behind me, and I heard the signs of him scrambling out of bed and dressing, but I was already gone.

Shoving my boots on, I went straight for the fields. No time to saddle a horse—I needed to move and work off the panicked anger simmering under my skin.

His words were true. I shouldn't have allowed his leaving to cut off such an important piece of myself. I'd held on to my anger at him for so long, but my true fury was at myself. Instead of showing any sort of strength when he'd left, I'd crumbled.

I'd lost Harlan, then threw my art away with him. I'd

lost time I could never get back, and I had no one to blame but myself.

My boots sank into the ground as I walked faster. It had been so rainy lately that the earth was soft. My feet took me toward the back of the property line and the mine. Probably because it was on my mind. But I wasn't stupid enough to go into the mine by myself. That was a recipe for disaster.

However, I could see the sinkhole on the border of Dominion Ranch. There was something appealing about a piece of ground that had gotten so furious it had simply given up and collapsed in on itself. Or at least that was how I chose to think of it in that moment.

I sensed Harlan when he came near. I'd known he'd come for me. I'd wanted him to. Because no matter how angry I was—at him, at myself, at life—the most elemental part of me wanted to be near Harlan Young.

For a second, I stopped and stared. He strode toward me over the fields as if he were in a movie scene, the morning sun painting him like the perfect cowboy. He was breathtaking.

I didn't say anything. I didn't know what to do about this storm buzzing inside me, threatening to destroy me from the inside out.

"You don't have to talk to me," he called. "And you can work this off whatever way you like—you can walk, run, scream at the sky, come over here and punch me in the jaw, whatever you need. But I'm not letting you wander around out here alone while that asshole is coming for you." He pointed toward Wayne's house.

I turned my back to him and doubled my pace. I wanted to do all of those things. And so many more.

But mostly, I wanted back everything I'd lost. The future Harlan and I should've had. The years I should've spent hearing his heartbeat under my ear. The paintings I should've created.

The ground under my feet was softer here, and I slid around while trying to go faster. A futile attempt to escape myself.

"Be careful," he called from behind me.

I kept going, not stopping until I was in front of the sinkhole, looking down into the darkness. This spot was deeper than I'd thought. The tunnel below was at least thirty feet down. The dark mass in front of me was a fitting visual representation of what I was feeling. I studied it in silence.

"Gracie, step back. You're too close."

I didn't turn. "We lost so much. We can't ever get it back."

"No, we can't. We can only move forward from here."

I felt some of the storm inside me begin to settle. I turned toward him. "You're right. I—"

I felt the shifting too late. My feet sank deeper into the mud, suddenly throwing my balance off. The overwhelming dizziness didn't make sense. What was happening?

The sensation of hollowness—the nothingness—under my feet was so acute, adrenaline flooded my system. There wasn't time to move. The ground was already crumbling. Straight down the three-story drop I had been staring into.

Harlan called my name, but he was too far away to do anything.

I hurled my body in the only safe direction—toward him. Too late. I hit the edge and slid, hands grabbing nothing but liquid mud. I couldn't gain purchase. The ground was slippery and broken. I felt the dirt jam under my fingernails as I dug in with all my strength.

The rest of the ground collapsed under my feet, my

grasp on the edge the only thing keeping me from plunging into the abyss. Harlan called my name again, but all I could think about was the fact that I was hanging over a ledge. If I fell, the impact would, at the very least, break my legs.

But he was here now. No matter what had happened in the past, Harlan was here. And because of that, I wasn't afraid. Nothing else seemed important.

Yes, my heart pounded. Yes, I feared the pain I knew was in my immediate future. But if I fell, Harlan would be here with me. He would find a way to save me.

Because that's what Harlan did. He saved people who didn't know they needed it.

"Grace."

Harlan's face appeared over the edge. I hadn't realized how far I'd slipped. He couldn't reach me. That didn't mean he wouldn't try.

I saw the grim determination in his eyes as he stretched down. "Can you reach for me?"

"No." The word was barely a gasp, but it was the truth. I had no leverage. My legs dangled into empty air, and for a moment, I forgot he was there. Visceral fight-or-flight panic ripped through me.

"Don't you dare let go," he said, disappearing for a moment.

When Harlan appeared again, it wasn't his face I saw but his legs. He was extending his legs down to me. It was risky, and we both knew it. There was every chance this ground wasn't stable enough to hold both of us and he'd fall with me. But he was going to try.

One foot appeared by my hand. "Grab me, Grace."

"I don't know if I can hold on."

"You can. And as soon as you have me, I've got you." His tone and his words left no room for doubt.

My arms cramped. I didn't have long. Quickly, I yanked my right hand out of the soil and secured his leg in the crook of my elbow. And then my other hand.

Harlan's breath hissed out at the weight of both of us. But he dragged me upward with pure, brutal strength, pulling himself away from the edge and forcing me up and over as well. As soon as my weight wasn't in the balance, he grabbed me and jerked me away from the edge. More ground flaked away and fell into the dimness.

I lay on the ground, covered in mud, chest heaving.

"Holy shit," Harlan said. He knelt beside me, leaning down to kiss me. The way his mouth covered mine—filled with desperation and relief—was the way I always felt around him but could never let myself truly admit.

I blinked away the tears that filled my eyes. I wrapped my arms around his neck and drew him down to me. He took out his worry on my lips, and I reveled in it as I released every piece of my earlier anger. My close call had brought the reality of our situation into stark relief. I should have learned my lesson after losing Charles. Tomorrow wasn't promised, and if I wanted any kind of future with Harlan, I needed to let go of the pain of our past for good.

"Don't do that again," he begged, voice ragged.

"I wasn't planning on doing it the first time," I said. It was an attempt at lightening the mood, but it didn't work.

Harlan pulled me up, then yanked me against him as if he was never going to let me go ever again. "I'm sorry." His breath sawed in and out of his chest as if he'd run a marathon. "I'm so fucking sorry."

I hugged him back. "You didn't make the ground collapse."

"Not for that." He pulled back to look at me. "I never said that I was sorry, Grace. I explained why I did what I did, but I never apologized. And you have no idea how sorry I am that I did that to you. That's what I was going to tell you. I am never leaving you again. I'm here with you, and I want to be in this together."

My breath caught in my chest. Not a single part of me doubted his words.

"There's more I want to say, but I'm not going to say it while we're here, covered in mud and terrified." He grasped my shoulders. "But I need you to hear more than just these words. I am never leaving you."

I didn't know who moved first, but it didn't matter whether he was kissing me or I was kissing him. Neither of us could stand to be apart.

And I could hear the words he wasn't saying right now. That he *loved* me.

The truth was, I was falling in love with my husband. But there was every possibility that I'd never fallen *out* of love with him in the first place.

"This isn't always going to be easy. I know that. You know it too. But I'm not going to walk away from it, even if you scream at me for a year." He pressed his forehead to mine. "I'm so sorry I left."

My breath shuddered in my chest. I'd never thought I would be here, and I never thought I would speak the words. But the second they left my lips, I felt as if the sword that had been hanging over my head vanished entirely. "I forgive you."

Harlan's arms tightened around me. I didn't dare open my eyes. Because I knew that his face would wreck me if I did. I let us breathe in the peace. The freedom.

"Do you forgive me?" I asked softly. "For the way I've treated you the past two years?"

He slid his fingers along my cheek and behind my neck. He turned my face up to his, and I finally opened my eyes. "There isn't anything to forgive you for," he said. "But if you need to hear it, then yes. I do. I forgive you."

I melted. The retreating adrenaline that dragged my anger away with it turned my legs to jelly, and I nearly collapsed into him. Harlan caught me and swept me into his arms, already walking back toward the house.

"You can't carry me all the way back."

"Watch me," he said in a tone that dared me to disagree. "But the next time you need to rage, please go somewhere where the ground is actually stable."

"Yeah, no kidding."

He did, in fact, carry me all the way back to the house. As if it was nothing. When he set me on my feet on the back porch, he was barely winded.

I looked down at myself. "Guess I need to shower before Nelson gets here." The whole front of me was slathered in mud and dirt, and Harlan was the same.

"Maybe. But I think it's a good look."

"You're only saying that because you want to wash it off me," I said with a laugh.

"It did cross my mind."

Harlan's phone rang, and he pulled it out of his pocket. "What's up, Grant?"

He listened for a couple of seconds. "Yeah, I can come help. I'll be there in a few minutes." Hanging up, he looked at me. "They need help with an injured horse. I should be back before Nelson gets here."

"It's okay, even if you're not," I said. "He was friends with Charles. I'll be fine."

Leaning in, he kissed me quickly. "I won't be taking chances like that. Lock the doors, please."

I watched him start to walk around the house. "You're not going to change your clothes?"

"It's an injured horse. And it's just as muddy over there.

I'll probably be muddier by the time I'm done. And then later, you can wash it off *me*."

He was still chuckling when he disappeared around the corner, and I rolled my eyes. The man was brazen. And I loved that about him.

I loved him.

I'd known that forever. And as he made me see he was who he'd always been, that love had come back to the surface. I wasn't ready to say it out loud, but the words lived in my soul.

Words spoken out loud or not, that ease and relief I felt in my chest? Those had been worth the wait.

## Chapter 21

*Grace*

I relaxed in the shower for a while since I still had some time. Now that the adrenaline had left my body, I felt where I would be sore. Tomorrow, my arms would be screaming, and I was certain I'd see a giant bruise across my stomach from where I'd landed when I'd tried to jump to safety.

But the hot water felt heavenly, and I thought there was a good chance I could convince Harlan to play doctor with me. Though my idea of him helping me with ice packs was probably different from how he would interpret it.

My laugh filled the bathroom with an echo. It was still strange to be able to think that way. Knowing that Harlan would be here, no matter what. The words he'd said out there were as much a vow as those he'd made to me when we got married. Maybe more binding.

He was never leaving me again.

That was something I could believe and trust. The

certainty of a future together settled over me like a blanket. I wouldn't be alone anymore.

Plenty of people would have thought I was crazy if I'd told them that I'd felt alone since Harlan had disappeared. But I had, although I hadn't been willing to admit it. No matter how difficult it would be for us to find a path forward—and we both knew that it wouldn't be easy—there was no way I was going back to that kind of isolation.

I dressed in clothes that weren't slathered in mud and threw the ones from this morning into the washing machine. Odds were I'd probably end up muddy again, but showing up to a meeting covered in dirt didn't exactly make a good impression.

I still had an hour until I was supposed to meet Nelson, but I couldn't think about anything else. All I wanted was to find out if this could help me. How much was it worth? Besides, we still had a day until Wayne's threatened deadline. He wouldn't do anything yet.

I pulled out my phone and dialed Harlan quickly. He answered on the first ring. "Are you okay?"

I laughed. "I'm fine. I'm heading out to the mine early because I'm having a hard time sitting still."

"Grace."

"Harlan," I said. "I'll be fine. I'll have my phone on me, and I'll take Dove. You can meet me out there when you get back, okay?"

The length of his silence told me that he wasn't happy about it. "Be careful, please."

"I will," I said. "And thank you for not freaking out."

"I am freaking out," he muttered under his breath. "I'll be there shortly."

It was a good thing he wasn't here to see the smile I desperately tried to hide. "See you soon."

Dove shook her head when I entered the stable. "Hey, girl. Want to go for a ride?"

She always did. Big Red was a good horse, but Dove was gentle, and I usually liked riding her more because she was so relaxed.

In the haze of my outburst this morning, I hadn't actually noticed that it was a beautiful day. Cooler than it had been recently, maybe because of the rain. There was quite a breeze, but the sun felt good on my skin. I couldn't remember a day in the past couple of years that I'd felt this…content. Even with Wayne bearing down on me and the ownership of Ruby Round up in the air, I felt *good*.

I shook my head. Life had a way of surprising you that way.

When we passed the fence, I left Dove at the same tree Harlan had tied the horses to the other day. They weren't comfortable with the tunnels under the ground. After the incident this morning, I didn't blame them.

Honestly, before all of this and Harlan discovering the mine, I'd never usually come out this far. The mountains towered overhead and were completely overwhelming. This close, it was easy to realize how small you were. And when you were underground, it was equally easy to imagine how much weight was above you, ready to collapse at the slightest provocation.

I picked my way toward the mine's entrance, taking my time since I had plenty of it. The view of the ranch from here was gorgeous. I wanted to come back and take some pictures. Hell, I might come back and paint it.

Coming over the hill from the west, I froze when the opening to the mine came into view. An unfamiliar horse was tethered next to the entrance, behind a bend in the rock that kept it hidden. Was Nelson here early?

But my stomach dropped when I saw the saddle. The

leather was stamped with a giant G. G for Gleason.

*Shit.*

We'd figured he knew about the mine, but why the hell was he here now? He had no rights to this place without official ownership. Was he stealing? Laying a trap?

I didn't know what to do. I could head back to the house and wait for Harlan to show up then come back to confront Wayne. But if I left right now, I'd lose any chance of finally having proof that Wayne was up to something shady.

Harlan would kill me if I didn't call him. I pulled my phone out of my pocket, and my heart sank. No signal. One bar flickered in and out of existence, not enough to get a call out.

Resolve slid down my spine and solidified. I'd been afraid of Wayne long enough. We'd needed proof this entire time, and this could be it. Moving with an almost comical slowness so that I wouldn't be heard, I made my way down the hill. The horse whickered quietly as I came close but didn't give me away. Thankfully.

How far inside was Wayne? The farther I had to go into the mine to find him, the more chance that he would see me.

My heart pounded in my chest so loudly I had to pause in the doorway for a second. But I could do this. I *would* do this. For Charles. For me. For Harlan. I wasn't going to let this bully of a man steal from me. Whether it was a single sapphire or my whole damn property.

The tunnel was dark beyond the natural light of the entrance, but I didn't dare use the flashlight on my phone. Instead, I kept my hand on the wall as I walked forward. I didn't make it all the way to the room with the branching tunnels—I heard voices before I got that far.

He wasn't alone. *Fuck.*

I risked the light on my phone for a few seconds to turn on a video recording. If he was talking, then I was going to listen. But right now, I could only hear the reverberant echoes of voices. I needed to get closer. I may not be able to get them on camera, but I had to do whatever I could.

Wayne's voice resolved into its normal sneering tone. "I don't care about your reputation. You're going to tell her that this place is worthless. Got it?"

There was a mumbling response I couldn't make out, but my stomach sank as I realized Nelson Barnes was already here with Wayne. I immediately realized I'd been completely wrong when I'd told Harlan that I would be fine alone with Nelson because he'd known Charles. He was already in my enemy's pocket.

"What does telling her it's worthless do? She's not going to sell off the mineral rights either way. This is a bad idea."

"If she thinks it's not worth anything, then maybe she'll give in and do it the easy way. She's close to breaking, even if she bought herself some time with that bullshit marriage."

Anger flared in my chest. Our marriage wasn't bullshit.

Seconds later, I blinked, realizing I actually believed that. Not only was I in love with Harlan, my subconscious mind had already decided our marriage was real.

I was so shocked by the realization that I missed what Nelson said in response.

"Charles had everything I needed. But I thought she would know where he kept it. Clearly, the bitch needs a little motivation. As far as I know, she hasn't found the safe-deposit box key. I tried to take it off him when he crashed the car, but he was supposed to be dead on impact. I didn't hit him hard enough, I guess. The ambulances were coming, so I didn't have time."

Ringing filled my ears.

I felt as if the mountain were spinning underneath me.

He had killed Charles.

I'd known Wayne was after the property. The mine. I'd just never thought he'd killed Charles to get it.

Air. There wasn't enough air in here.

This changed everything. Harlan needed to know. And Charlie. Wayne had admitted to murder, and I had it recorded.

"Well, you should have made time," Nelson said. "Because this is much harder. You promised me an easy payout with this when you called this morning. But whatever you think Grace Townsend is, she isn't stupid. She's going to be able to see that this mine isn't empty. It's clear as day."

"You think I don't know that?" Wayne growled. "And you'll get your money. All you have to do is not fuck it up. She'll be handing me the keys to the place tomorrow. If she doesn't, she already knows that I'm going to take it by force."

I heard a sound that told me Nelson still wasn't pleased. "Fine. But you need to leave. She's going to be here soon, and given everything, her seeing you isn't a good idea."

A laugh filled the mine, low and sinister. "As much as you're right, I wish I could see the bitch's face when she realizes everything—and knows I've won."

Footsteps scraped on the ground. They were coming straight toward me now, on their way to keep up appearances. I had to get out.

It was harder on the way back, hearing them behind me, just talking about nothing now. They were moving faster than I was because I had to keep quiet. Every time I glanced back, I felt as if they were closer.

Light appeared in front of me, and I took what felt like my first breath since the moment I'd heard Wayne's and Nelson's voices. But I couldn't relax. I couldn't let them see me. At all. I had to make it to Dove and ride like hell. The chances of my doing that were almost zero. She was too far away.

Their voices were right behind me, and in seconds, they were going to be able to see me. I didn't have the luxury of sneaking anymore. I ran.

The horse was so startled as I rushed by that it barely had time to make a sound. Dove was down the hill, and right then, she felt as if she was an entire lifetime away. Behind me, Wayne's horse finally reacted to my passage, and I heard the sounds of surprise. And then the shout when they saw me.

Adrenaline poured through my body for the second time today. But unlike this morning, Harlan wasn't here to save me. This was far more dangerous than a couple broken legs.

My lungs and legs burned with the effort of running down the hill. I had to make it. I didn't have another option. If Wayne caught me, I didn't know what would happen.

Sounds of galloping sounded behind me, but I didn't look back. I couldn't. I pushed myself harder. Dove was close, but I didn't know if I could make it to her in time. It would take a miracle.

I heard the sound of the gun before I fully registered it, and I hit the ground. My body skidded over rocks and into the grass, and I kept rolling to get some distance. The shot that rang out went nowhere as Wayne rode past me.

One more chance. He had to turn around to catch me now, but he was definitely going to catch me.

"Mrs. Townsend!" he bellowed, trying to wrangle his

skittish horse. My only advantage. The horse hadn't been prepared for what it was being asked to do, and it reared when Wayne tried to turn.

Launching myself off the ground, I ran for Dove. There was no way I could make it back to the house now. But there was something else I *could* do. Because Harlan would come looking, and if I wasn't here, he would tear the world apart to find me.

I shoved my phone under Dove's saddle and ripped her reins loose. I smacked her on the rear. And again when she didn't move. "*Go.*" Her ears went flat with fear. Wayne was coming, and it was the sound of the other horse that made her finally run.

He didn't chase her. She wasn't what he wanted.

The thud of him dropping to the ground was shockingly final. "Got you."

I didn't say anything. I wouldn't give Wayne Gleason the satisfaction of knowing I was terrified. But my body didn't agree with that plan. I backed away from him as he approached, well aware of the pistol in his hand. Until I was backed up against the tree and I had nowhere else to run.

"You know you're trespassing," I said, shocked at how calm my own voice sounded.

He laughed again. A copy of the sinister tone I'd heard a few moments ago. "What are you going to do about that?"

"I don't know," I said. "But you need to leave right now, Wayne. Before I press charges."

Wayne looked at me, his stare making my entire body go cold. "I gave you a chance," he said. "I told you to take the easy way out. This isn't the easy way."

I barely saw the gun coming before the butt hit my temple, and everything in the world went black.

## Chapter 22

*Harlan*

I disconnected the call with Grace, not happy that she was going to be wandering the property alone. But this wouldn't take long, or so Grant had said. Hopefully that was true and I could get to her quickly. Maybe I was over-reacting, but until the whole situation was resolved, I didn't want her to be alone.

Grant waited near the stables with one of Resting Warrior's trucks and the horse trailer. Cori, the vet, stood near him. I recognized the look on his face. I'd seen it on Lucas's face often enough, and I was sure they'd say the same of me. The man was crazy about Cori.

She smiled too, leaning against the truck as if she was meant to be there. If I weren't as eager as I was to get back to Grace, I'd back off and give him some more time. Grant had his demons, as we all did, and it was good to see him smile.

But the whole reason he'd called me was that

always went in twos when we could. We each had enough in our pasts to make us more comfortable that way. Grant had an injury that held him back, though he didn't like to admit it. And moving a horse like we were here to do could make it flare up in an instant. He loved working with the animals, but it wasn't always easy for him.

"Hey," I said, coming up to them.

"Hi, Harlan," Cori said. "Good to see you."

I nodded. "What's going on?"

Grant sighed. "Turns out Grace's piece-of-shit neighbor didn't actually take care of that horse from the other day. Surrendered him. Cori found him a home down the road, but I wanted backup."

"Sure thing," I said.

The animal hadn't been abused; that was clear. We'd received enough abused animals at Resting Warrior to recognize the signs. But it was also clear Gleason was a negligent animal owner. Yet another reason for me to dislike the man.

But Grant had kept his word. Once we got the horse into the trailer—easier said than done with a horse that was both skittish and healing—the place we were dropping it off was only a ten-minute drive. I'd driven past the ranch plenty of times but had never met the owner. They were nice, and getting the horse out of the trailer was a hundred times easier than putting him in.

"Thanks," Cori said with a grin. "I had been hoping he'd let this horse go when I saw him the other day. A nice animal like this doesn't belong with a guy like him."

"You're telling me."

Cori stroked the animal's neck. She reminded me of Lena, with her open laugh and quirky hair colors. "You found this place awfully fast."

"Yeah." She shrugged. "But when you're the vet, you

pretty much always know when people are looking for new animals. And the Smiths are excellent owners. Even though this guy won't be ready to work for a bit, I know they'll take good care of him."

"I'm sure they will," Grant said. "Hell, this was the easiest placement we've ever had. I should come to you for help more often."

"And maybe for some other things too," I whispered.

Cori turned away to check something in the stall, and Grant elbowed me in the side. "Stop."

"But it's so much fun." Yeah, we were brothers. Twelve-year-old brothers.

I'd always known Grace was the woman for me. No drama there. But watching my brothers-in-arms fall in love was entertaining as hell.

"Anything else you need to take care of?" I asked Cori.

"Nope, that should be it. We can head out."

"Thanks," I said. "Don't mean to rush things, but I need to get back to Grace."

Grant grinned. "Hot date?"

"I wish," I laughed. "No, an appointment at the ranch I told Grace I would be there for."

That was one way to put it.

Leaving her had been easier, knowing that Gleason had dropped the horse off. It meant for at least part of the morning, he had been away from his house, and that made me feel better about Grace being alone there.

"Thanks for this," Grant said. Softly enough that Cori didn't hear. I knew what he meant.

"Any time. Now, do you want me to try to get you more time with her?"

Grant raised an eyebrow. "I told you before. She's my next-door neighbor. She's taken, and we're nothing more than friends."

"The look on your face when I walked up on the two of you tells a different story."

He glared at me. "Not a word to her."

"Wouldn't dream of it." I raised my hands in surrender. "Say, how was Gleason when he dropped off the horse?"

Grant frowned. "What do you mean?"

"When he surrendered the horse this morning, how did he seem? He gave us some bullshit deadline for tomorrow and…" I trailed off when I saw Grant's face. "What?"

"He wasn't the one who dropped it off."

Everything inside me went cold. "What?"

"It wasn't him. It was a ranch hand. One who made sure to tell me who the horse belonged to, though. Very intentional about that."

Shit. *Shit.* All my instincts screamed at once, and every shred of peace and calm I'd managed to grab hold of vanished. He'd sent someone else to drop off the animal. And Wayne Gleason had been here long enough to know at least the basics of our operation. If he knew there was a good chance I'd be called away…

My mind shifted into tactical mode, the one way I could fight the sudden panic. "You drive," I said, jumping back into the truck and pulling out my phone.

"Everything okay?"

"I hope so," I said as I called Grace.

No answer. Shit.

I called her again. Signal was spotty out in the fields at best, but I knew that wasn't it. I felt it in my gut.

"What's going on?" Cori asked.

Clearing my throat, I admitted, "I don't know. But I have a bad feeling about it."

"Tell me."

I had no reason not to. In fact, the more people who

knew about this, the better. I called Grace's phone again while I gave Grant and Cori the brief rundown of what had happened. I should have told them before, but I knew Grace didn't want everyone knowing her business. Our business. Now, I didn't care.

"Are you fucking kidding me, Harlan?" Grant asked, pushing his foot down on the gas. "Your wife is being threatened, and this is the first time you're telling me? Telling us?"

He practically slid into the Resting Warrior driveway, as much as you could towing a horse trailer. Cori opened the door. "I'll give you two a minute. Harlan, if you need anything, please let me know."

"Thanks." I waited until the door closed before I spoke. "I had it handled. You know Grace. She's barely let me back into her life. I wasn't going to risk that by telling everyone her business behind her back. I have to go."

"What do you need?" Grant asked.

"Check the cameras. Wind it back and see what happened, if there's anything to see." Her phone went to voice mail again. "And track her phone."

"Got it."

I didn't stop to look back to make sure he was doing what I asked. I trusted that he would. Now that they knew, none of the men would take chances with Grace.

My phone rang when I was barely three minutes away from Resting Warrior. It was Daniel. "Hey."

"You want to fill me in?"

"I'm assuming Grant already did that."

He made a sound of annoyance. "And when were you going to tell the rest of us?"

"I don't have time to listen to a lecture. If you're going to rip me a new asshole, save it for later. I'll let you beat it out of me on the mat. I have to go."

"Are you sure anything is wrong?"

My instincts told me there was. It didn't matter that it didn't make sense. The timing on this whole situation was too convenient, and I wouldn't put anything past Wayne Gleason. "Yes. I'm sure."

"Okay." Daniel's voice was all business. "We're working on the phone and the cameras. The second you know what's going on, you tell us. Do you hear me? No more hiding this shit. You know that's not a part of the deal."

He was right. Other than some specific details of our pasts, we had an unwritten arrangement that we didn't hide things from one another. Especially stuff like this. But I'd worry about that later. "Will do."

I hung up before he could try to pull me into any further conversation. The road was barely on my radar. Grace's number appeared under my fingers, and I pressed it. I knew she wasn't going to answer, but calling that number was the only thing I could do until I got there. So, I called. And I called again.

Instead of going to help Grant, I should have called one of the other guys. I should have told Grace not to go out there alone, despite thinking it was safe. I should never have let her out of my sight for a second. When was I going to learn? I'd let her out of my sight for ten damn years.

When I found her—and I was going to find her—I was going to glue us together if that's what it took. After I dealt with Wayne Gleason.

One more call, one more soundbite of Grace's voice telling me she couldn't come to the phone right now. I shoved down the panic. She was fine. I was overreacting. There was no signal in the mine.

She was fine.

I drove faster.

## Chapter 23

*Grace*

It felt as if my brain was trying to pound its way out of my skull. Without reaching up to touch it, I knew I had a knot on my temple, swollen and throbbing. Wayne hadn't held back when he'd hit me.

Not that he would. He'd been waiting a long time to do that.

Quiet, tinkering sounds entered my ears, and I opened my eyes. Rocks formed the ceiling, lit up from a dim source. Dread immediately pooled in my stomach. I was in the mine. I was sure of it.

But I had no idea *where* in the mine I was. We already knew this place sprawled for miles. How far back into the tunnels had Wayne taken me?

My skin crawled at the thought of his hands on my body.

I tried to move but couldn't. Metal cuffed my wrists almost too tightly, and I felt another set on my bare feet.

Where were my boots? The light in the corner wasn't bright, but it showed me the ground in relief, and I saw the marks where I had been dragged and dropped.

Somehow, that was almost worse than Wayne carrying me.

The man himself was the source of the sounds. His back was to me as he crouched over something. I heard a soft scratching and then a ticking. I must still have been woozy from his hit to my head, because I didn't feel good.

Oh no.

I rolled onto my side in time to vomit on the ground, spilling out nothing but bile. Between Harlan this morning, our fight and reconciliation, and this, I hadn't eaten. There was nothing to throw up. But vomiting wasn't a good sign. I definitely had a concussion. Maybe worse.

Wayne turned toward me, and I shoved those thoughts away. I could survive a concussion. But there was a good chance I wouldn't survive whatever Wayne had planned.

"You're up," he said.

"No thanks to you."

His rough chuckle slithered across the walls. "Well, forgive me, I didn't think you'd let me march you all the way in here of your own free will. Besides, can't give you any ideas about where you are or hope that you can make it out. You can't."

I started to shake my head but stopped immediately. The pain and dizziness were too much. But I slowly leaned against the nearby wall and worked myself into a sitting position. This felt better, even if I wasn't actually any better off.

"What are you going to do, Wayne? Leave me here to starve? They're going to come looking for me sooner or later, and when they find me dead and cuffed, there will be an investigation. It'll take a long time to get your hands on this mine while it's tied up in a hundred miles of red tape."

He glanced at me before looking back at the small machine in front of him. His body still blocked most of it from view, so I couldn't tell what it was. "You know anything about mines, Mrs. Townsend?"

"It's Mrs. Young, and I know enough."

"So you know that the reason mines sometimes blow up is that there are pockets of gases in the walls. When they get carved out, the gas seeps into the open spaces, the oxygen drops, and that's when things get a bit more interesting."

"Canaries," I said, leaning back against the rock wall. Why did I feel so weak? It was a bump on the head and some dragging. I was stronger than that. "That's why they used them."

"Correct," he said, shifting his weight so I could see a little more of the machine.

From my vantage point, it looked like a kitchen scale. A device with a little screen and a metal plate on top. Wires connected to it snaked around the lamp that was on the ground and into the darkness of the hallway beyond. More wires ran around the edge of the room, but I lost them because they blended into the rock itself.

"But it's modern times now, so we don't need canaries. Not when we have little beauties like this."

I didn't ask him what it was. I had no doubt he was going to tell me. He didn't disappoint.

"It measures the composition of the air and sends alerts to a phone if you want to set it up that way. No need to kill a canary over something like that anymore."

A laugh fell out of me, and it made me dizzy. The echo came back to me from down the dark passageway. Wherever we were, we were far underground. "Ironic."

Wayne lifted an eyebrow. His face was more sinister in the half-light. "Is that so?"

"You're not willing to kill a canary, but you're going to kill me. You haven't circled back around to it yet, but we both know that's why we're here."

"I did underestimate you," he said with a laugh. "Let me be clear. I'm perfectly willing to kill a fucking canary. I'd kill every animal on both your ranch and mine if it would get me what I want. But it won't. Getting you out of the way is the only thing that will do that."

"What's one more murder, right?" He stared at me. "I heard you say you killed Charles."

"He was stubborn. Like you. When that sinkhole opened and we figured out what was down here, I offered to buy the land from him, and he said no. I upped my offer three times, and he still said no. So, I didn't have any choice. *You*, however—" Wayne stood, suddenly huge, throwing shadows like the nightmare he was "—you have had choices, Grace. I gave you time. I tried to go the easy way. You could have let the state take Ruby Round and give it to me. You could have sold it to me.

"But no. You had to go the hard route. Fact of the matter is, I need you gone, and if you won't get out of the way, then I'm forced to remove you."

Panic stirred under the nausea. I pulled harder against the handcuffs, but there was no way out of these chains. "But you're still back to the problem of them finding me down here and locking this place up for longer than you're willing to wait. If there's anything I've learned lately, it's that you're impatient."

"There won't be an investigation," he said, pointing down at the little machine. "Because I've had some modifications made to this little beauty. This part of the mine is full of methane. Down there on the ground, you're probably getting some good lungfuls of it."

Oh God. Was that part of the dizziness? I wasn't getting enough oxygen?

"When the methane builds up enough, there's a little mechanism in here. A lighter. It ticks over that threshold, one little flame, and *boom!*" He shouted the word with vicious glee. "You're gone, and there's no question about foul play. Accidents happen all the time in mines. It was on your property, you were exploring it, and you should have known better than to be wandering these tunnels alone."

I felt sick. That was a really good plan. And it would work. "How long have you been planning this?"

"A while. It was my last resort. I had hoped you would see reason."

"You know that Harlan will know what you've done," I told him. "There's no way he won't. And I swear on whatever god or piece of land you like, Wayne. He will kill you." The words took more energy than they should have, and they didn't sound nearly as convincing as I'd hoped they would.

"Another thing you shouldn't have done," Wayne said. "If you'd left him out of this, he would have been fine. Now I'll have to take care of him too. If you're lucky, I'll find him in time for you to say goodbye."

He slung a bag over his shoulder and stepped away into the darkness. Panic seized me, and I tried to get to my feet to go after him, but I couldn't. My limbs weren't working the way I wanted them to, and if I somehow managed to get up, I still wouldn't be able to take a step.

Wayne then dropped the bag on the ground and riffled through it. Metal clanked, and he muttered something I didn't understand. "I need you to stay put," he said. "And if you can't accept that fact, then I'll take care of it."

He held a thick chain. One that was clearly meant for large cattle or machinery. With ends that screwed tight around whatever they were hooked to. And that chain was going to be hooked to me.

I screamed. If there was any chance I was close to the surface and could be heard, I would take it. And I fought; I kicked out at him with everything I had left in me.

It wasn't enough.

Hits landed on his legs as he dragged me back toward the wall, and the grunt he made when I managed to make contact was so satisfying, I did it again.

Pain burned through me, starting in my stomach. And again. One more time. I had no air in my lungs—it was all forced out as he landed kick after kick to my ribs.

Coughing hurt.

"I should have known you'd fight in a situation that's impossible to win," he said, quickly attaching the monster chain to the restraints around my ankles. "And if I didn't need it to look like you died of natural causes, I would kick you until you stopped breathing."

Wayne attached the chain to a loop of iron in the wall I hadn't seen before. He really had planned all this. "I'm pretty sure the chains are going to rule out natural causes," I snarled.

While Wayne had never been a friend, he had been relatively nonthreatening in the past. He could even be charming when he needed to. Now, the look in his eyes was pure death. He grabbed my neck, pressing it into the ground until I swore I felt my spine groan. "You really are a bitch," he spat, the warmth of his spittle hitting my face. "I'm pissed that I can't kill you right now. You deserve every inch of pain that I'd give you for trying to take everything away from me."

He lifted me by the throat and slammed me down into

the dirt. Gravel dug into my scalp, but I didn't move. I shouldn't have fought. Now I could barely breathe, and I was on the verge of vomiting again.

"Consider yourself lucky," he said, leaving me and stalking to the lantern. "Oh, and don't bother trying to escape. Even if you somehow manage to get free of those chains, there's no way out. I'll be making sure of that."

The word was out of my mouth before I could stop it. "Explosives?"

"You bet. As soon as the flame ignites, the whole place goes up. More than methane. So don't worry about them finding the chains. That's nothing a little TNT can't fix."

Oh fuck.

Oh *fuck*.

I didn't move, not able to take my eyes off the lantern's light as it faded down the path and disappeared around a corner. Eventually, that was gone too, and the only spark of illumination in this place came from the machine. A little green light to tell me that it was still there, waiting for me to suffocate to death.

Wayne had planned out every detail.

The dark suddenly became close and thick. Invisible hands reached out and grabbed me. My breathing hitched up a notch. I was going to die. Here. I was going to die, and I would never see Harlan again because I'd been such an idiot.

All I could do was hope that Harlan got his hands on my phone and the proof of Wayne's crimes. Because that was all he needed to take the bastard down for good.

As for me? I really didn't see any way out of this.

## Chapter 24

*Harlan*

Grace was nowhere.

Absolutely fucking nowhere.

She wasn't in the house or any of the outbuildings. She wasn't in any of the fields. Dove was still missing, and I'd called everyone I could think of to see if she'd gone into town. Anything to take the horrible knowledge out of my gut that she was in trouble, and once again, *I hadn't been there*.

First my father, then my men, and now Grace. I was going to explode.

Would she have gone into the mine? Of course, with Nelson, but the guy's truck wasn't here.

I dialed his number.

"Nelson Barnes."

"Hey, Nelson." I schooled my voice into something comfortable and breezy. "How did the assessment go?"

"Fine." He cleared his throat. "You two have got a

216

really nice piece of property there. I'm sure you'll be happy with the results. Grace knows everything, but I'll send over the full report tomorrow."

That didn't add up. The assessment itself should have taken longer. "Okay, thanks. By the way, did Grace say she was going anywhere when you left?"

"No." I could practically hear the man shaking his head. "Nope. She was fine when I left. Stayed out by the mine."

"Thanks, Nelson."

I slammed the screen of the phone with my thumb way too hard. The only reason he would mention she was fine when he left her was if she was, in fact, *not* fine.

My phone rang, and I didn't look at it before answering. "Yeah."

"It's us," Daniel said. "Found the phone. It's six miles due east. Still moving."

"That's not her," I said.

"How do you know?"

"Come on, Daniel."

Jude's voice rumbled in the background, but I couldn't make out what he said.

"Talk it out, Harlan. You need to."

I huffed out a breath. He wasn't wrong. Even though he knew the same things I did, I needed to say it. "The phone is on. If it was with her, she would have answered if she had signal. A horse from the ranch is missing. It's probably the horse."

"Good. Nothing on the cameras. Too much wind and too many branches got in the way. We see Grace for a few frames going toward the mine, and we see a few frames of her running back. That's it."

"Fuck." I was desperately trying not to panic. "She's in the mine, Daniel. I know it."

"How?"

"Because I *fucking know*." The words echoed across the ranch. There wasn't any part of me that doubted it. I knew she was in the mine like I knew there was air in my lungs. I wasn't sure what Nelson had to do with it, but she was in those tunnels. "I'm going to get her."

"No, you're not," Daniel said. "We're on our way. Don't go in there without us, Harlan. We do this shit together. I mean it. We need safety equipment. Gas masks. I'm sending Grant and Cori to get the horse. Thirty minutes."

"Make it twenty," I said.

I stalked into the house. On the off chance she wasn't underground, I needed to look and see if I could find anything. Any sign that she'd been taken elsewhere—or had been *forced* elsewhere.

If I hadn't been living here, I might not have noticed the subtle differences. Just like the first time her house had been broken in to, a couple small things were out of place.

A drawer wasn't quite shut on one of the end tables. A light was on in the bathroom. And in what was now Grace's office, the papers she'd left on the desk had been moved.

Something on the desk didn't look right. My memory wasn't perfect, and I was out of practice cataloguing the exact state of things in a place. Something was off from the last time I'd seen it. But what?

I zeroed in on the top drawer. Barely a fraction open. There. That was it. It wasn't meant to be like that. I opened it. Grace had put the safe-deposit box key right there so she wouldn't lose track of it. And now the key was gone.

My phone was in my hand before I fully realized what I was doing. "Daniel."

"Yeah?"

"I need you to track Wayne Gleason's phone."

"Why?"

He couldn't see me, but I shook my head anyway. "Just do it."

Daniel sighed but relayed the order. "I want you to tell me why, Harlan. You're my brother, but I need a better reason to break the law."

"I'm pretty sure that he broke in to Grace's house again and took something. And if Grace is in trouble, it starts with him."

I heard his hesitation. "What are you thinking?"

"Right now, I'm not thinking anything. I'm going to ask the man some questions."

"Tracking says he's at his place," Jude said from the background.

"Great."

Daniel sighed. "We're still on our way. Please don't do anything stupid, Harlan."

"I'm not."

"Remember that Grace doesn't benefit from you beating the hell out of him."

I grabbed my keys and headed back out to the truck. "I beg to differ on that one. But I'm not planning on beating him up. Yet."

"Harlan—"

"Get here." I ended the call and revved up the truck. Then I stopped for a second and breathed. Daniel was right. I needed to know exactly what I was going in there to do. My gut *was* telling me to beat the hell out of him. But if he had anything to do with where Grace was…

My vision tinted red, thoughts spiraling to dark and terrible places. If she was in as much trouble as my instincts screamed she was… If I didn't get to tell her I still loved her—had always loved her... If she died alone—

I slammed that train of thought to a stop. I couldn't allow myself to entertain an outcome like that. Grace was my *wife*. My wife. I wasn't going to be in the wrong place at the wrong time.

She was mine.

Throwing the truck into reverse, I turned and spewed pebbles under my wheels as I headed for Dominion Ranch. It was only a few miles away, but those few miles felt like the longest stretch of road in the goddamn world.

Dominion Ranch had none of Ruby Round's charm. It was darker, like its name. The sharp architecture and drab colors stood in stark contrast to each other. Knowing Gleason, I wasn't exactly surprised. The only things he cared about were power and money.

There weren't any cars in front of the house, and it felt almost vacant. I got out of the truck anyway and banged on the door. "Gleason." My voice resonated through the air. "If you're in there, you better get your ass out here."

Nothing. Not even the vague sense of movement you sometimes got when someone was about to open the door. He wasn't there.

Quickly, I rounded the house, but the barn doors were shut. There were no signs of life on this ranch, except for cows in distant fields.

"Where is he?" I barked into the phone when they picked up.

"Phone still says right on top of you."

Damn it. "Okay. I'm coming back."

He'd left his phone here on purpose. So that I would come here. Or, at the very least, not know where he was. The fucker.

My phone protested under my grip. I had the urge to

call Grace's phone again because I still hoped against hope I was wrong. But the fear I'd barely been able to keep at bay crawled up my throat and spread its icy fingers.

I didn't have time to waste. Gleason or not, I needed to be back at Ruby Round now. There wasn't a chance in hell I was letting someone else go into that mine after her. If Grant and Daniel tried to hold me back, I'd have to remind them, again, that I'd graduated first in my class at BUD/S.

Road disappeared underneath my tires. I was going way too fast, but I didn't care. Charlie wasn't going to stop me right now. It had been almost thirty minutes. They should be there now, setting everything up.

Screeching metal tore the world apart.

Glass shattered and everything spun.

The passenger side of my cab crumpled like an accordion as the truck plowed straight into me. I never saw it coming. All those thoughts occurred in a second, and then I was flying, letting go of the wheel and protecting my face and head. The truck flipped, and my stomach swooped under. Another flip and I registered the pain.

I wasn't sure where the pain was coming from yet. It was originating from everywhere and nowhere. My head, for sure. Maybe my leg.

My truck slammed to a stop against a tree. If it hadn't been there, I would have kept spinning into the base of a rock formation. The sudden silence and absence of movement were jarring. What the hell had happened?

Grace. I needed to get out of the truck. It wasn't that far. I could walk.

What was that noise?

Crunching footsteps sounded around the driver's side. Moving felt like too much at the moment. Everything was heavy. "I'm okay," I called to whoever was there. The driver, I guessed. What had happened?

My nerves were sending me warnings, and I couldn't focus on the message. Hell, my eyes could barely focus from the adrenaline and the pain. *Get it together, Harlan.* Grace needed me.

I shoved the truck door open and groaned. I shouldn't have been going that fast. But it didn't matter now. I'd catch a ride or run.

Pushing out of the truck, I turned and came face-to-face with Wayne Gleason.

Everything suddenly clicked, and the things I hadn't processed before came spiraling through my mind. The truck barreling out from the hidden drive and not trying to avoid me had been *aiming* for me.

Wayne had a shovel in his hand, and I had nothing. No weapon. I wasn't stupid enough to think all he had was a shovel.

"Gleason."

"Young," he said, seconds before he lifted the shovel. I wasn't an idiot. I knew he'd go for my head, and I dove under his first swing. The crash had put me off-balance. In my rush to make it back to Ruby Round, I hadn't grabbed a weapon. In general, I didn't need one, but I wished I had one now. I was sure Gleason was packing.

"What did you do with her?" I asked, squaring up against him now that I was free of the truck. Fuck, my ankle throbbed. I must have hit it, or something in the truck had. My whole body felt as if I had surfaced from too much time under water.

"You'll find out soon enough."

I looked him dead in the eye. "If you hurt her, I will kill you." Since leaving the SEALs, I'd gone to great lengths to put myself in a position of not having to kill. But this threat didn't bother me. However, Grace… If he'd put his hands on my wife, I'd wipe him from this earth without a second thought.

The bastard smiled. "You think I didn't plan for you too?"

"You can try." He swung at me, but I moved away from him easily. Even off my game, I was still a SEAL. I'd fought in worse conditions than this. Conditions that didn't have my wife's life at stake.

Gleason kept coming as if it took no effort at all. He backed me toward the road. I was going to have to get closer to him, but the shovel had reach, and I didn't want to take a hit like that.

"You guys over at Resting Warrior think you're better than the rest of us. But as long as you stayed over there, that was fine. I had everything handled until you had to put your nose in my business."

I kept backing away. Not out of fear, but in an attempt to see if I could gain an advantage. "I don't think I'm better than everyone else," I said. "But I am better than you."

Keep him talking. His arrogance and ego were weapons I could use.

"You know what? You can walk away. Or I'll cut you in on the deal. All you have to do is pretend none of this ever happened. I know you only married her so she could keep that property a little longer."

I laughed. "You don't know shit, Gleason."

"Maybe not. But I know enough." He didn't seem like he was in a mood for more conversation; he lunged at me with the shovel.

Gleason's jacket felt open, confirming my suspicion that he was armed. "Why the shovel, Gleason? Are you afraid you won't be able to hit me? Is your aim that bad?"

The sound of a car reached me. Good. Perfect. Wayne wouldn't do this in front of a stranger. I heard a honk, and I glanced back long enough to identify the driver. My stomach plummeted. It was Nelson Barnes. Fuck.

*Fuck.*

I should have been back at the ranch by now. Daniel and the rest would sense that something was wrong. I could take these two men at my best, but my head was still swimming from the crash.

Running wasn't an option with my ankle like this. And if I did, Wayne would use his gun.

Turning so I could see both of them at once, I tried to think. "You've gone to an awful lot of trouble to get me alone, Gleason. And you could have killed me already. So get on with it."

The man chuckled and looked down at the ground for a second. It was an opening, and I took it. Ignoring the pain and dizziness, I launched myself at him. Under the shovel and through his guard, tackling him to the ground. The shovel went flying, and I moved as fast as I could, pinning him and punching him in the face. Again and again.

I needed him unconscious so I could deal with Nelson.

The click of a barrel made me freeze.

Gleason shoved me off him. "Don't shoot him yet. I need him."

"What does it matter? They're not going to be able to tell." I could hear Nelson's voice shake slightly.

"I'm not taking that chance," Gleason snarled, retrieving the shovel. "Stick with the plan, Barnes. We're almost there."

"Fine."

I could still make it out of this. They needed me. For something. That was leverage, at least. But the barrel of the gun touched the back of my head, and I didn't dare move. The man holding the gun hadn't liked me from the beginning. I wasn't going to antagonize him further.

"You going to enlighten me?" I asked.

"I'd rather not," Gleason said, nodding to Barnes.

I didn't have a chance to react. I barely got a foot under me when I felt a pinch in my neck, and the world swam in and out of focus. The drug wasn't designed to knock me out; instead, I was no longer in control of my body.

"Don't worry," Gleason said, malicious laughter filling his voice. "You'll be awake again soon enough."

It felt as if I was drunk enough to black out while still being alert. This was bad. I pushed up onto my feet and went down again. "We've wasted enough time," Gleason said. "We need to get moving."

Those were the last words I heard before metal cracked down on my skull and made everything disappear.

## Chapter 25

*Grace*

The dark reached for me. I felt it. My eyes kept swinging back to that single point of green light as if it were a lifeline. Ironic, since it was that light that would kill me.

I could tell the air was thinner now. My breaths felt shallow. How long had it been? How long was it going to take? Sitting in the dark made my thoughts spiral. I could almost hear Harlan's voice telling me to hold on. That he was coming for me.

Because he was. I knew that.

But I also knew that Wayne wouldn't stop. There was a chance—

No. I couldn't think like that.

But what other choice did I have?

If Harlan didn't reach me, I was going to die. Was that what people meant when they said their life flashed before their eyes? Mine certainly was.

I should have painted more. Harlan had a point—I'd

allowed that passion to abandon me. It had hurt, but maybe I could have gotten past it.

After Charles died, I wished I hadn't cut myself off so fiercely. I wished I'd let Harlan in sooner. Because I'd known how he felt, and I'd thrown it back in his face every chance I got. I'd been too proud to hear him out. If I had and had known the truth sooner…

A little sob ripped out of me. If I'd let him in, maybe we would have been together sooner. Maybe I wouldn't be here at all. Maybe I would have gotten the chance to tell him that I loved him with actual words instead of sitting in the dark, sending the thoughts toward him and hoping he felt them.

Heavy thumping sounds came from the direction of the tunnel. Grunting. What the hell was that? It echoed, and it sounded like some kind of monster was crawling toward me. But I couldn't be entirely sure I wasn't imagining the sounds.

The darkest part of my soul wanted this to be over, to pass out and wake up somewhere better. I didn't want to spend hours trapped in my own thoughts and longings and regrets.

A bright light came down the tunnel. One single point, blinding me. What? The beam slanted away, and I saw enough to make out the shapes of two men wearing gas masks and hard hats with head lamps. They carried something between them.

The sound of the voice through the gas mask was ominous. "You're still up, I see. Well, don't say I never did anything for you."

They dropped the thing they carried in a heap, and the light passed over him enough for me to see. *Harlan*.

"What did you do?" My ragged voice sounded weak, almost slurred.

"Nothing. Yet," Wayne said. It didn't sound like him, but I knew it was. A monster in a mask and goggles. The other smaller man… I blinked into the light. It had to be Nelson. He was the one with him, right? He had to be helping.

I kept looking at him. "You don't have to do this."

The light shining in my eyes was too bright for me to see his face beyond the gas mask. But it didn't matter. He said nothing.

Wayne led the way out of the tunnel, and Nelson lingered for a second. I felt him looking at me. But again, he said nothing before he followed Wayne out of sight.

"Harlan," I said. He was here, and that gave me a kind of clarity despite the fuzziness in my head. "Harlan."

I wasn't steady on my feet. I'd already tried that to see if I could reach better air when I stood. I didn't last long. The aching in my head along with the dizziness were a one-two punch that had me back on the ground in seconds.

With Wayne and Nelson gone, the darkness was once again absolute. "Harlan."

I crawled toward him and reached out. He was there, and breathing, but not moving. I stretched out as far as I could; my hands barely touched him. I shook him gently. "Please," I begged. "Wake up."

If he woke and could catch them, maybe we had a chance. I didn't see handcuffs on him. But if Wayne hadn't restrained Harlan…then he was absolutely sure that we couldn't get out. No way would he have left Harlan free otherwise.

The ground rocked underneath me, and I was glad I hadn't been standing. Pebbles pelted me from the ceiling. A roaring boom raced through the tunnels. What had Gleason done?

Harlan jerked under my hands. "What?" His voice sounded groggy for one second and then alert the next. "Hello?"

"Harlan."

He moved out of my reach before I could react. I heard him scrambling and staggering on the loose gravel then he landed hard beside me. "You're here." His words weren't any clearer than mine. What had they done to him?

His hands were on me. Everywhere. Checking to see if I was hurt. But I heard the soft sounds of pain that he tried to hide. "Grace."

For one brief second, I let myself forget where I was and what was happening. I let him lift me from the ground and hold me close. In the darkness, his lips found mine, his kiss desperate and deep.

"Are you injured?"

"My head…" I tried to form coherent thoughts, but it wasn't going well. "It won't matter. Both of us are hurt, and there's no way out."

"How do you know that I'm hurt?"

"You fell," I said. "And I know you wouldn't go down without a fight."

"I'm glad you know that."

I felt him shake his head. "They gave me something. My head is cloudy, but it was enough to take me down. I'm going to get us out of here."

"We're in the mine."

"I figured." He moved away from me. I heard a quiet scraping sound as he made his way around the room to get his bearings.

"Harlan, there's no getting out."

"Of course there is."

I shook my head before I remembered that he couldn't

see me. "No. There's not. I'm pretty sure what woke you was him blowing up the tunnel."

"Fuck," he cursed under his breath. "We have to check at least."

I couldn't stop him. The echo of his careful footsteps faded as he slowly went down the passageway. And I heard another curse from far away. I knew it.

Tears flooded my eyes despite my not wanting them there. "Harlan."

"You were right. It's blocked."

"TNT," I said. "He told me as much. And there's more. Once that little machine over there senses the oxygen drop, this room will explode."

"We can make it." His voice was close now. "I'm sure we can move enough rock to get out, even in the dark." Harlan knelt beside me. "Come on."

Slowly, I found his hands and guided them to the metal on my wrists. And we fumbled together as I directed him to the chain. "I'm not going anywhere."

"I'm going to kill him."

I ignored his words and the way he touched the metal, trying to find any weakness. Instead, I drew my hands up his body until I found his face and pulled it close to mine. I'd wanted this chance, and now I had it. "The only thing I wanted to tell you is I love you. In actual words. I didn't want to die without you knowing that."

"We're not going to die." His voice held all the conviction mine did not.

"He planned everything. There's no way out of it." I didn't want to give up. Not now that I'd found Harlan and we were together. I wanted a *life* with this man who'd sacrificed everything to keep me safe. More than once. Hopelessness robbed me of my strength. My lungs felt hollow, and my limbs were weak.

If I was going to die, I would rather do so in the arms of the man I loved than any other alternative.

"Grace," Harlan said. "Gracie, listen to me."

He leaned forward and pressed his lips to my ear. In the darkness, his voice felt like an anchor. I could pretend we were in our bedroom and not awaiting certain death. "I didn't wait all these years to die without getting to spend real time with you. We are not going to die in here. You hear me? I've waited too long to hear you say you love me. I'm not going to say it yet. I'm going to say it when we're under the open sky and safe. And you know without a shadow of a doubt that this is forever.

"You're my wife, and I don't ever want that to change. You are my *wife*, Grace. It wasn't always about helping you. It was always about forever."

A tear spilled over, and I was glad he couldn't see it. Every part of me wanted to believe him. "Tell me, Harlan. Please."

"I will. When we're out of this." Harlan pressed his forehead to mine then pulled away. "Just hold on."

## Chapter 26

*Harlan*

My head pounded. Whatever they had injected me with wasn't strong, but it had been enough to get me down here. The bastard wanted me to know the way he killed me. But I wasn't going to let that happen.

I wasn't.

Everything ached, and I felt a sharp pain in my ankle as I made my way back down the hallway to the obstruction. Of course he'd taken my phone, so we were entirely without light. It didn't matter. I wouldn't let it matter.

We'd trained in darkness. A part of me was glad it was me down here rather than Noah or Jude. They'd been held in darkness—to the point where it was paralyzing. Now that I was here with Grace, and she was alive, I could do anything. Everything in my soul was relieved that I hadn't been too late.

I spent a moment to reach out and get the layout of the collapse. There was movable ground here. It would take time, but I could get us out. I had to hope I could move quickly enough that the device he'd planted wouldn't go off. If I had a light, maybe I could disarm it. Or I could blow us both sky-high. I had never been on the bomb squad, had never wanted to be. My skills lay elsewhere.

Slowly, I started to clear debris from the top and moved rocks and dirt away from the collapse. Frankly, we'd been lucky everything hadn't collapsed right on top of us.

Dread pooled in my stomach. I had no way of knowing how much of the tunnel had fallen in on the other side. For both our sakes, I hoped Gleason was greedy enough to be careful and not blow up more of the mine than he had to.

I wanted to go back down this tunnel and scoop up Grace and hold her. Make love to her even though it was dark and impossible to see, so we could be together one final time. But I wasn't going to give up on us. By now, the guys would have figured out something was wrong, and they'd be looking. They would find us and help.

I removed more rocks and dirt, slower than I wanted. I slid and stumbled going back and forth, tripping over rocks that had tumbled out of the pile. But I thought I was making progress. Or I hoped I was. Time was impossible to measure without any kind of light.

With aching slowness, I tried to climb the pile of rubble. One foot at a time to make sure I didn't make it worse. There was no break, no sliver of light. Only more dirt and more rocks. Perched here, I saw no sign that I could break through. Maybe I couldn't. Maybe there was too much ceiling bearing down and every inch of dirt that I'd dug out would be replaced by more.

I shoved the thought out of my head. As long as I had breath in my lungs, I wasn't giving up on us. I was finally in the right place at the right time. I would not fail.

The problem was the air in my lungs was definitely

getting thinner. It took more and more strength to move the rocks, and I was spending longer resting in between each trip.

"Harlan." Grace's soft voice reached me.

I moved toward her like a moth to a flame, keeping myself oriented with one hand on the wall. "I'm here."

She was on the ground, leaning against the wall. I almost tripped over her. "I'm here."

"I don't feel right."

Panic seeped into me as I lowered myself beside her. "You're okay." I gently pulled her against me, grateful for both the way she felt in my arms and the rest from clearing debris.

"I don't think I am."

Grace's hand found my chest, and she curled her fingers into my shirt. That tiny gesture was everything. It was hard to believe that we were here now. "I've got you."

She drooped against me, exhausted. It took every bit of discipline the Navy had taught me to keep the fear out of my voice. "When we get out of here, we're going to head out of town for a while. Wherever you want to go. We could go to Vegas again if you wanted. Or Mexico. Hell, we could go down to Missoula. Anywhere there's a hotel and room service. Somewhere we don't have to come out of the room the entire time that we're there.

"I want to hear about every detail of your life. Everything that you haven't told me. And I'm going to tell you everything I haven't told you. I'm going to make love to you in every way you can think of and probably some ways you haven't even considered. When we come out of that room, wherever it is, we'll know each other better than any other person on earth."

Grace held me closer. "That sounds nice."

The blankness in her voice terrified me. It was as if she

heard me but wasn't listening. "When we get out of here," I said softly. "When we're safe. I'm going to get that engagement ring I bought for you. I want you to have it and wear it."

Sitting there, I felt the pull on my body. The air was worse here. And she'd been sitting in it for who knows how long. "Come on, Grace. We have to move you."

She didn't fight me as I moved her, as I pulled her with me toward the tunnel as far as the chain could go. If I ever saw Wayne Gleason again…

I laid her on her back and stretched her as far as I could. Maybe the air was a little better closer to the tunnel. I hoped the best of it hadn't been taken already.

"Grace?"

"Yeah." It was barely a breath. A soft sound.

I leaned down and covered her mouth with mine. Only a brief kiss so I didn't steal her air. But I needed her to feel it right now. Terror gripped me, and though I still had hope, I wasn't going to take any chances. "I love you," I told her. "There's not a day since I met you way back in high school that I haven't loved you. No matter what happens, I need you to know that."

Her only response was a slow exhale. Her breath was still even, and when my fingers found her pulse, it was steady. But she didn't have much time.

"I love you," I said again, more for myself than for her.

The tunnel seemed longer this time, and the collapse in front of me far larger. But I couldn't stop trying. I wouldn't. Even though I knew I didn't have much more time myself.

One rock after another. And another. And another. Only able to feel, I had to hope that I was making a dent. The rocks slipped more easily from my sweaty palms.

The top.

I had to keep taking from the top.

My sweaty hand slipped from the rock I was using as leverage, and I went down. Was it possible for rocks to be comfortable? Because right now, they felt like a feather bed.

No.

That wasn't right.

I shook my head, but it didn't help clear my cloudy mind. What was I doing? Why was I resting? I needed to keep moving if we were going to get out.

Slowly, I turned and crawled higher up the pile. Maybe I could push the rocks down and spread it out. That would work, right?

It might. But I couldn't think. I tried to lift the next stone, but it slipped from my grasp. My fingers didn't want to work the way I needed them to. That was all right. All I needed was to rest. Only for a few minutes. Then I'd start again.

～

"Harlan."

The voice came as if out of a dream.

"Harlan, can you hear me?"

Whose voice was that? I couldn't tell. It wasn't Grace's. Her voice was the sweetest in the world. This voice was rougher. Darker.

No.

A swirling pit opened in the bottom of my dreams. The place I went when I realized I was too late. That I would always be too late. Despite being in the right place at the right time, I had still been too late.

"Harlan, I swear to God." Panic mixed with anger in that distant voice. "If you're in there, you have to tell us."

In where?

I forced my eyes open to nothing but darkness. Where was I?

It slammed into me with the force of a boulder, but my body still didn't want to move. I was on the rock pile. The oxygen must have dropped. Or the methane had risen. I only knew my mind was fuzzy and thoughts slipped in and out of it like fog.

Grace.

Where was Grace?

"Harlan? *Grace?*"

That voice. Voices. More than one. I recognized them. "Hello?"

"They're in there. Hold on, Harlan, we're coming for you."

"I was resting." I knew my words weren't loud enough. "Just resting."

I barely heard the muffled sounds of rocks being moved, but I did hear it. "Be careful, dammit. We can't have another collapse if we want to get them out of there."

It was easier to drift and maybe let go. My team was here. They would rescue me, but something hovered at the edge of my consciousness that I couldn't let go of. Something they needed to know. I couldn't remember. It kept slipping away every time I reached for it.

"Harlan? *Harlan.*" The words were coming from above me now. "We broke through. Can you make it up here?"

Broke through? What?

My body felt as if it weighed a million pounds, but I moved it. I felt an urgency under my skin, some kind of panic I didn't understand that made me move. I climbed the pile of rocks in the dark, following the pinprick of light that was visible at the ceiling. "Hello?"

"Thank God." Grant was on the other side. "Here."

The hole was only big enough for his hand, but he

shoved something through. A mask and a long canister. I caught a whiff of air from that hole where Grant was, and it was enough to remind me how to put the mask on.

Oxygen flooded my body and my senses. It felt as if a tsunami-sized wave had crashed me back into myself. Everything returned in a rush.

"Oh shit."

"There he is," Grant said, not to me. "You alive in there?"

I inhaled again and let the mask go so they could hear me better. "Barely. I need a flashlight and more oxygen for Grace."

"You got it."

He started to disappear, and I stopped him. "Grant, we don't have much time."

"What are you talking about?"

"Gleason. He wired this place to blow when the methane builds to a certain level. There's a device in here. I don't know how to disarm it. And if I was that far gone…"

Grant swore and relayed the message as he passed me a flashlight and then another oxygen mask. "Go get her. We'll keep digging."

"We don't need a hole that big, just enough to get the hell out of here."

"Yeah."

I slid down the rocks, nearly stumbling over myself. My brain was catching back up, but my body wasn't quite there yet. How close had we come to death?

I couldn't ask that question yet. We were still in plenty of danger.

In the room where Grace was, I looked down at the device again. Shit. The light on it had been green before.

Now it was orange, and I didn't need to imagine what happened when that little light turned red.

I hit my knees next to Grace. Shit, I'd forgotten she was chained. The lack of oxygen had wiped that small detail from my memory. She was so pale it terrified me, and her pulse seemed weaker than before.

Gently, I placed the mask over her face and secured it. "Grace, baby, you have to wake up. I have to get you out of here."

She stirred slightly when she heard my voice, but nothing more. Not even enough for the chains to rattle. Fucking hell. Now that I had a flashlight, I could get a look at the device that could end all of our lives.

I checked the screen on the front of it, and my stomach plummeted. Ninety-five percent. I didn't know how long it would take for the guys to dig out that hole, but in the meantime, I didn't know how much the hole would affect the buildup.

Could the machine be fooled? I didn't know. And I didn't dare to touch it in case moving it might set off the spark. Likewise with unhooking what was clearly the fuse.

Explosives were always unpredictable. But TNT was a whole different ball game.

"Grace," I said again. "I need you to wake up, okay?"

Nothing in response.

"Goddamn it."

I sprinted back to the collapse and up to the hole, my ankle throbbing. "Hey."

"Yeah?"

"I need bolt cutters."

It was Daniel this time. "Bolt cutters? I don't think we have any. Maybe we have something else that can work. What do you need them for?"

I barely kept a grip on my anger. "Because that animal chained her to the wall."

The little that I could see of Daniel's face darkened. "I can send someone to get some."

"We don't have the time for that. The display on the device says ninety-five percent. I don't think this tiny hole is going to stop the kind of gas buildup that's in the room. Do you?"

He shook his head.

"How long have you been looking for us?"

"When you didn't show up after thirty minutes, we went looking and found your truck. It didn't take us long to figure out what had probably happened. We called Charlie and had him put the word out to look for Gleason. But we've been scouring these tunnels for about four hours. This place is way bigger than we thought."

Four hours. Shit. I must have passed out for longer than I imagined. Not only that, but if the mine really was that big, it didn't surprise me at all that Gleason would kill for it. A sapphire mine this size would be worth millions.

"I need anything you have that can cut metal."

"Give me a second."

I heard voices, and Jude's face appeared. "You okay?"

"Been better."

He grunted. "Yeah."

Daniel appeared beside him and held up a brick hammer. "Do you think you could break the chain?"

The tool was flat and sharp on one end like a chisel. "Do I want to know why you have *that* but you don't have bolt cutters?"

He raised an eyebrow. "Is now really the time to be asking that question, buddy?"

He was right; the fog was still clearing from my brain. I shook my head. "It's worth a shot."

Daniel passed the hammer through the small space, and I retreated. It wasn't much, but I had to get her free. I *had* to. For once in my damned life, I was exactly where I needed to be, exactly when I needed to be there. I wasn't about to become the biggest cosmic joke in the universe by dying when I'd finally accomplished that.

"Gracie. You awake?" I was still hoping she'd open her eyes and start to move, and I shoved away the thoughts that she might have gone too long with too little oxygen. The possibility that she was alive but had been robbed of who she was.

*Not the time. Focus, Harlan.*

I flashed the light over her wrists and ankles. He'd made the cuffs tight. There wasn't much room between them, and I was still shaky enough that I didn't trust my arms not to hit her. The big chain was the better option.

Quickly, I checked the device. Ninety-six percent. *Fuck.* Okay. I could do this. I could do this.

The chain was thick. I needed to find a piece of it that was weaker than the rest to help me. But there wasn't time to spend looking at each link for the imperfections in it. Instead, I picked one away from Grace's feet, and I hit it with all my strength.

Nothing.

Again.

Nothing.

I lost myself in the banging of the chain, and though I was making marks on the link, this wasn't moving fast enough. "Harlan," one of the guys called.

"Yeah."

"We're almost there. It'll be a tight fit, but we can get you out soon. Maybe ten minutes."

I wasn't sure that was enough time. "Okay," I called back, out of breath. It would take a while for my lungs to bounce back. Right now, it felt as if I'd run two marathons back-to-back. I'd been here before but only on a mission. In the field—in battle. Which this was, in a way.

The metal rang out under my hands. I wasn't making a dent the way I needed to. I *needed* it to.

Ninety-seven percent.

Exhaustion meant nothing to me. Not when Grace was in danger. I jogged back down the tunnel. They hadn't lied —the hole was bigger. Not huge. And it might hurt, but it could be big enough for both of us to get through one at a time.

But that was only if I could get her free.

"Did it work?" Daniel called up from the bottom of the pile. I could see them now. My brothers. All forming a line to help take down stone after stone without causing a collapse. They'd installed some emergency supports too.

"No. Ninety-seven percent."

"Maybe we can release some oxygen into the air," Noah called. "Will that make it go back down?"

"I don't know. And I don't know if it will be—" I stopped mid-sentence, and they all looked up at me.

Daniel stepped closer. "What is it?"

"It wouldn't matter," I said, the realization dropping through me like a stone into still water. The ripples were endless. "Gleason wants the mine. He wouldn't leave anything to chance. That was the trigger, but there's no way it's not blowing up anyway. A timer. A detonator. Something."

Curses filled the air. They knew I was right. Gleason had been playing all of us for too long, and he'd been ready each step of the way. He was smart. He would have made sure to have every contingency covered.

"Get her," Daniel said. "Now."

I ran back down the tunnel, and this time, I didn't

bother with the chain. This tool was a chisel, so that was what I used it as. The stone around the wrought-iron loop was tough, but the metal spike had to have been inserted in there somehow.

*Yes.*

It wasn't fast, but it wasn't nothing. Rock broke away from the wall in flakes and chunks as I struck the surface. "Grace. Gracie. Baby." My words punctuated my movements. "I need you to be awake. I need you to be alive. Stay with me."

One breath to check the device. Ninety-eight. I attacked the wall with everything I had. Rock rained down on the ground until I screamed at it. I kept going until I felt the metal bolt move a fraction.

"Yes."

Again, right there, and it moved. This was what I needed. Exactly. It shifted with every hit, and I missed and crashed into the wall when it fell out. The pain was nothing. I pushed it aside and dropped the hammer. Grace was the only objective here. I scooped her into my arms.

She was still breathing, but her body looked lifeless. The heavy chain slowed us down, and I had enough light to see that the device was at ninety-nine percent.

We were so close. But I was slow, and everything felt heavy, even with the oxygen.

I reached for every ounce of strength I'd ever had. I was not letting Grace die here. I made it the last few steps.

"We're here," I said, dragging her up the collapsed rocks and trying not to let her fall into anything dangerous. "We're here."

"Okay."

"She's unconscious," I said. "Help."

Hands reached through the hole, and I gathered what little strength I had left to lift Grace all the way. To maneuver her shoulders into the hole. Her mask scraped the ceiling. "Do you have her?"

No answer came. "Do you have her?" I asked again. The desperation was clear in my voice.

"We've got her."

I felt the moment her weight shifted fully from me to my team. To the men I trusted with my life. And Grace's life. Her legs went through the hole limp and still chained. I gathered the heavy iron links and threw them through the hole after her.

"Okay, Harlan. Get your ass through here."

It was a much tighter fit for me. Tighter still because I was weak and wasn't managing my panic well. My chest was too thick, and I felt stuck. "I need help."

In moments, Jude and Noah were there. They heaved, and I didn't care that they nearly pulled my arms from their sockets. It worked. I tumbled headfirst onto the stones and came up dizzy. I might have hit my head. "Where is she?"

"Daniel has her. They're already moving." Jude said.

"Okay, we need to go."

We didn't bother to stay for the tools. They could be replaced. We couldn't be. I tripped more than once in the dim light our flashlights cast, but my brothers managed to keep me upright and moving.

Holy hell, how far inside this mine were we?

We caught up to Daniel and Grant. I wanted to take Grace from their arms, but I knew they were stronger than I was right now. Her safety was more important than my need to have her close. I didn't know how much TNT Gleason had planted and how much farther we needed to go to get clear.

How much time did we have?

The ground shook beneath us, followed by the roar of

the explosion. A cloud of dust raced toward us. All of us were thrown to the dirt, the blast large enough that, for a moment, the ground felt like jelly.

But the roof didn't cave in on us.

"Everyone okay?" Daniel asked.

I heard groans of assent.

That was close, but we were alive. We'd gotten her out.

## Chapter 27

*Grace*

Everything was blurry. I thought I heard Harlan's voice and a banging sound, but I couldn't be sure. It was as if I was stuck in a dream world, moving both in slow motion and way too fast at the same time.

Where was I?

At one point, I felt arms around me. And I sensed brightness after the dark. But I couldn't quite place the feeling or claw myself back from the haze that had settled over my mind like a veil.

"Grace."

There. That voice was clear. His voice. The only voice I wanted to hear.

"Come back to me, Grace, okay? You can't leave me now. Not after everything."

*I'm not gone.* I wanted to say the words, but they didn't make it to my lips. It was as if I was paralyzed.

Things slowly became clearer, and I heard Lena's voice. "I swear to God almighty, Grace. If you don't wake up, I'm going to find your spirit in the afterlife and kick its ass."

That made me smile. Of course Lena would say that.

"Hey, wait." Those arms around me got tighter. "Grace. I know you're in there. Open your eyes for me, baby."

My eyelids felt as if they weighed a million pounds each, but I did it. Blazing brightness shone down on me. I couldn't see anything, and I winced. The light hurt; darkness was better.

"There you go."

Harlan. Harlan was holding me. I forced my eyes open again, and this time, there was shade. The brightness was the sun, and I could see the open sky. We weren't in the mine anymore. Harlan's face was so close.

I saw a plastic mask over my nose. Oxygen? Why? "What happened?"

My voice sounded strange in my ears. Weak, yet resonant. Things hurt. My head and shoulders. Somewhere on my leg.

Harlan leaned down and pressed his forehead to my own. "We're out. We got out."

I reached for him, but my hands stopped short. Memories assaulted me hard and fast. The mine and Gleason and the handcuffs. My feet wouldn't move either. Panic rose up in me suddenly, raw terror I wasn't able to control. "Get them off. Get them off. *Get them off.*"

"Hold on," Harlan said. "They're getting the bolt cutters. They'll be here in a couple of minutes, and then they're coming off. I promise."

He pulled the mask away from my face, and I got true, fresh air. It smelled like home and him. It was amazing how those two things could suddenly mean the entire world to me.

"I can't—"

Harlan's hand on my cheek calmed me down. "Breathe with me."

I did. In and out evenly until the panic started to fade. But it was still there, gripping my chest. I wanted to be able to move. Being trapped—I didn't ever want to feel that again.

"Here they are," he said.

Lucas came into view with the giant clippers, and Harlan moved me so he could reach the metal that kept me bound. "Hold still."

I did.

"We'll have to wait for handcuff keys to get them all the way off, but you'll be able to move."

That was all I wanted; it was all that mattered. My feet were first, and I stretched them once they were free of the cuffs and the cursed chain, still holding entirely still until I heard and felt the snap between my wrists. I wasn't the one who moved first. Harlan had me up and pulled against him as if no one was else here.

His lips met mine, and it didn't matter that I was still short of breath. I needed his kiss more than I needed air. Literally. "I love you, Grace. I love you more than anything, and…"

I kissed him back. Until I collapsed against his chest, still exhausted. "What happened?"

Harlan's swallow was audible. "We got out. It was close. There was an explosion. Right now, we don't know how much of the mine was destroyed, but we're alive, and that's what matters."

"How close?"

He leaned down, tilting his head against mine. "It doesn't matter."

I tightened my fingers in his shirt. "How close?"

"Close." His voice was thick with suppressed emotion. "I thought I was going to lose you."

Sirens sounded in the distance. "They're here!" Lena's voice cried out again.

"Don't let go of me," I said into his shirt. Terror suddenly gripped me. It felt the way it had before—when I'd found out he'd left and I'd realized I would never see him again. It wasn't rational and it wasn't real—he was here. But I still didn't want it. Being in his arms felt like the only safe place left in the world. "Please."

"I won't," he whispered so only I could hear him. "I meant it when I said it, Grace. I'm never leaving you again."

EMTs approached and knelt beside us. They smiled when I said I didn't want to leave Harlan. But they checked me. My wrists and my ankles. Harlan shifted me in his lap so they could look at where Wayne had hit me in the head. Where he'd kicked my ribs. They took my vitals.

"You're still going to need to come to the hospital so we can get some scans on your head and check your ribs and lungs, but it seems as if you're in pretty good shape." The female EMT tucked her equipment back into her bag.

"You have to get checked too," I said. My voice was still rough, but Harlan heard me.

"I'm okay."

"We should check you out," the EMT said. "But we can wait until we get to the hospital."

Harlan kept his arm around me, and I felt it tighten a fraction. "That's fine."

One of the other EMTs came over. "We have a stretcher—"

"No." Harlan didn't let the potential fear of our separation enter my head. "No, I've got her."

He had to be exhausted, and yet he stood with me in his arms as if it was the easiest thing in the world. I turned my face into his chest. All our friends were here, but I didn't want to see them. Embarrassment had taken root in my chest. I should have been smarter or fought harder. Instead, I had caused all of this mess.

"What do you remember?" Harlan asked quietly. "Before you passed out?"

I shook my head and stopped suddenly because it ached. "Not much." That was the truth. But I still had a few memories. "You said some...really nice things."

"Do you remember what I said about the ring?"

That made me look up at him. "What ring?"

"Your engagement ring."

I blinked. "What?"

"The one I bought for you. I told you I'm going to give it to you. Because I want you to have it. And more than that, I want it to mean something."

He climbed into the back of the ambulance with me and laid me on the padded gurney. Turning to the EMTs, he said. "Can you give us a second?"

It was the first real look I'd gotten of him. Harlan was streaked with dirt and grime, and exhaustion clung to his frame. But his eyes were entirely focused on me, and there was no doubting his sincerity or passion. "I know you didn't marry me because you loved me. And I know things have changed between us since then. But I don't ever want to assume anything."

He took my hand, and I lost the little breath I had. "I love you," he said slowly. "I've never stopped loving you. Ever since all the way back when, you've been it for me.

And I'll keep saying it until you believe me. I'm not leaving you again."

I couldn't speak. All I could do was squeeze his hand.

"This probably isn't the best place to ask. But will you stay married to me?"

"Yes." I nodded and tried to pull him closer. He crouched by the gurney in the ambulance and kissed me. It was soft. Sweet. So perfect it made my chest ache. "I'll stay married to you or get remarried to you. All I want is you."

Harlan's smile blinded me. "Good. Now let's get you to the hospital."

I rolled my eyes as he nodded to the EMTs. I didn't want to be in the hospital, but I knew none of my friends would let me get out of it. I hadn't been to the hospital since Charles died.

Now that I knew *how* he'd died—

"Harlan."

He squeezed my hand. "Yeah."

"Did you find my phone?"

"I think they found Dove and grabbed it, yeah."

A new, different kind of panic gripped me. "I need my phone. You need to get whoever has it to bring it to the hospital."

"Grace, what's going on?"

"Before they grabbed me—"

"I wasn't going to ask you about that until you were ready. But what happened?"

I took a long, slow breath. "There was a horse already at the mine's opening when I got there—after I'd called you. Wayne and Nelson were inside. Talking about me. I recorded them because I thought maybe I would finally have proof Wayne was trying to undermine me. Instead, I recorded him saying…" My voice caught in my throat. "He admitted to killing Charles. Or trying to. Charles was meant to die instantly, but he didn't. I wasn't fast enough. I only managed to get the phone to Dove and set her free."

Harlan reached for his phone and swore. "Can I borrow a phone?"

With wide eyes, the EMT handed Harlan a phone. They probably hadn't been expecting to find out about an attempted murder on this run to the hospital. Then again, they had been called to the scene of an explosion.

He dialed quickly. "Did you guys find Grace's phone?" A beat. "Bring it to the hospital. Meet us there. As soon as possible, okay?" The call clicked off, and he handed the phone back to its owner. "Thanks."

"Seemed important," the guy said with a laugh.

Harlan smiled. "A bit."

The ride to the hospital wasn't long, but I filled Harlan in on some of the details before I'd been dragged into the mine. He told me about getting hit and the missing safe-deposit box key. I was fine—we both knew it. But now that I was safe, I was exhausted.

They rolled me into the hospital, and Harlan didn't let go of my hand. One good thing about living in a smaller town, all hands were on deck as soon as we showed up. We got a room in no time, and the nurses helped me into a gown while Harlan met Daniel for my phone.

I was so tired. "We've got some tests we need to do," the nurse said. "And the doctor will see you after."

"Any chance I'll be able to take a nap somewhere in there?"

She smiled. "Yes. Soon."

Harlan stepped back into the room, along with Lena and Evelyn. "Hey," he said and crossed the room to me. We'd only been apart for minutes, and he still leaned down and kissed me. Kissed me as if he'd just gotten home from war.

I had a flashback. A while ago now, at that family dinner. Where Lucas had wrapped Evelyn up in his arms and kissed the hell out of her, a need sparked by what they'd been through together. I'd been envious.

But now, that was what we had. After everything we'd been through together, past and present, Harlan and I were going to be like that. And right now, I didn't care if we ever grew out of it.

"Will you be okay with Lena and Evelyn here?" he asked gently.

"Where are you going?" The panic started to creep in again, though it had lessened now. Harlan looked at me. I knew. "You're going after him."

"Yes."

There was no point in asking him not to go. If I thought the doctors would let me out of the hospital, I would ask to go with him. But Wayne had killed Charles. And he'd tried to kill Harlan and me. My neighbor was dangerous. "Please be careful."

"I'm not going alone, and Charlie already knows."

"Okay."

He pulled back and looked at me. I memorized his face. "I'm coming back to you. No question." I nodded, and he kissed me again before he was gone.

Lena sat on the edge of my bed. "He'll be okay."

I swallowed. "I know."

"And if you weren't in the hospital, I would *pound you into the ground* for making us worry so much."

Evelyn stood back and smiled. She'd been in my position, and her scars told the tale. "If you don't want to stay here in the hospital, Evelyn, I understand."

"I'm okay, Grace. But thank you. Besides, Lucas left me here. And we already have one Resting Warrior on a rampage."

The three of us laughed together. "I guess I do have one now, don't I?"

"You do," Lena said. "And you owe us all the details you've been holding back."

"After her scans," the nurse said, appearing in the door. "She can tell you after."

I laughed again, the tension banded around my chest loosening. We'd be okay, and Harlan would come back to me.

## Chapter 28

*Harlan*

I didn't want to leave Grace. But Charlie had called before he could get to the hospital. Wayne had been spotted, and they'd followed him. Not to a bank, but to a tiny credit union on the edge of town. It was purely local. So small that it was really only used by the older generation of ranchers who had no confidence in a bigger banking system.

Charles didn't have any accounts there; I knew from Grace's exploration and Charlie's confirmation. But it made sense that might be a place he would put something important he was nervous about.

The bank manager had been instructed to stall but to let Wayne into the safe-deposit vault after some delays. Charlie was on his way, but he'd been on a call out past Garnet Bend and wouldn't be there before us.

I started to play the video on Grace's phone again. She was right. It was a clear confession to attempted murder.

But that wasn't the part that made me see red. It was the shaky footage from when she'd run and fallen. From when that animal had chased her. When he'd *shot* at her.

The tension in the truck was palpable. Because Lucas and Daniel felt the exact same. We'd left Grant and Noah at the hospital just in case. Though, if they were here, they'd feel the same, too.

Wayne's actions weren't exactly a surprise. Anyone who treated their animals with such disdain was likely to treat those they thought of as lesser the same way.

"You should let us go first."

I didn't bother to respond to that. There was no way in hell.

We pulled up to the credit union. No cop cars in sight. They were told to wait so they didn't scare Gleason off, but they'd be here soon. And I was fine with that because I wanted to have a few words with the man.

"Harlan, wait," Lucas called after me. But I was already out of the truck and pushing into the bank. The place was small enough I didn't need to ask directions. There was only one door to the back, and it was already open.

The front door chimed as I went through it, and the older man on the staff stepped into the doorway and smiled. "Oh, hello. Can I help you?"

I pushed past him. In the time it would take me to explain who I was, I would lose any element of surprise. Shock registered on Gleason's face a second before I grabbed him. "You son of a bitch."

"Mr. Young." He was surprisingly calm. Smirking. "I guess I didn't try hard enough."

"I'm used to people coming after me," I said, holding him against the wall by his shirt. I was in his face the way I had wanted to be for months. "Hell, I welcome it. Come after me all you want. But you come after my *wife*? All bets are off."

"You were there when I warned her," he said, anger showing through now. "The bitch didn't get out of the way. She got lucky, but she somehow didn't learn her place out here."

After everything he'd put us through, I snapped. My fist crashed into his face, and I didn't give a shit about the pain. The couple of punches I'd gotten off earlier weren't enough. Everything he'd put Grace through—all the pain and fear. Killing Charles. Chaining her to die. Every single instance played through my mind.

He was on the ground, and I was vaguely aware of shouts in the room. People trying to pull me off him. But I wasn't fully present. All I could think about was making him feel a fraction of the pain and fear he'd caused Grace.

Lucas banded his arms around my chest, and Daniel joined him, pulling me off Gleason. "Let him go. He's already going to jail."

Gleason glared up at me from the floor. "I'm pressing charges."

"Yeah, go ahead," I spat. "See how far that gets you."

I lunged at him again when he laughed, but Lucas caught me. "Enough, Harlan."

I let out a frustrated groan, and I turned to the table with the box. Inside was everything we'd needed this whole time. Grace and Charles's marriage certificate. His will. The documentation of Ruby Round's mineral rights. A few other documents, and a small bag filled with uncut sapphires.

So Charles had known. And he had planned to tell Grace. I wasn't entirely sure why he'd chosen to keep such important documents here, but we had them now, and that was the only thing that mattered.

I looked over at the man who ran the bank. "These belong to my wife. She's in the hospital, and I'll be taking them to her."

Cops came through the door to the bank, and Lucas's hand fell on my shoulder. "Speaking of that, let's get back to your wife before you get arrested."

They dragged me out of the vault, but I didn't leave until I saw the cops put the cuffs on Wayne Gleason. It was the most satisfying thing I'd ever seen.

"Get in the truck," Lucas said quietly. "Now."

This time, I did, and we left the bank as more police cars pulled into the parking lot.

"Were you going to kill him?" Daniel asked. He didn't sound angry. More amused and curious than anything.

I rubbed my hand through my hair. I was still covered in dirt and sweat from the mine, and I desperately needed a shower. Everything ached. "Honestly? I hadn't thought that far ahead."

"That's for damn sure," Lucas said with a chuckle. "Can't say I blame you, though."

Daniel agreed. "He had it coming. I'm glad it's over."

"It's not over until he's in prison," I said. "Permanently."

"He's headed there now," Lucas said. "You think Charlie won't lock his ass up and conveniently lose the key?"

I hated to bring it up, but I had to. "You and I both know that jail isn't always the end of it, Lucas."

He went quiet. Looking back on the incident with Evelyn's stalker wasn't fun for any of us. We'd nearly lost both of them. First, when the stalker had taken Evelyn, and again when he'd bought his way out of jail and attacked Lucas. "That's a fair point." His voice was rough.

We pulled into the hospital parking lot, and Lucas

already had a hand on my shoulder. "Let's maybe walk this time."

"There's nobody I'm rushing to beat the hell out of in here."

Daniel smirked as he closed his door. "Yeah, don't pretend you're not dying to get to Grace's room at full speed."

He wasn't wrong. I did want that. But we hadn't been gone that long. She was probably still getting checked out. Too late, I realized that was why they had me slow down. They guided me into a room with a waiting nurse. "I'm fine."

"Sit down, Harlan." Lucas crossed his arms, making it clear I'd have to go through him. "Let them make sure you're okay, so that when you get to Grace, you don't have to leave."

I couldn't argue with that. But I was afraid to stop moving. My body was hanging on by a thread, and momentum was really the only thing carrying me forward.

But I let them check me. Almost everything was superficial. I was going to have bruises, but nothing had been too badly injured in the crash other than my sprained ankle. Though my truck might have other ideas about my definition of "badly injured."

Unlike Grace, I didn't have my head scanned. I hadn't been unconscious for as long, and I was lucid. They told me to keep track of any symptoms and come back if I showed signs of confusion. I wouldn't need to. Gleason hadn't hit me hard enough for that. He'd wanted me to wake up in that mine.

"Free and clear?" I looked at the doctor.

"Seems that way." She smiled. "I'll be along to see your wife shortly."

I didn't think I would ever get tired of people calling

Grace my wife. Every time I heard it from a person who wasn't me, my whole body swelled with both pride and relief.

"Thanks, Dr. Gold," Lucas said. The woman was the same doctor who had tended to Evelyn. One of the best in the area.

Daniel swore as we approached Grace's room. Two police officers waited outside the door. One I recognized from that day at the ranch with the broken fence. "Edgar," I greeted him. "This about Gleason?"

The man shrugged, though he looked apologetic. "He's pressing charges for the assault."

I nodded. The charges wouldn't stand. Not after the evidence we provided for the charges we were going to press against *him*. "Will you give me five minutes to speak with my wife?"

"Sure."

"Thanks." I looked at my friends, my chosen family, silently thanking them before going in to see Grace.

# Chapter 29

*Grace*

The head scans were fine. The doctor hadn't confirmed, but the technician said as much. My ribs were cracked and bandaged, but there wasn't much else to do for them. All I could do was wait. Exhausted. And I couldn't stop thinking about Harlan.

Where did he go? Did he find Wayne? What was he going to do?

Lena and Evelyn were still here. They were making sure I wasn't alone, even though there was nothing wrong with me. Everyone fussing over me made me uncomfortable, and I just wanted to go home with Harlan.

The man himself walked through the door, and all I could do was stare, trying to see if he was hurt. He looked okay. Perfect. But there was blood on his knuckles, and he limped a little.

"Lena, Evelyn, I need a minute."

They didn't hesitate. I saw Evelyn startle as soon as she

left the room, and Lucas intercepted her with an arm around the waist.

"Did you get him?"

Harlan sighed. "Yes. And he had these." He set a pile of papers in my lap. "Well, not that he had them. But the box was already open. Everything you were looking for."

"Oh my God."

He wasn't lying. It was everything I'd been searching for the past…since Charles died.

"And this." He added a bag of uncut sapphires to the pile. "So the one he sold wasn't a fluke. Charles did know."

I nodded. I figured he had once Wayne admitted to killing him. Or I'd guessed. "Ruby Round is safe, then."

"For as long as you want it." He reached out and took my hand. I stared at that hand. The one with his wedding ring on it.

"But what happened? Where is he?"

"He was arrested."

Slowly, I swallowed. "Then why is there blood on your hands?"

A grim smile. "Because we got there before the cops, and I may have beaten the hell out of him."

"Harlan," I gasped. Not in anger—not in the slightest. Honestly, I wished I'd gotten to see it.

Edgar, the deputy, stepped into the door. "Mr. Young?"

"Harlan, what's—"

He leaned closer. "Gleason is pressing charges for that same beating. It won't stick, but they have to arrest me now."

"Wait, no."

"It'll be okay." He kissed me quickly before standing. "I'm ready."

Edgar already had the handcuffs out, and I had a visceral reaction to the sight of them, shuddering. The feeling was still far too familiar. "You can't take him, Edgar."

"I'm sorry, Mrs. Townsend, but yes, I have to." He started reciting Harlan's Miranda rights, and I was nearly out of the bed to follow before Lena came back in to stop me. In the back of my mind, I made a mental note to change my name as soon as possible. I only wanted to be Mrs. Young from now on.

Harlan had never taken his eyes off me. "I love you. It's going to be okay."

"I have to go after them," I said to Lena.

"Grace, you're in nothing but a hospital gown, and the doctor hasn't seen you yet. Don't worry. As soon as everything is sorted out, he'll be back with you."

That deep, irrational terror boiled up from the base of my spine. I couldn't let him leave. "But—"

A loud voice boomed from the hallway outside. "What in the actual hell is going on here?"

This time, I was able to slip past Lena to the door, where I stopped. The scene was chaotic. The Resting Warrior guys were spread along the hallway, and it only took one look to see they didn't approve of Harlan's arrest. Harlan was cuffed and being held between Edgar and another officer. Evelyn was curled against Lucas's side, and there, facing down everyone, hands on his hips, was Charlie.

He glared at his deputy. "I asked you a question."

"Gleason pressed charges."

"Has the paperwork gone through?"

Edgar shook his head. "Not yet. But it will soon."

"Then there aren't charges yet. And if you think that asshole will have the privilege of pressing charges, you've got another think coming."

I was glad I wasn't on the other end of that tirade. But

suddenly, I was. Charlie looked straight at me. "Grace, are you pressing charges against Wayne Gleason?"

"Yes." My answer was immediate. Of course I was. And I wouldn't be the only one. Harlan would too, and the state of Montana for whatever the name of the crime was for intending to kill someone and having them die of those injuries.

Charlie pointed at Harlan. "You too?"

"Absolutely," Harlan said. "Assault, kidnapping, and false imprisonment, at the very least."

"Let him go."

"Charlie…" Edgar said.

The police chief shook his head. "They survived an explosion. Let the man go home with his wife. It's not like we don't know where he's going to be." Charlie looked at Harlan again. "Don't disappear on me, okay?"

"I won't."

That was a promise I knew with absolute certainty Harlan would keep. Because he wasn't leaving me again. I finally believed that. Entirely. Wholly.

Harlan Young was my husband.

The strangeness of the situation had started to wear off, and a deep sense of rightness had begun to settle into my soul.

They removed Harlan's cuffs, and three seconds later, I was in his arms. I didn't care that everyone was watching him kiss me. I didn't care that my ribs ached because he was holding me so tightly. I didn't care that the stylish hospital gown left my bare ass flapping in the wind. Harlan was mine, and I was his.

"I hate to interrupt," a female voice said. All our friends laughed. The doctor had walked up in the middle of all the commotion. "But I think you might be eager to get out of here."

"Dr. Gold," I greeted her. "Can I?"

She smiled. "I don't see why not. You need rest more than anything, and you can't get that here. Give us a few minutes for the discharge paperwork, and your husband can take you home."

"Thank you."

I pressed my face into Harlan's chest and pretended we were the only two people in the world. This was where I wanted to be. Always.

"Harlan?"

"Mmm." A single resonant sound.

I looked up at him. "Take me home."

The only thing Harlan and I had energy for when we got home was to shower and sleep. And even that had been a struggle. We barely bothered to dry ourselves before crawling into bed, Harlan wrapping his arms around me.

We slept long and deep. The sun was fully up and shining when I opened my eyes the first time. I immediately closed them and sank back down into the bed. The second time, I could tell it was afternoon, and my eyelids felt less like they were weighed down with cement.

Harlan's breath ran along my shoulder. He was *here*.

Now that I'd finally let my mind accept the possibility, I was addicted to it. He was here, he was my husband, and this was our life.

Slowly, I turned over in his arms until I could tuck my head under his chin.

"Good morning." His voice was a low rumble.

"Whatever time it is," I whispered. "I can tell you it is definitely not morning."

His laugh vibrated through our bodies. "It's our morning."

"I'll take that."

"How are you feeling?" He rolled me onto my back so he could see my face.

I took stock. Everything felt fine. I was still tired, and I was sure if I touched any of the scratches or the bumps on my head, I would have some pain. And if I took too deep a breath, I hurt. But overall, I was fine. After Evelyn, I knew exactly how lucky I'd been. "I'm good. And you?"

"Fine," he said. "More than fine. I'm with you."

His kiss covered my smile.

"Grace," Harlan said when he released me. His face was uncharacteristically serious. "The first time I lost you, I knew you were safe. And that was all I wanted. This time, I almost really lost you."

"But you didn't."

One shift from him and he was over me, body stretched along mine, holding himself above me so he didn't crush my ribs. "I know. But I'll never forget how close I came. I don't ever want to feel that way again."

I didn't either, but I didn't know how to say it. He would have to live with that memory forever, just as I had to live with the years after he'd left. "We both have our scars."

Harlan kissed me. It was a kiss that was leading somewhere. What we'd both wanted to do the moment we'd left the hospital but had been too exhausted for. But now we were already naked, and I could feel him hot and hard between our bodies.

He dragged his hands down my sides, reaching to capture my hands with his, weaving our fingers together. I took the moment to look at him. Perfect. Handsome. Mine.

Lifting my hands up, Harlan pinned them to the bed

and kissed me harder. This kind of trap was the kind I loved. I slipped my knees around his hips, trapping him too. "Two can play at that game."

"You don't think that's exactly where I want you?" His grin was wicked. "Look what you've done."

Harlan rocked his hips, and I gasped as his hardness pressed up against me. Heat raced through me like a wildfire, and I grew wet from the anticipation and the sensation of having him so close. The knowledge that this didn't have an expiration date.

"I could slip into you." He rocked again, that delicious friction making my eyes flutter closed. So slow. So careful not to hurt me. But turning me on fiercely.

"Do it," I said.

He froze. "Just like this?"

I knew what he was asking. He was bare—no condom. That wasn't something I was afraid of anymore. I'd always envisioned having children with Harlan, and I didn't much care if it was now or later. "Just like this."

A groan left his lips, and he kissed me, slowly moving his hips and driving me crazy. His smooth, steady movements teased me. I wanted more. "Please."

"You're my wife," he said. "Now and forever. And now that I have you all to myself, I want to take my time."

I moaned and arched into his hold. "Take your time in round two. You know there'll be one."

"Yes, there damn well will." But instead of speeding up, he ducked his head to draw his lips along my jaw.

"Harlan," I begged. "I need you."

He pulled back and shifted his hips enough, then he was there. Harlan's eyes were dark as he looked down at me, but then he closed them and groaned. "You feel so good."

This was a brand-new feeling. Brand-new friction. Like

this—without anything between us—he felt bigger. Harder. I squeezed down on him just to hear him and the sound he made when he was close to losing control.

I vibrated with need. "Let me touch you."

All I wanted to do was feel him. I ran my fingers down his arms and back up to his shoulders. I gripped him to bring him closer. Strong muscles flexed beneath my palms, and I scraped my nails down his skin. I wanted to tell him to go—to move—but I couldn't find the words.

My husband.

This was everything.

Harlan's hands moved down to my hips, and he pushed off the bed. The dark look in his eyes told me he was ready. I was more than ready. I wanted all of him.

Fully accepting him, fully accepting us, had unlocked something in me. I needed him like I needed my next breath, and Harlan gave me everything, while at the same time so careful of my injuries and not causing me pain.

After only a few thrusts, I went over the edge. A glorious free fall into pleasure that ripped my voice from my lungs and all control from my body. It writhed and stretched and took me. A living thing that had a mind of its own.

Harlan's rhythm faltered. Every stroke still drove me higher, but now I felt him and that heat. Curses fell from his mouth. One more stroke. Another. And another.

Then he called out my name like I was the center of his universe.

Slowly, he lowered himself back down onto my body. Kisses on my neck turned into him kissing me, and we got lost in each other, still connected. "I love you," he whispered. "I don't want you to go a day without knowing that. You already had too many days without it."

I gingerly wrapped my arms around his neck and lifted my mouth to his. "I love you too. No matter what."

We lay in silence for a while, coming back to ourselves and catching our breath.

"Thank you," I said.

"For what?"

"For saving me. For saving this ranch. For being willing to give up everything to do that."

Harlan moved, pulling us to the side so we faced each other. "That's nothing."

"It's not."

"Compared to what I'm willing to do for you, Grace? It's nothing."

I didn't have words to say to that.

"Whatever you want to do, I'm here for it. If you want to paint? Do it. If you want to turn Ruby Round into the best damn cattle ranch in the world? I will help you. It doesn't matter to me because I'm here for _you_."

Tears pricked my eyes, and I had to look away. "I want you to have what you want too."

His hand on my cheek brought me back to him. "I have everything I want right here."

I was the one who kissed him this time, and we got lost in each other. For round two. And round three. Because now that we had each other, we had all the time in the world.

## Epilogue

*Grace*
   *Three Months Later*

The wind ruffled my hair as it rolled in over the back fields, and I reached out to keep my brushes from sliding off the table. Again.

It had been a while since I'd painted outside, and I needed to get a cup to put the damn things in if they were going to keep rolling off. But the ability to paint out here? There really wasn't anything like it.

I felt *good*.

The past three months had been nothing but good, and I couldn't remember a time when my life had been this blissful for this long.

Sighing, I leaned back and looked at the mountains. In the distance, I could see movement at the base of them. Right where the entrance to the mine was. It was a full production over there now, and based on an assessment that wasn't a trap, it would be for a good, long time.

How that mine had stayed unknown for so many years was still a mystery, but that mystery would take care of us forever. I wasn't complaining.

After everything that had happened here—Charles and Wayne, getting to know Harlan again—I'd gone back and forth for a while on whether I wanted to stay. Harlan had his house at Resting Warrior, so we could live there. But in the end, this felt like our home.

I didn't have any desire to run the ranch the way it was meant to be run, so we sold the remaining cattle, bought a few more horses, and decided to keep it as it was. A beautiful piece of land that belonged to me. To us. With the mine, Harlan and I would have more than enough money to live.

As his name passed through my head, the door opened behind me, and he appeared. "You're back."

"I am back." He stooped to kiss me. There was no such thing as quick kisses between us by unspoken agreement. We never knew what life would bring, so we would never rush our pleasure. Or the chance to show our love.

And every time he kissed me, I still saw stars.

He sat beside me. "That's beautiful."

"Thanks." The painting was just of the view beyond our house, but it was good practice. The more serious pieces I was working on were inside where I didn't have to think about them for a while. Painting had come back to me as if I'd been struck by lightning. I couldn't get enough. And Lena had conned me into agreeing to an art show in town. If I wasn't careful, she was going to box me up and mail me to a bigger city so I could do a show there.

I looked over at my husband. "How did it go?"

"As well as it could have gone, I guess." He shrugged. "I'm glad he wasn't there."

Another week, another statement or testimony to give.

That was how it felt, at least. But I was fine with that. Wayne Gleason—when we finally got through the inevitably lengthy trial process—would be going to prison for a very long time. With the evidence we had, it was open-and-shut. Nelson Barnes was being charged as well, though he likely wouldn't get as much jail time.

The delicious irony in all of it was that the state took possession of Dominion Ranch, and the property was now for sale the way Wayne had wanted Ruby Round sold. It wasn't kind, but I wished I could have seen his face when he was told.

Harlan had been officially deposed today. Mine wasn't until next week.

"I'm glad he wasn't there too," I said. "The last thing we need is for you to launch yourself across the table at him."

"Don't tempt me," he said, but he was smiling. "Did Lena call today?"

I rolled my eyes and picked up a brush. The motion made my engagement ring sparkle. Harlan had gotten down on one knee and asked again, despite knowing my answer. But I'd never taken off the wedding ring.

I never planned to.

"Yes. Twice," I said. My best friend was a force of nature, and besides the art show, she was planning our wedding. Since we were already married, we didn't need to concern ourselves with the legal side of things, so a party seemed like a great idea. Only, Lena's idea of a party and mine were very different.

She was making the cake, planning the invitation list and decorations, and she called at least once every day to check on something or get my opinion. It had become a running joke, and she knew it.

But I secretly loved it.

I'd always wanted a wedding to Harlan, and now I was going to get to walk down the aisle to him. I couldn't wait for him to see me in my dress. A couple more months, and it would feel even more real.

It was late fall, and the air was growing colder. Another breeze hit me, and I shivered. Harlan stood and peeled his leather jacket off his shoulders. I loved feeling its weight. And it smelled like him. Cedar and campfire smoke.

"You don't have to," I said. "I was thinking of going in anyway."

Harlan smiled. "For tea?"

I made a face. "You know me too well."

"I don't think that will ever be true," he said with a laugh and disappeared through the door. He still made me tea because he made it better than I did. I secretly watched him whenever I could and followed his steps exactly. It never tasted exactly the same.

While I gathered the canvas and paints, I took a deep breath of the fresh mountain air. On days like this, I loved the way it felt. I still woke sometimes in the night with memories of pitch-black darkness and not enough oxygen. But Harlan was there every time I did, and slowly, those nightmares were coming less frequently.

My husband had nightmares of his own. I didn't think either of ours would ever go away entirely, but as long as we had each other, I wasn't worried about it.

I set the supplies and canvas down inside and went back out for the easel. "I've got it." Harlan scooped me up into his arms from behind and then grabbed the easel.

A laugh burst out of me. "I think I can manage the five steps into the house."

"Ah," he said. "But can you manage all the steps all the way upstairs?"

"And why would I be going upstairs?"

He set the easel down and made a face like he was thinking. "Well, I was about to put on water for tea. And then I had a thought."

"Oh?"

"Tea is almost always better when you're snuggly and sleepy."

I hit his arm. "That's when *you* like tea. I like it all the time."

Harlan pretended I hadn't spoken as he walked us toward the stairs. "And thinking about being cuddly and sleepy made me wonder if maybe you wanted to push the tea back. Just a little."

Desperately, I tried to fight my own smile and failed. "I could be convinced. If you make it worth my while."

"Oh, I will," he promised. "First with my mouth, and then with everything else."

We'd been married for months, and he still managed to make me blush. "In that case…" I gestured up the stairs.

He took them two at a time, which had me dissolving into laughter before we made it to the bed. "I love you," I managed. But his mouth was already on mine. His own words were whispered between kisses and peppered along my skin.

I didn't need him to say them. He showed me every day. In bed. Out of bed. Every touch, every look, every action.

This was a simple life, but it was all I'd ever wanted. After everything we'd been through together, I was happy. And Harlan and I had already planned one thing for our wedding—the vows we would make. Never to be separated again.

•••

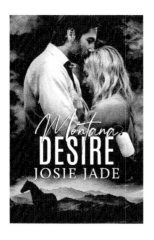

Thank you for reading MONTANA DANGER! The Resting Warrior Ranch series continues with MONTANA DESIRE, Grant and Cori's story. Grab it **HERE**.

## Acknowledgments

A very special thanks to the Calamittie Jane Publishing editing and proofreading team:

Denise Hendrickson
Susan Greenbank
Chasidy Brooks
Marci Mathers
Tesh Elborne
Marilize Roos

Thank you for your ongoing dedication for making these romantic suspense books the best they can be.

Also by Janie Crouch

Baby

Storm

Redwood

Scout

Blaze

Forever

INSTINCT SERIES (series complete)

Primal Instinct

Critical Instinct

Survival Instinct

THE RISK SERIES (series complete)

Calculated Risk

Security Risk

Constant Risk

Risk Everything

OMEGA SECTOR SERIES (series complete)

Stealth

Covert

Conceal

Secret

OMEGA SECTOR: CRITICAL RESPONSE (series complete)

Special Forces Savior

Fully Committed

Armored Attraction

Man of Action

# Also by Josie Jade

See more info here: www.josiejade.com

## RESTING WARRIOR RANCH

Montana Sanctuary

Montana Danger

Montana Desire

Montana Mystery

Montana Storm

Montana Freedom

Montana Silence

## About the Author (Josie Jade)

Josie Jade is the pen name of an avid romantic suspense reader who had so many stories bubbling up inside her she had to write them!

Her passion is protective heroes and books about healing…broken men and women who find love—and themselves—again.

Two truths and a lie:
- Josie lives in the mountains of Montana with her husband and three dogs, and is out skiing as much as possible
- Josie loves chocolate of all kinds—from deep & dark to painfully sweet
- Josie worked for years as an elementary school teacher before finally becoming a full time author

Josie's books will always be about fighting danger and standing shoulder-to-shoulder with the family you've chosen and the people you love.

**Heroes exist.** Let a Josie Jade book prove it to you.

## About the Author (Janie Crouch)

"Passion that leaps right off the page." - Romantic Times Book Reviews

USA Today and Publishers Weekly bestselling author Janie Crouch writes what she loves to read: passionate romantic suspense featuring protective heroes. Her books have won multiple awards, including the Romance Writers of America's coveted Vivian® Award, the National Readers Choice Award, and the Booksellers' Best.

After a lifetime on the East Coast, and a six-year stint in Germany due to her husband's job as support for the U.S. Military, Janie has settled into her dream home in Front Range of the Colorado Rockies.

When she's not listening to the voices in her head—and even when she is—she enjoys engaging in all sorts of crazy adventures (200-mile relay races; Ironman Triathlons, treks to Mt. Everest Base Camp...), traveling, and hanging out with her four kids.

Her favorite quote: "Life is a daring adventure or nothing." ~ Helen Keller.

Printed in Great Britain
by Amazon

24923341R00169